Reyanna's Fire

Book 2 of the
Forge Born Duology

By Whit McClendon

Copyrights

Reyanna's Fire

Copyright © 2018 by Whit McClendon

ISBN-13: 978-1-7326300-1-7
ISBN-10: 1-7326300-1-1

Cover Art by: Wicked Smart Designs
Copyediting by: Michelle McClish
Published by: Rolling Scroll Publishing, Katy, TX
Website: www.jidaan.com

To join my mailing list to be notified when a new novel is published, go to
http://www.jidaan.com/contact

You can also Like my Facebook page!
http://www.facebook.com/whitmccauthor/

Dedication

This book is dedicated to pugs everywhere. I love pugs. They're sweet, loving animals who exist for almost no other purpose than to hang out with you, love you, and be loved by you. I've always been a 'dog person' so having a canine character play a prominent role in my stories was really no surprise. Mastiffs are basically enormous pugs, so although Beauty is definitely a fighting dog (and pugs are somewhat less ferocious), she's got a loving heart, as all dogs do.

If you're looking to fall in love with a pug (especially if you're in the Houston area), wander over to http://www.pughearts.com/. *Pughearts Pug Rescue of Houston* is a non-profit organization entirely devoted to helping these sweet little dogs to live happy, healthy lives, and find forever homes.

If you get a chance, give a pug a hug.

What Has Gone Before

The years after the war with Mordak had been peaceful. The Guardians, wielders of the ancient, magickal spears known as the Jidaan, had gone their separate ways and settled into more quiet lives.

More than two decades after that conflict, a young woman, a human, grew up in the Weya village of Allinshae. Trained as a Weya Ranger in the ways of bow and dagger and leaf and stream, she was content with her life. To her, the Guardians were legends, old stories told by her adoptive parents and the LorMage of the village.

Without warning, a powerful vision reached across the continent and whelmed the remaining Guardians to their knees, and Reyanna as well. In it, the Guardians recognized their companion, Gart, and they knew that something dire was afoot. Kiran and Layton made their way to Guardians Keep in their search for answers, battling Air Daemons along the way.

After consulting the village elders and the LorMage Calliana, Reyanna, too, learned that Gart was the central figure in her vision. The most powerful of the Guardians, and something of an enigma, Gart had been facing a threat of immense power in the vision. Reyanna decided to make her way to Guardians Keep with former Weya Ranger Ginn as her guide.

Kiran and Layton arrived at Guardians Keep only to find Nessar unconscious, stricken by the vision. After helping him recover, the trio discovered Gart's notes, revealing his dangerous plan. Obsessed with his long-dead wife, Gart was determined to call her spirit from the netherworld, risking an apocalypse in the process. Armed with that knowledge, they sought out a Weya LorMage to tell them where to go in order to stop him. Their path led them to the lost, underground city of Corria, in search of a massive diamond with mystical powers. They knew that Gart needed it for his ritual, and with it, they could prevent him from reaching his goal. They had no idea that the subterannean creatures who had scoured the life from Corria centuries ago were still there and very much alive.

Gart had chosen Nimshi as the first stop on his quest, however, and discovered that the ancient temple was far more dangerous than his research had indicated. He bested the undead High Priest that guarded the Blood of Nimshi, but was ambushed by two sorcerers, Barovius and Arkhan. Beauty came to his rescue, but was brutally stabbed by Barovius before the two men escaped with Gart's Jidaan of Storms.

Meanwhile, Reyanna and Ginn are attacked in the forest by a deadly half-human wolf-beast. Someone had sent a sorcerous Joining of man and wolf to stop her, demonstrating that her quest was more important than she even knew. Reyanna's magick, long held at bay inside her, emerged to destroy the beast, though she had little memory of the event. Afterward, she and Ginn continued on their way, meeting Teryn, a preistess of Rowann. Sister Teryn was a spider rider, having just come from the colony of Kulcania the Spider Queen. When they are attacked by ruffians on the road and Teryn is wounded, Reyanna continued on Teryn's mount, the enormous spider, Drusilla.

Tired, Reyanna stops at an inn for the night. She is visited by the shade of the evil sorceress, Melidia. When Melidia threatens to stab her, Reyanna's power erupts from her body in searing flames, disrupting Melidia's shade and sending her away. Unfortunately, Reyanna's mind was overshadowed by her power, and her awareness had fled. When the innkeepers sons burst in to help her, she nearly killed them and burned down the inn before losing consciousness. Taking pity on her, the inkeeper's wife, Vania, had her carried to a safe bed, where she waited for the young woman to awake. She had a lot of explaining to do...

Chapter 1

"Quick! Get behind that wall!" Kiran leapt over a huge chunk of debris, skirted another tumble of fallen stone, then disappeared behind a moss-covered wall. She reappeared an instant later, urgently beckoning Nessar and Layton to join her. The pair scrambled around the obstacles somewhat less gracefully and ducked behind the barrier with her just as another ear-splitting howl erupted from within the cave they had just escaped. The ground rumbled and shook as something monstrous pulled itself out of the underground chasm in search of whatever had disturbed its slumber.

They managed to put some distance between themselves and the cave opening, but were still barely a quarter of the distance across the ruined city of Corria. Breathing heavily, Nessar scanned the surrounding walls. The passageways they had found had all been filled in, but surely there was another way out, even if they had to climb all the way to the top. Unfortunately, he doubted they could climb fast enough to avoid whatever they had awakened. "This could be a problem," he said dryly.

Kiran kept peering around the corner of the wall, searching for the source of all the noise. "You think?" Not bothering to look away, she continued, "I hope you can 'thief' your way out of this and take us with you. I don't know what's coming, but...oh...oh yeah, that's bad."

The beast that emerged from the cave was easily the biggest living thing Kiran had ever seen. It resembled the creatures that had attacked them inside, possessing the same white, pebbled skin, eyeless face with long, slitted nostrils, and sharp claws. However, it was obviously a breed apart; it was ten times as large, and far more muscular in the body. It also sported a long, thick tail ending in four sharp horns that stuck out at odd angles. It had to stoop until it cleared the confines of the cavern. Then it stood to its full height, roaring a challenge to the world outside.

"I agree, that sounds like it's all bad," Layton murmured.

1

Kiran snapped her head around to regard him. "Are you back to normal yet, Layton? We could really use your Gates, man!"

Layton grimaced and shrugged his shoulders. "Sorry," he said sheepishly. "I'm still pretty confused."

Kiran rolled her eyes at him in disgust. "Ugh! Nessar, have you got any ideas that will get us out of here? That monster hasn't moved yet, but it's trying to catch our scent, and when it does, I'm not sure how long I can Ward us against it. We either have to get out of here or kill the thing. Right now I feel like a mouse discussing how to kill a mountain lion, so escape sounds better."

The creature roared again, then slowly began to edge away from the cavern opening, its great weight vibrating the earth with each ponderous step. It methodically moved its head from side to side as it snuffled at the air, searching for the intruders.

All right, I have a plan, but you're not going to like it. Nessar's voice echoed in Kiran's mind, startling her. She heard Layton's sharp intake of breath and guessed that he, too, had heard Nessar's silent speech. Fortunately, Layton had the presence of mind to keep quiet, else they might have alerted the creature. *Kiran, can you use a Ward to make some noise over to the north, far away from us? To distract that beast while we go the other way?*

Kiran thought for a moment, then replied, *Sure, I can do that. I can use it to nudge one of those wall fragments so that it falls down. That'll attract its attention, I bet.* Kiran felt Nessar's approval through the magickal link they shared.

Perfect. When you do that, I'll use my Gift to cover us. We'll head over to that toppled building there. Nessar pointed one gnarled finger at a huge pile of rubble that looked to have once been a tower. Part of the stone spokes overhead had broken away and crashed down upon it at some point in the past. It had fallen in a heap, with much of the structure leaning against one wall of the sinkhole. *That will get us part of the way out. The rest will take some elbow grease, but we can do it.*

Kiran saw instantly that Nessar intended for them to clamber atop the rubble, then resort to climbing up the vine and tree-lined sides of the depression to escape. Using the demolished building as a ramp would create an expedient shortcut, provided it did not fall to the ground, killing them all. She wanted to say something sarcastic, but for the life of her, she could not think of a better idea, so she simply nodded. Suddenly, she frowned. *Are you going to be able to use your Gift to cover us and climb out at the same time? That's heavy work, old man. I swear to Rowann, if you pass out from exhaustion and fall to your death, I'm going to kill myself and come on after you to kick your old arse!*

Layton managed a weak chuckle, then caught himself. Nessar raised one bushy eyebrow at Kiran.

Yes, little lady, I'm perfectly capable! Now distract that thing so we can get a move on. It's going to be dark soon!

Kiran shook her head ruefully at her old friend, but turned her attention to the structures farthest away from where they were headed. A crumbling wall caught her eye and she willed her Jidaan to life, hoping that the pulse of her magick would not alert the massive creature. Focusing her power just behind the distant wall, she created a Ward roughly the size of a large shield. Once she was certain that it was solid, Kiran slammed it into the wall as hard as she could, sending bricks and dust everywhere with a huge crash.

The creature instantly turned towards the sound and burst into motion, heedless of the structures it destroyed in its rush to find the intruders. It plowed through anything it could not step over, brutally shoving everything aside as it moved.

Let's go! Hurry! Nessar's voice echoed in Kiran and Layton's minds. They felt the tingle of power wash over them as Nessar hid them with his Jidaan, their bodies disappearing completely from sight. *Stay close, or that beast will hear you! Grab hold!*

Layton reached out to where Nessar had been and felt soft flesh before it jerked away from him.

Not my eye, you snot! Here! An unseen hand grabbed Layton's wrist and guided it until the younger man had a firm grasp of Nessar's leather belt. Layton felt Kiran's hand on his back for an instant, then it slid down and

3

grabbed his own belt. *If everyone is ready, let's move!* The trio set out for the fallen tower as fast as they dared.

Behind them, the creature had reached the wall Kiran had pushed over. It roared a challenge, the fearsome noise echoing through the sunken city, beating on the escaping Guardians' eardrums as they ran. They kept their eyes on their goal, ignoring the rumble of crashing stone as their pursuer destroyed everything within its reach as it searched for them. A cloud of fine, white rock dust from the destruction drifted through the city, clouding their vision and irritating their lungs, but they ran on.

Stay close! Nessar's voice echoed again. *I can still cloak us if we stick together! Let go and climb as fast as you can!*

The old man nimbly sprung onto the pile of rubble at the base of the fallen tower, moving from stone to stone like a billy goat. Kiran and Layton stumbled along behind him. It had been years since they had been forced to climb anything, much less at speed, but Kiran found her rhythm quickly. Layton, usually the most fit and agile, was still groggy and fighting through a fog of pain. Kiran could sense his confusion and unease, especially as they climbed higher up the leaning tower.

Exhilarated, Nessar bounded along the rubble until he reached the spot where the structure had made contact with the earthen sides of the deep, cylindrical sinkhole in which the city sat. Although the rest of the climb looked to be over a hundred feet, the rock was porous and craggy, not to mention covered with vines and shrubs, all of which offered hand and footholds aplenty. Nessar grasped the thick stem of a nearby shrub and hauled himself towards the wall, shifting into a vertical climb.

Below, Kiran navigated the sloping side of the fallen tower as quickly as she could. Climbing great heights had never been her favorite activity, but she was determined to give a good account of herself, regardless. She stayed focused and kept moving. Being unable to see or hear her footsteps on the slanted stone threw her off at first. Finally, she reached out with her magick as Brunar had once taught her, using it to sense the terrain ahead. Once she could feel the rough stone that surrounded her, she was able to tell secure footholds from loose stones. Encouraged, she picked up speed.

Suddenly, she felt a burst of terror from Layton as a shower of rocks exploded from an outcropping just ahead and to her right. Instinctively, she reached out with her magick and sensed Layton's plight. He had stepped poorly and debris had shot out from underneath one of his feet, leaving him to windmill his arms as he frantically tried to keep from falling to his death.

Kiran shifted the angle of her run to intercept him, but before she could get close, she heard Nessar's voice in her mind.

Gotcha, snot rat! The old man had monkeyed down and covered the distance like lightning, latching one gnarled hand onto Layton's wrist with a vice-like grip. *One of these days, I'm going to have to teach you to climb! That's two you owe me, Junior...now keep your feet under you!* Kiran felt Layton's heart begin to slow as he regained his composure. *Keep moving, both of you! If that thing heard the noise he made just now, we...uh oh.*

The loud roaring of the enormous, sightless beast, followed by the crash and rumble of its bulling through the stone ruins toward them, confirmed their fears. It had heard them, and it was heading in their direction.

Move it! No time to waste, we've got to get higher than it can reach!

Sprinting as fast as they dared over the sharply sloped ascent, they quickly reached the vertical wall of the sinkhole. Handholds were plentiful, but the climb was straight up. Moving with a speed born of desperation, they pulled themselves up the wall, praying all the while that they could climb out of the creature's reach in time.

Hands abraded by the rough bark of shrubs and vines, faces stinging and scratched from sharp branches and twigs, they climbed toward the fading light up above. The loud, heavy footsteps of the creature drew near, and soon, it was below them. If any of them slipped and fell, they would likely be swallowed whole if they had not already been shredded between the thing's sharp fangs. It roared again, and they could feel its hot breath buffeting them from below even as they struggled to keep from jamming their hands over their ears to shut out the noise. Ears ringing, they climbed on.

The beast's enormous bulk shook the earth as it maneuvered around the rubble of the fallen tower. It snuffled wetly at the air, trying to gain a sense of its prey. Suddenly, the thing roared in triumph, for although the Jidaan cloaked them perfectly, it could not hide the scent they left behind once their trail fell outside the mystical weapon's influence. The beast tried to scramble up the steep ramp of debris after them, but the angle was far too acute for its great size. It howled again, this time in anger.

Without warning, the huge creature whirled in place, lashing out with its thick, horned tail. It slammed into the top of the tower with incredible force, shattering the damaged structure and sending jagged shards of rubble in all directions.

A fist-sized lump of rock struck Nessar's shoulder, blinding him with agony and disrupting his focus. He, Kiran, and Layton suddenly appeared, as if out of thin air, as the protection of Nessar's Jidaan of Stealth was lost to them. They continued climbing upwards along the side of the sinkhole as fast as they dared. A bright blue Ward burst into existence, forming a shield around them as Kiran engaged her own Jidaan.

Layton reached Nessar first. The old man was cradling his left arm close to his chest, his face a clenched mask of pain as he held stubbornly to an exposed root.

"Come on!" Layton said, grasping the thief by his belt in the back. "I've got you! We're almost out of its reach now. We've got to keep going before it spots us!" The ache in Layton's head intensified, but he ignored it as best he could. "Let's go!"

As if in answer, the creature below bellowed again, and this time, they could feel the heat of its breath as it faced them directly.

"I'm pretty sure it's found us, Laytie dear!" Kiran called out as she threw herself at the next jutting root above her. "Come on, move it! I can protect us for now, but the sooner we can reach the top and be out of here, the better!"

6

"I'm all right," Nessar grunted to Layton, opening and closing his left hand. "Took me by surprise, is all. Just give me a boost to get me going; I'll do the rest."

Layton grunted with effort and heaved the older man up to the next handhold. Nessar grasped it with both hands, gritting his teeth through the pain. Although his shoulder was on fire, Nessar was true to his word, and he hauled himself upward again, gaining speed as he went. Layton stayed close by to keep an eye on him, and Kiran scrambled up right behind them. The circle of sky overhead, broken only by the stone spokes that caged the city below, seemed to beckon the Guardians, and they climbed with every ounce of strength they could muster. Their hands blistered and bled, and new welts appeared on their faces, but they ignored all those superficial hurts and kept moving.

The creature slammed its powerful tail into the wall again and again, attempting to dislodge them. The impact caused the three friends to slow, but they were finally too far up the wall for the resulting tremors to disrupt them. Still they climbed, not wanting to let down their guard until they knew they were safe. They climbed until they were no more than fifty feet from the top of the vertical cavern, then Nessar turned and looked down at their pursuer.

The monster had its eyeless face turned up towards them, and its long, slitted nostrils sniffed the air for signs of their presence. It grunted as if frustrated, then it stepped carefully away from the fallen tower, away from the wall the Guardians clung to with all their might.

"I think it's given up!" Kiran exclaimed. "Ha! Couldn't get us, you big ugly beast! Take that!" Nessar groaned at her words, concerned as always that she was putting the cart before the horse.

The beast below squatted down on its haunches, hunching down as low as it could and presenting its broad back to the tiny humans up above. They heard it groan, and then there was a grotesque ripping sound.

"You have got to be kidding me," Kiran said, then she started climbing for all she was worth. Nessar and Layton continued to stare for a moment longer before following her prudent example.

Two long slits had ripped open in the creature's back, and a pair of bony appendages had emerged, spreading out on either side of the beast. Wet, leathery skin unfurled as it stretched across the slender bones. It moved its wings gently at first, as though they had been dormant for so long the creature had forgotten how to use them. Then it opened them to their full, impressive width. It flapped its wings once, then again with more authority, each time sending a rush of wind up the vertical tunnel.

The third blast of air was strong enough to freeze Kiran, Layton, and Nessar in place as they struggled to maintain their holds.

"This is bad," Nessar commented.

"You think?" Kiran retorted. "Keep moving; we're almost there!" She scrambled upwards again, desperate to reach the top.

The beast below unleashed an ear-splitting bellow of triumph. Still roaring, it crouched low for an instant, then sprang into the air. Dagger-like teeth gnashed and snapped, and massive claws clicked together in anticipation of rending the flesh of the tiny, arrogant intruders. It had scented them now, and eagerly anticipated the taste of their sweet, coppery blood, the crunch of their bones. It flapped its powerful wings, reveling in the full use of its long-dormant limbs.

The wind from the creature's wings was fearsome, and Layton struggled to hold on to a thick root with one hand and a tiny ledge of stone with the other. The pain in his head made it difficult to focus, but he knew he had to keep moving. He pulled hard on the root and shifted his other hand higher, trying to find another hold. The root gave way, and he felt himself falling away from the wall. He turned to see Nessar's wide eyes staring at him as he fell.

No! Layton! The terror in the old man's mental voice was scrawled across his lined face as well. Desperate to save his old friend, Nessar lunged as far as he could in an attempt to grab him. He fell short, and Layton was out of his reach in an instant. Layton felt one of Kiran's hands frantically grasping at his trousers as he hurtled past. For an instant, he thought she would succeed, but then he heard the cloth rip and he continued to fall.

Well, damn. Layton's only thought was one of disappointment. He still had no idea what was going on, and now he would die before he found out. He looked downward in that instant and saw the horrifying creature almost upon him, its fanged mouth opening wide to catch him.

And then, Layton's fall suddenly ceased. He froze in mid-air, supported by nothing he could see. A subtle golden glow became visible around his arms, and as he recognized the tingle of magick, he found himself rising again, moving quickly out of the beast's reach. As he rose he saw that Nessar and Kiran had also been surrounded by the golden glow, and they were floating away from the wall, rising with him through the air.

Awaiting them at the top of the circular walls of the sinkhole was the dark figure of a man. His features were hidden by a wide-brimmed floppy hat, and his arms were raised in front of him. The magickal glow emanated from his hands, and he guided the floating trio up and out of the deep cavern that held Corria.

They cleared the top of the steep walls of the sinkhole where they were deposited unceremoniously on the ground with a thump that knocked the wind out of their lungs. They gasped, trying to catch their breath so they could warn the newcomer about the enormous beast that pursued them. Nessar rolled over and retched, while Layton lay silent.

"Wait! That thing is coming!" Kiran croaked as she tried to suck in a decent breath.

Unperturbed, the man quietly walked over to his right, near the base of one of the huge stone spokes that spanned the hole. Below, the creature howled its defiance and anger, and they could hear its approach as it beat the air with its massive wings. The man raised his arms and the golden glow appeared around his hands again, brightening in intensity until it was difficult to view. It churned and writhed as it grew, almost a thing alive. Finally, the magick leaped out from his hands and surrounded a portion of the stone spoke. Kiran heard a low grinding sound, and then felt a resonating crack as a long section of the spoke broke away from the main, detaching itself and floating in the air, guided by the stranger.

Just then, the beast's head rose into view, larger than a hay wagon, and its massive wings whipped the air into submission to keep it aloft. Its eyeless face instantly focused on the man, scenting him easily from so close. It roared a challenge.

The man answered. Without a hint of alarm, he gestured sharply with both arms. The floating beam of stone responded by slamming itself into the side of the creature's misshapen skull.

Its roar turned into a bellow of pain. Black blood spurted from several spots on the creature's hairless head, and it immediately dropped out of sight below the sinkhole's edge. The man stepped closer to the edge and peered down into the pit. With another sharp gesture, he sent the huge chunk of stone hurtling after the creature. Another loud impact, felt more than heard, reached Kiran, followed by another inhuman bellow of agony. The man stood silently for a few moments, still peering into the ruined city below. The beast's horrid screeching became more distant. There was a rumbling of stone, likely many of the structures below collapsing under the weight of the creature and the huge piece from the spoke. The stranger watched silently for a few moments, long enough for the noises below to finally cease. He nodded to himself, then slowly turned toward the recovering Guardians. He made an absent motion that reminded Kiran of dusting one's hands off after a task well done, then slowly began to walk towards them. His face was still hidden by the brim of a hat that seemed older than the hills. He stopped right in front of her and offered her one of his hands. She took it and allowed him to help her to her feet.

"Well, you three seem to have found some trouble," the man said in a tired voice, both distant and familiar.

Kiran brushed dirt from her shirtfront and thighs as she rose. "You can say that again, mister..." she looked up into his face just as he raised his chin up to meet her gaze, and Kiran's words died on her lips as shock overrode her brain. She was staring directly into a startling pair of icy blue eyes. Although she had not seen those eyes in nearly two decades, she knew them well enough. He looked much as she remembered him, although he now had a scruff of pale blonde whiskers growing around his cheeks and chin, and the lines in his face were deeper and more plentiful. Beneath the piercing blue of his eyes, there were smudged, dark hollows. Gart looked as quick and wiry as ever, but his posture slumped enough to betray his exhaustion. He was tired, bone tired. That much was obvious.

Gart sighed. His voice was calm and quiet. "Good to see you, Kiran. I certainly didn't expect to find my fellow Guardians here." His eyes narrowed a touch, just enough that Kiran felt her stomach go cold. "So then…why might the three of you be here, of all places?"

Kiran did not answer right away, and that hesitation cost her.

Gart nodded wearily. "I thought so. I'm sorry about this. I truly am." His cobalt eyes flashed gold as he called on his magick again.

Kiran drew in a breath to protest, but never got to speak the words.

Chapter 2

Reyanna opened her eyes and stared at the plank ceiling overhead. The smell of charred wood and smoke was irritating her throat, and she took a hitching breath as she sat up. She coughed until she felt better, then she looked around the unfamiliar room, trying to remember why she was there. A brief chill raised gooseflesh on her bare shoulders, and she realized that she was naked, save for the blanket and sheets. The window nearby showed that the sky was still dark, dawn yet an hour away. Rain pattered soothingly against the walls and roof of the inn. The room was dimly lit by a lantern that sat on the nearby desk, and her pack sat next to it, looking somewhat rumpled. The room resembled the one she had slept in, but was not the same.

"Begging your pardon, ma'am," a rumbling male voice spoke up from the darkness of a far corner.

Reyanna gasped in surprise. "Who are you? Where am I?" She saw her dagger on the desk next to her pack, and she leaped for it, suddenly not caring in the least about her nudity. She snatched it up and turned in a fighting crouch, looking for a way out.

From the shadows, Geoff's voice was startled. "Whoa, whoa, easy now, miss Reyna!" He eased into the lamplight, palms raised to show he had no weapon. "I wouldn't hurt you, no ma'am. I'm hoping you'll return the favor, what with all you already did to our inn last night."

Reyanna frowned, still holding the dagger in a fighting stance. "What do you mean? How did I get in here? This is not the room I went to sleep in."

Keeping his hands where Reyanna could see them, Geoff slowly pulled the chair from the corner, turned it so that the back faced the girl and sat heavily in it, his arms draped tiredly over the chair's back. He was exhausted from working half the night to get a covering on the damaged roof so that the rain would not come in and ruin everything. He groaned in relief as he settled his weight onto the wooden seat. "No, it ain't. You pretty much destroyed your own room with fire and then tried to kill my sons as well.

12

We would ordinarily be quite put out by such a thing, but well, we were just so surprised by it all that we decided you might have an explanation. You seem a nice enough young woman. Why would you do that to our place? To us?" As he spoke, a stern glint came into his eye. Geoff was a kind man, but he wanted some answers.

Reyanna was shocked into silence for a moment. "I..." she stammered. "I did *what?*"

"Tried to burn us out," Geoff replied without hesitation. "And then tried to throw fire at my boys when they came to help." His brow wrinkled in thought for a moment before he continued. "They said they heard you scream, so they went to see what was wrong. To help you," he emphasized. "For their trouble, they nearly got cooked like roast boars." He took a deep breath to calm himself before continuing. "You came floating out of that burning room, all aglow with some kind of flaming magick holding you up. I've never seen anything like it. You were glowing and your eyes were full of fire. You had this smile that was frightening to see, lass. You nearly killed us all, but for some reason, you didn't; you held back. Then you passed out right there in the hallway, and all the fire went away. *Poof!*" Geoff gestured at the sound. "It was all gone. Fortunately, the damage wasn't nearly as bad as I feared, though my sons are more than a little nervous to be in here with ye." Geoff leaned forward and shook his head gently. "Truth be told, I'm a lot nervous to be in here with ye, but...are ye all right, girl?"

Tears had begun to run down Reyanna's face at Geoff's words. She had nearly killed innocent people. They had only been trying to help, and if what Geoff said was true, she had attacked them and nearly burned down their inn. Suddenly, a hazy memory surfaced and she gasped. "That woman! She tried to kill me!"

Geoff frowned defensively. "What woman? Vania? Nay, lass, she only sat with ye afterwards. She took care of ye!"

Frustrated, Reyanna finally lowered the dagger. "No, kind sir, I'm sure that your wife was exactly as you say, though I can't remember that part at all. There was another woman; tall, with red hair and pale skin. Green eyes. I..."

she struggled to remember. "Yes, I woke, and she was in my room with me. She's the one who tried to kill me! With my own dagger, no less!" She gestured with the blade, then resheathed it and placed it back on the desk with a sigh.

Geoff's voice betrayed his doubt. "There was no one like that at the inn tonight, not that any of us saw. And Baylen was dozing in the common room downstairs at the time. No one could have come in either door without him hearing them. We saw no one like that come out of your room either." His face clenched as though it pained him to speak further. "There was only you."

Reyanna turned away from him and put both hands on the desk, unmindful of the view she was presenting. She was confused and angry. She *knew* that someone had been in her room, just as sure as she knew that the sky was blue. She would never forget that lovely, yet hateful face. What was more troubling was the fact that she could not remember what happened next. Reyanna suddenly knew that she had to get away from Geoff and his family as quickly as possible, lest something else happen.

"Um," Geoff cleared his throat. "Would you mind if I got you some clothes? If Vania comes in here and sees me staring at your bare behind, she'll whip mine, no doubt."

Reyanna blinked for a moment and looked down at herself, suddenly remembering that she was still unclothed. In spite of it all, she laughed even as her tears were still drying on her face. She whipped the blanket from the bed and wrapped it around her shoulders, covering herself. "Geoff, I can't tell you how sorry I am about all of this. I would be much obliged if you could find me something suitable to wear so that I don't get you in trouble, and so that I can be on my way as soon as possible. I don't want to bring any more trouble to you or your family." She leaned over to rummage in her pack and found the hidden pocket within where she kept most of her coin. She produced four gold pieces and tossed them to Geoff, who caught them and held them up for inspection, staring at them in awe as they gleamed in the firelight. "I cannot possibly take back what I did. I don't remember it at all, and I wish I could. You have treated me much more kindly than most would have. I never meant to harm anyone, I hope you believe that. I hope the gold will at least help you rebuild."

Geoff pocketed the gold with a decidedly happier look on his face. "Milady, it most definitely will. I'll go get you some clothes!" He bolted from the room, barely taking the time to shut the door behind him.

Although deeply worried, Reyanna could not help but smile at the man's eagerness. She sighed, then rummaged in her pack and pulled out the map she had been given back in Allinshae. Although the pack had gotten wet, its oiled surface had kept most of the water away from the contents, and the map was not even smudged. She spread it carefully out on the desk and tried to pinpoint her position.

"It looks like another three weeks," she guessed, calculating the distance to the mountain range Teryn had indicated. Then she amended her estimate, "More like half that on Drusilla." She rolled the map again and secured it in her pack just as a knock sounded on the door. Reyanna turned away from the desk just as Vania entered the room.

"I've brought you these things, dear," Vania said. She was nervous, but polite as she handed over a small pile of clothing. "The trousers are Baylen's from when he was younger, but I think they will be a good fit. You weren't wearing a dress when you came, and mine won't fit you, I daresay."

Reyanna took the clothes and set them on the bed. She folded the blanket and laid it carefully aside, then began to dress herself. "I'm so sorry, Vania," she began.

Vania shushed her. "No need, girl. My Geoff told me what you said. I don't know what happened to you, but I watched you sleep afterwards and I can see you now. There's no evil in you. I can't say I know what happened to turn you into that...fiery thing," Vania shuddered. "But in my heart, I know you mean no harm."

Tears were in Reyanna's eyes as she adjusted the belt she had been given.

Vania continued, "I hope you don't mind my saying, though, that I'd prefer it if you 'meant no harm' somewhere else. Far away from here, if possible."

15

Reyanna gawked at Vania for a moment and then the two women burst out laughing and fell into a hug. "I'll do that, Vania. Far, far away."

Chapter 3

Nessar rolled over with a groan and found himself face-down in the dirt. His head was aching as though it would burst open at any moment. He slowly pushed himself up to his knees and then sat back on his heels, squeezing his eyes shut against the fading light. A few deep breaths later, the pain finally started to ebb, and he looked around. Layton and Kiran lay on their backs nearby. They were silent and unmoving.

Nessar lurched to his feet and rushed to Kiran's side. He fell clumsily to his knees and shook her as gently as his fear allowed. "Kiran! Baby girl, can you hear me? Wake up! No time for sleeping!"

Just then she grunted and sat up, wincing in pain. "Ow. I'm fine, you old coot. Just...give me a moment to catch my...my breath." She pressed a palm to her forehead. "Goddess, that aches something awful."

Nessar sighed with relief. "Thank Rowann. I thought for a minute there that you'd been...never mind. What happened? We were climbing for our lives and then something grabbed us and we floated up here. I landed hard enough to knock the sense out of my head," he said, somewhat sheepishly, "but I thought I heard you talking with someone. Then the lights went out till just now."

Kiran cast a sideways glance at her old friend. "Right. That was Gart."

"Gart? He was here?"

"Yes, and yes." Kiran got to her knees and crawled to where Layton still lay unconscious. She touched her fingers to his neck and was reassured to find his pulse steady and strong. "He must have knocked us all out somehow. I didn't even have a chance to put up a Ward, nothing. One second we were talking, and then I woke up to your wrinkly face. I don't even know how he did it." She shook her head in wonder. "He must have been after the same thing we were." At the thought of the Heart, she whirled on Nessar. "Cripes! Do you still have it?"

Nessar slapped his hands to his chest, only to find that he was no longer wearing his backpack. He whipped his

17

head around and spotted it lying on the ground a few yards away. He groaned. It looked flatter than it should have. He crawled over to it and thrust a hand inside to rummage for the Heart.

"Nope," he sighed. "Gart must have taken it with him. Blast!" Nessar threw the backpack down in disgust and sat on the ground, wrapping his arms around his knees. "Well, at least he saved us from that overgrown lizard-thing down there. Nice of him, really."

Kiran got to her feet and eased over to the rim of the massive hole. She looked down at the ruined city below and carefully pulled herself back from the brink before speaking. "He didn't kill it, I don't think. I see some black stuff that could be blood down there, and a lot more damage than we could have done, but it must have crawled back into the cavern."

Nessar barked a curt laugh. "Well it can stay there. I'm quite happy up here, thank you very much. Now we've got to figure out where Gart's headed. We have to find a way to stop him."

"If he sees us coming, I don't know what we can do. He laid us all out with a thought. He wouldn't even let me try to talk to him." Kiran said sadly. She and Gart had never been terribly close, but she had considered him a friend over the years. She folded her arms and frowned, thinking. She nodded at Layton. "If wonder-boy there would come back to himself, we might be able to surprise Gart. Maybe use his Gates to appear behind him and clout him in the head or something. Even that would be risky, but if Gart's strong enough to knock us unconscious like that, we may have to do it from as far away as possible."

"Right, right," Nessar reluctantly agreed. He had spent the most time with Gart over the years. He was angry and hurt that Gart had made choices which made it necessary for them to consider doing him harm. Even so, Nessar knew the risk to the world was too great if Gart made a mistake during the ritual. They had to do something. "Let's see if we can rouse Layton. Whether he's back to normal or not, I'd just as soon not have to carry him to his horse. We need to get moving."

"To where?" Kiran said as she walked over to Layton and knelt down beside him. "Do you know where he's headed? Nimshi?"

Nessar pulled his journal out of his backpack and thumbed through it. He was silent for a time, then replied without looking away from his book. "Actually, no. We should head for this Shrine. That's where he's going to have to end up to cast the spell."

"Why not try to head him off at Nimshi? Keep him from getting that other stuff, the Blood?"

"Three reasons: one, we don't know if he's already been there. If he's already found the Blood, then he'll be on his way to the Shrine for sure now that he's got the Heart as well. If not, then we'll be able to wait around for him and think of a better plan to stop him. We can't take the chance that we'll miss him by going somewhere he's already been."

Kiran grunted in agreement. "Mmhmm. You're right on that one. Heavens forbid that the world go to Hel in a handbasket while we're bumbling around Nimshi when he's already come and gone."

Nessar counted on his fingers. "Secondly, the eclipse is approaching. If he went straight to Nimshi when he left Guardians Keep, then came here afterward, that makes more sense.

Kiran nodded. "True, true. What's the third reason?"

Nessar grinned. "It's closer."

Kiran chuckled. "I can't argue with that kind of logic, old man. Let's see if we can rouse Layton. I hope to Rowann that he's back to his old self, or it'll be a race to see if we can catch Gart before he reaches the Shrine." She leaned over Layton and gently slapped his cheeks. "Hey. Are you in there? Wake up."

Layton's eyelids fluttered and opened. He looked up at Kiran for a few seconds without comment.

"Remember me? It's Kiran, your old sparring buddy. Are you in there yet, Layton?"

Layton squeezed his eyes shut and opened them again as he tried to focus. He gazed into Kiran's pale green eyes and saw her brows furrow with concern, then looked past her into a sky slowly purpling into twilight. His head ached fiercely. Finally, he spoke. "We're not in the museum."

"Correct."

"We're in the forest above the city?"

"Also correct."

"How did we get here?"

"It's a long story. And you were no help at all, you bum."

Layton frowned and sat up. "I didn't just Gate us here? What happened? Is everyone all right?"

Kiran sighed and threw her head back for a moment, relishing the sense of relief that washed over her. "Thank Rowann." Then she looked back at Layton and patted him soundly on the shoulder. "We'll explain on the way. Come on, we've got to try to get to the Shrine before Gart does." She stood and brushed the dirt off her clothes briefly before continuing. "Glad to have you back, man." Her words were curt, but Layton felt the warmth behind them. She was glad he was unharmed, and that reassured him somewhat.

Nessar's gravelly voice called out. "If you would be so kind to get us back to our horses, Layton, that would be just peachy. We've got ground to cover, lad, hop to it!"

Layton got to his feet and prepared to engage the power of his Jidaan. He still had no idea what had happened, and his head was aching dreadfully, but otherwise, he felt whole. The last thing he recalled was killing three awful-looking creatures outside the museum down below. To himself, he muttered, "Well, at least we didn't run into too much trouble down there." Layton engaged his Gift, then created the portal that would take them back up to the ridge where their horses awaited.

Chapter 4

Melidia slapped the serving girl across the face. Blood spattered onto the stone floor, blending with the steaming tomato soup the girl had brought on a tray. She fell to her knees, badly bruising them before landing painfully on one shoulder. She cowered, holding her shattered face and crying through bloody fingers as she held her broken nose.

"Get out!" Melidia screamed, enraged. She had come from her scrying room and was not happy with what she had seen. Not happy at all. "You clumsy cow! Get down to the kitchens and get me some beef and wine, not that filthy slop!" Although completely enraged, Melidia gained a slight sense of satisfaction at the sound of the girl's nose breaking, and the sight of her crawling in terror and pain on the floor did lift her mood.

Tears and blood ran down the girl's face, but she pulled herself together as best she could. "Yes, M-mistress!" she stuttered as she gathered the broken pieces of the bowl and other debris, loaded them on the tray and scuttled out of Melidia's bed chamber as quickly as she could manage.

Still furious, Melidia grabbed a vase from a nearby end table, and threw it at the door as it closed behind the girl. It shattered with a satisfying crash, spraying shards everywhere. Whirling, the sorceress turned and stalked towards the window. She placed her smooth palms on the rough stone and leaned out into the night. The stars above looked like diamonds laid out on black silk. She had always loved the night. The best things always happened under cover of darkness. The cool air washed over her exposed neck and chest, calming her at last.

She had known that the young woman was important somehow; she had been appearing in her scrying visions for months. What Melidia had not foreseen was the enormous power that resided within the girl. Indeed, she doubted that the girl, herself, even understood what she was capable of. The burst of magick she had manifested should not have been able to hurt Melidia, as her presence there was mostly a spirit-shadow. However, Melidia had sent enough of herself through the magickal link to be able to hold a dagger, and Reyanna's magick was of a magnitude Melidia had never seen before. Had she not severed the connection the instant that Reyanna's power had flared, she could have been irreparably damaged, maybe even killed. As it was, the skin on Melidia's right hand, the one that had held the dagger, was still aching deeply. She shuddered to think what might have happened to her had she physically been there and tried to kill Reyanna in person.

Get a grip, she thought to herself. *This can be salvaged. If I can't stop the girl, then I can still send Arkhan and Barovius through a portal to intercept Gart before she finds him. Surely they can take him this time; he doesn't even have his Jidaan! I've got to get the Blood from him before he uses it in that infernal ceremony to call that woman of his. If he burns it all up, I can't use it to aid Balroth, and there's no way I'm passing up this chance!*

Melidia closed her eyes and calmed herself further by imagining what it would be like to rule the world at the right hand of a Daemon-God. She would be his! And would speak with his voice. The entire world would bow to Balroth, and as such, to her as well.

Those overgrown monkeys thought they could kill him...bah! They only destroyed his physical form! She laughed at the Augenan, the primitive but powerful ape people from the jungles of Triagga. They had struck the final blow with the Tugan, an enormous battle-axe forged in ancient times from material that had come from a falling star. When Mordak had fallen at Alverton Falls, his death had unleashed a torrent of Balroth's energy on Talwynn, giving the Daemon-God the foothold he needed to create a tunnel between worlds. When he had stepped through, all of Talwynn had quivered in fear. Melidia shuddered, remembering the exquisite moment Balroth broached the barrier and manifested his physical form, towering over all, his head in the clouds. It had not lasted long, though. One of the damnable apes had flung the axe through the air, and the token of power had struck true. Upon slamming into Balroth's forehead, his entire physical body had disintegrated.

At the time, she had thought him dead. She had collapsed and wept openly on the floor of her scrying chamber, despondent in her loss. She raged against Brunar and the Guardians, and against the Weya, too, for taking part in the conflict. The Augenan, as well, were responsible, and would one day feel her wrath. At that moment, though, it had felt like her very soul had been scoured from her body with the loss of her Daemon-God.

In spite of her pain, Melidia had eventually picked up the pieces and carried on. There were plenty of petty intrigues and dalliances to fill her time, and she flung herself into them. Her nights were filled with the cries of those whom she used for her vile experiments and rituals of dark magick. None of it was ever enough, but for a time, such things sufficed.

Years had passed, and one night, she had fallen into her bed, too tired even to wash the blood of her latest diversion from her hands. She drifted into a fitful doze, a place of welcome nightmares. That was when she heard the voice. *His* voice. A faint but unmistakable whisper in the night. At first, it was the barest hint of him, just a vague sense of his remembered presence, floating through her subconscious. In time, the voice had gained strength. His presence had become more tangible, more *real* in the world of her dreams. Finally, he appeared to her, and although he was still a shadowy version of what she had known before, it was undeniably Balroth. He spoke to her, explaining that although his physical body had perished, his essence had been drawn instantly back through the corridor, back to his former prison world. She rejoiced, ecstatic to find that her love and master had survived. In turn, he made wild promises, seductive insinuations, and began once again to guide her steps. She was beside herself with the knowledge that he had not perished at Alverton Falls. Not only that, he needed her help. Mordak had failed, he said, and only she had the power to make things right.

Melidia took another deep breath, then turned away from the window. She went back into her casting room and closed the door. In one corner, she had erected a tall folding screen to obscure the item she had placed there. Now she moved the screen aside and gazed upon her prize.

Standing as still as a statue, his body covered in a faint scarlet glow, was a man. He wore only a light pair of breeches, leaving his upper torso naked. He was a magnificent specimen, well over six feet in height, weighing close to three hundred pounds of sculpted muscle. His jaw was strong and square, and his long blonde hair was braided into a single plait that hung over one shoulder to drape down over his thick chest. Melidia gazed lovingly at the silent, unmoving figure and slowly traced one delicate finger along the line of his jaw, then down his neck, along his shoulder and down along the swells of muscle in his arm. She found herself purring slightly as she did so. The body was perfect for Balroth; she knew he would approve. The mind inside the body was gone, long since ripped away by Melidia's foul arts, but the body was healthy and strong, a young warrior in his prime. It just needed a spirit, a consciousness, to animate it.

Once I have the Blood, I'll be able to bring Balroth into his new body. A smile finally appeared on her face. *I will be his bride, and together, we will rule everything!* For a time, she lost herself in blissful, ambitious daydreams as she gently caressed the body that would eventually belong to Balroth. Then she heard the daintiest of knocks on the door outside. The serving girl had returned. Melidia's stomach growled at the thought of food, and she sighed.

Arkhan and Barovius can intercept Gart before he reaches the Shrine, she thought. *He doesn't have the Jidaan anymore, so he's bound to be less dangerous. Together, they can subdue him and take the Blood. I'll find a way to deter the girl. I don't know why she has figured so prominently in my visions, but with that kind of power, she will have to be dealt with. I won't let some little girl, no matter how powerful, stand in my way!*

Melidia knew of something that might work against the girl. Everything pointed to the Poravian Mire; all of her visions were clear on that. Whatever else happened, all of her plans would come to fruition deep within the dark and swampy borders of the Mire. Dangers untold, both living and otherwise, awaited there, but she knew how to master them. Ancient Poravia had once been a paradise, but something had happened long ago to corrupt the land and every living thing in it. There were old and slumbering evils there, things that made even the strongest Mages think twice about entering. A chill ran up Melidia's spine as she realized that she had decided to awaken a nightmare.

Part of her recoiled from the idea, but the longer she thought about it, the more certain she became. It was dangerous, incredibly so. *Arkhan and Barovius won't approve, cowards that they are,* she thought, smirking at the idea that they had any say at all in the matter.

She stared at the still figure in the corner for a moment longer, her gaze lingering over his thick, brawny muscles. Then Melidia carefully replaced the screen and headed for the door. Her sly smile remained. In spite of the obstacles, she knew she would end up getting what she wanted, as always. The two lesser sorcerers, Barovius and Arkhan, were putty in her hands. They would serve their roles perfectly before she killed them both. Soon, the world, and everything in it, would be hers.

Chapter 5

Gart jerked awake just before he slid out of the saddle. Bessie snorted at him as if amused. Through the link he shared with Beauty, he sensed her concern even before her gentle whine reached his ears. "I'm ok, girl. I just..." he struggled with his words for a moment, still groggy. "I just nodded off there for a bit, that's all. I'm all right."

Beauty's *whuff* made it clear that she was not at all convinced, but she went back to watching the trail ahead and listening for interesting animals in the forest nearby.

Gart shook his head and lightly slapped his cheeks to wake himself up. He reached one hand behind his saddle to feel the reassuring lump made by the Heart of Corria in his bedroll. Finding it, he let himself relax slightly. The Blood, he knew, was still safe in its flask in his backpack. He had everything he needed to perform the ritual, if he could just stay awake long enough to escape the pursuit of the friends he had left unconscious at Corria. He had covered his tracks well, and the fact that his immediate destination lay in the opposite direction as his ultimate goal worked in his favor. Even if the others knew he was headed to the Poravian Mire in the west, they could not know that the portal Gart would use to get there was east of Corria.

He had been driving hard the last several days, and the constant stream of magick he had to maintain to keep Beauty alive was wearing on him. He needed sleep. *Can't afford it,* he answered himself. *Got to reach the portal as soon as I can.* He guided Bessie up a slight rise and pulled her to a halt. The trees had thinned as he slowly left the forest behind, and Gart turned to look at the distant peak that marked the location of the sunken city of Corria.

He had hated using his magick against his fellow Guardians, but there had been no alternative. He had temporarily cut off the blood flow to their brains as quickly and painlessly as possible, but that did not mean he enjoyed doing it. Remorse bloomed in him for a moment, making his heart ache.

Beauty *whuffed*, as if commenting on his thoughts. Gart sensed a definite feeling of disapproval from his companion and he frowned down at her where she walked alongside Bessie.

"Hey, you know I didn't want to hurt them. But they had something I needed, and I couldn't..." he trailed off as his thoughts jumbled momentarily. He shook his head again and continued. "I couldn't let them stop me. Understand? This is important. I have to see Gennie."

Beauty growled softly, then allowed the growl to turn into a massive yawn. She did not fully understand why Gart needed to do what he was doing, only that he felt strongly about it. She sensed his unease, though, his inner conflict over hurting his friends. That bothered her, and she was not afraid to express it. She growled again and barked quietly, just once, to let him know of her concern for him.

Gart read her mind through the link of his magick, and sighed. "I know you're worried about me, but this is just something I have to do. Understand?"

Beauty ignored him. She was so closely connected through his magick, she could feel quite clearly that something was amiss in Gart. She could not identify it, so for now, she would simply carry on. She loved him dearly, but much of what went on in his mind was a mystery to her. She only knew that she would protect him at all costs, no matter how strange his thoughts might be to her.

All of this, Gart perceived as a muddle of emotions and faint visions, and he sighed again. Her simple, pure love of him was humbling. He turned his eyes back to the east. The land rolled gently, covered with grass and trees too sparse to be called a forest, and in the distance he could see the terrain become more rocky and jagged. Although he was already tired, he reached out with his magick, searching for a particular landmark. It took him only moments to find the tall cluster of rocks that hid the ancient portal he needed. His research had been very clear on its location, and if it still functioned properly, it would transport him to within a few days ride of his final destination. The network of portals functioned very similar to the magick of Layton's gift of Gates, but these portals were fixed, and they covered much greater distances than Layton had ever been able to traverse. Spanning the breadth of a continent could be as easy as walking into one door and out of another. The ones he had used already had been relatively simple and quick, but there was always a chance something might go wrong. The scrolls had been unclear on a few things regarding the next passage.

The portals had lain mostly forgotten, scattered across the face of Talwynn in hidden coves, secluded grottos, and even a few in underground caverns. Some had been destroyed over the centuries, but Gart had only needed a few of them to work. It had only taken him three months to figure out how to pronounce the invoking words properly, but now, he could travel across the Realm almost at will, depending on how far from a portal he found himself. It would take him well into the night to reach the next portal his magick had revealed, and he would be exhausted by then, but he knew he had no choice.

He urged Bessie down the far slope and mentally called Beauty to come along. She trotted ahead, giving Bessie plenty of room to navigate the incline, and Gart's heart gave a little lurch as he watched the massive dog run. She got to the bottom and turned in a circle, throwing a happy bark back up at them. He loved seeing her like that. She felt his approval and burst into a run, enjoying the feeling of moving her muscles, the air in her face, the pure joy of being alive.

And through the link of his magick, Gart felt it too. He hoped he could find a way to heal Beauty completely. *After I see Gennie*, he added. *Yes, after I see Gennie, I'll take Beauty somewhere to heal her. She'll be fine.*

Thunder rumbled in the distance, but Gart did not notice.

Chapter 6

Reyanna wiped her tears on the sleeve of her borrowed shirt. Vania finished wrapping a bundle of food in a cloth and tied it tightly. "Take this with you," she said. "The gold you left will more than pay for it." The older woman handed it to her, and Reyanna took it gratefully.

"Thank you," she said, sniffling. "Again, I'm so sorry about all this. I don't know exactly what happened."

Vania raised an eyebrow. "You'll want to see someone about that, then. The Priestesses of Rowann, maybe? They know the ways of magick, then, don't they?" Vania wiped her hands on her apron, more out of nervous habit than because anything was on them. "If I were known to catch fire while I was sleeping and turn into some kind of..." she waved her hands in the air, "whatever that was you turned into, then I'd definitely want to figure out how to control it." Vania sighed, then sat down heavily on one of the kitchen stools. She suddenly looked left, then right, as if making sure no one was nearby. Then she leaned toward Reyanna and whispered. "My grandmother had the magick, too, she did!"

Reyanna's eyes widened in surprise. "Really?" she said, only to be shushed immediately by Vania. Reyanna lowered her voice and repeated, "Really? How so?"

A mischievous gleam appeared in Vania's eye as she spoke, and Reyanna could see a hint of the little girl Vania must have once been. Her whisper was tight, but excited. "Why, she saw things before they happened. She always knew when people were coming to visit. And she could move things without touching them, but that left her very tired. The most wonderful thing, though, was that she could talk to me without ever opening her mouth. I could hear her words in my head, and she could hear mine. It was something only we could do together, and I loved it!" Vania's eyes shone as she thought of her dear grandmother.

Reyanna's brow furrowed for a moment, and then she looked up at Vania. *Was it like this?*

Vania's eyes flew wide and she gasped in surprise. "Yes! It was just like that!" Her hand fluttered to her neck as she recovered from the shock of hearing Reyanna's voice in her mind, clear as a bell and twice as loud. "Oh, my stars, you gave me a fright. That was so much louder than Gramma!" Then she laughed. "I should be frightened of a girl who turns herself into a fire-daemon, but my Goddess, you remind me of her, of my grandmother. You don't look anything alike, not a bit, but..." she trailed off, searching for words. "You feel like she did. When I sat next to her, it felt like heat coming off a stove, but it didn't hurt. But you're much, much stronger. Does that make sense?"

Reyanna finished lacing up her backpack. "It does, I think. And I agree with you. I'll seek out someone who can help me. I don't want anyone else hurt because of me." She kept her eyes focused on her pack so that Vania would not see the fresh tears that she was holding back. "There's something I have to do first, but then I'll go straightaway." She sniffed again and then gave Vania a huge hug. "Thank you for understanding, Vania. Say goodbye to Geoff and the boys for me. I need to go as quickly as possible." She thrust her arms through her pack and walked towards the door.

Vania got up and followed after her. "Are you sure there's nothing else you need? I can ask Geoff to help you."

Reyanna pushed through the kitchen door and walked through the common room of the inn. A number of dirty, tired men were there, resting while others worked on the damage upstairs. Geoff and his sons were nowhere to be seen, but Geoff's voice echoed down the hall where he directed workers who were helping to repair the damage she had done. She felt her cheeks flush with shame at the thought. All eyes turned towards her and a hush fell on the room. Stories had been told and opinions shared, not all of them correct or favorable toward Reyanna. She felt a swell of emotion from the men gathered there as something dangerous began to form. One of them, a dark-eyed, burly fellow with a long beard pushed his chair back with a loud scraping noise and stood up. His eyes locked on hers and did not look away.

Vania came through the door just behind Reyanna and immediately felt the atmosphere in the room. She saw the big lout standing there, murder in his eyes as he stared at Reyanna, and she called out, "Hey there, Rupert, leave off! She meant no harm! Leave her be!"

Reyanna headed for the front door, but another man stood up and stepped in front of it, barring her way. She stopped in her tracks. Rupert's voice was clear in the still of the room. "She's a daemon," he stated simply, his intense gaze never leaving Reyanna. A mumble of agreement rose from the other men in the room, all of whom had seen the damage she had done. They'd had ample time to build her up in their minds, and now they saw her as an evil sorceress at best, surely up to no good. "Can't have the likes of her around here." He drew a giant knife from his belt as he started to make his way towards her. Others stood and drew their own weapons, mostly hammers and tools they had brought to help rebuild the inn.

"Here now, you all sit back down! She's a nice girl, didn't mean nothing!" Vania tried desperately to calm them, but the men had their blood up and they ignored her. "Geoff! Geoff! Come help!"

Reyanna glanced at the approaching mob for only a moment, then focused her attention on the man at the door. He was a grim-faced fellow with missing teeth and the heavily-muscled arms of a blacksmith. Reyanna took a deep breath, let most of it out, then stepped forward and efficiently kicked the man squarely in the crotch. His eyes widened in surprise and pain, and his knees buckled, no longer willing to support him. Reyanna reached out and grabbed one of his thick-fingered hands, stepped close to him and whirled like a dancer, viciously twisting the man's wrist. Using his own weight to her advantage, she threw the groaning man directly into the nearest group of oncoming thugs, knocking three of them down and giving her a bit of breathing room. Before the men had come to rest on the hardwood floor, Reyanna burst through the door and out into the street beyond.

Rupert made his way through the men, not bothering to look where he placed his big boots, and kicked open the door to the inn. Still ignoring Vania's pleas, he stepped outside into the faint light of dawn, the other men close behind him. The rain had stopped and the sun was peeking through the clouds in the east, a beautiful sunrise of purple, pink, and orange. Rupert spotted the girl running across the empty field towards the trees to the west. She was fast, but she'd never make the trees if Rupert had anything to say about it. He just needed to be close enough to throw his knife.

"Daemon-witch!" Rupert screamed, and the cry was taken up by many of those behind him. He broke into a run, determined to catch her and make her pay for what she had done. The crowd of men came rushing across the field, yelling war cries all the while.

Reyanna ran until she was almost to the forest, but then she slowed to a stop just short of the trees and turned to face the oncoming mob. She stood there quietly with her hands at her sides, waiting. There was no fear on her face, only sadness.

The men came on, howling in rage, makeshift weapons raised high. Their eyes were wide with excitement and anger, and all of them were intent on catching up with the young woman, catching her and making her pay. Rupert shifted his grip on his knife, preparing to throw it.

Up above Reyanna, the leafy canopy suddenly erupted as Drusilla burst through the branches above Reyanna's position. Lightning-quick, the enormous beast crawled down the thick tree trunks, then covered the distance between the forest and Reyanna in the blink of an eye. The spider then reared up behind the woman, showing off her long fangs and spreading the first two pairs of legs wide. The spider hissed loudly, a sound Reyanna did not even know Drusilla could make.

The angry mob skidded to a halt in the field. To a man, their faces filled with shock and fear, their fury fading away into nothingness at the sight of the enormous spider. Reyanna's voice drifted across the clearing, loud and strong in spite of the tears she was holding back.

"I'm sorry!" she said. "I meant no harm! I've left enough gold to pay for all the damages, and I'm leaving right now. You won't see me again. Don't try to follow me, though," her voice turned to steel. "I'm no daemon-witch, but I can defend myself. I don't want trouble, and neither does my friend here." Reyanna had coiled up her rage and sadness and then imagined it flowing down through the ground and out towards the now-terrified men. The resulting tremor was more than she had expected, and the earth trembled hard enough that many of the men staggered, trying to stay on their feet. "Now, go!" and she abruptly stepped forward, aggressively pointing towards the inn.

They fled. Rupert clawed and elbowed his way into the lead and Reyanna saw him disappear into the inn before any of the others. His knife lay forgotten, gleaming in the damp grass of the field. In spite of her anger and frustration, she managed a weak laugh.

"Thanks, Drusilla," she said as she turned to mount the big spider. "You showed up in the nick of time. Those men weren't nearly as understanding as Vania and Geoff were. And I don't know that whatever happened in there wouldn't happen again if they attacked me."

Drusilla sent her back a vague feeling of reassurance as she lowered her bulky body down to the ground. Reyanna slipped one foot in the stirrup and hoisted herself up into the saddle. She took a moment to be sure she was buckled in and seated properly before telling Drusilla she was ready. Instantly, the huge spider spun and raced back up the tree trunks to climb on top of the thick canopy of leaves, out of sight of anyone who might be traveling in the woods below. Reyanna settled into the odd rhythm of the spider's gait and tried to enjoy the cool dawn air.

She wondered what it all meant. Her heart was heavy at the thought of all she faced, and she still had so little idea of what was going on. The vision, the man-wolf attack, the way her magick seemed to be growing within her and even taking control at times. It was enough to make her head spin. All she had ever wanted was to fit in with the Weya Rangers, to live her life tending the forest and keeping the peace. Now, it appeared that destiny held something much greater in store for her.

A rueful smile crossed her face. *Whether I like it or not, it seems.*

Chapter 7

"How long do you think it'll take us to get there?" Kiran asked. The three of them had been riding for two days, using Layton's Gates to leapfrog across the land wherever possible. The forests had made it more difficult for Layton to find a safe place for them to emerge, so they had to ride on until a better situation presented itself. The trees surrounded them on all sides, majestic and towering sentinels that had always soothed Kiran, but made Nessar nervous. Born and bred in the city of Rualtha, he had never been comfortable in the deep woods.

"It depends on how often Layton can move us forward," Nessar replied, reading from his notebook as he rode. "If the rest of the way is heavily forested like this, then it'll take us at least another week. Any chance we can speed that up, we should take it."

"I'm sorry I can't be more help," Layton offered. "I can make a lot better time on flat ground, but the trees make it too dangerous."

Kiran laughed. "Hey, I'm just glad you're back with us at all." Genuine relief was evident in her voice, but she quickly needled him again. "Although, you seem to be slacking off lately. I mean, we should practically be there already!"

Layton chuckled. He knew Kiran's heart better than he ever let on, and it touched him to know that she had been so concerned for him. Not that he'd let her know that. "I know, I get one little head injury, and I'm suddenly loafing on the job. I'll try to carry my weight from here on out."

"That's what I like to hear!" Kiran's grin widened. "Finally, a little enthusiasm!"

Kiran cast a sideways glance at her old friend. As one of the only two Guardians who had been in a fighting profession at the time of their Choosing so many years ago, she had at first seen Layton as a rival. As soon as she heard his name, she recognized his reputation as the Weaponsmaster, and had immediately gone on the defensive. Although his skills were, indeed, legendary, he harbored no arrogance whatsoever, a fact which actually had galled her even more. He had been a quiet, enthusiastic, supportive, and kindhearted person, which was intensely frustrating as she strove to not like him.

In time, she had gotten over her initial insecurities and they had become close friends during the war with Mordak. Adventures afterwards had cemented their friendship, and as much as it pained her to admit it, Kiran had been heartbroken that Layton's injury might have stolen his memories and even his entire identity. She might have admitted the depth of her feelings under extreme torture, but a simple admission of gladness would have to suffice in the meantime.

They emerged at last from the forest onto a hard-packed dirt road. "Aha!" Nessar exclaimed. "If I read this map correctly, this road will lead us to a river that will help us make a lot better time. Especially if Layton can't be bothered to Gate us any faster than this." He ignored Layton's protests and continued, "If we can find a boat, that is."

"Boat or no," Layton suggested, "I can move us faster along the banks of the river by line of sight as long as there's room between the water and the tree line. It will definitely be easier than the forest we've just been through."

Kiran turned her horse and urged it into a westward trot. "That's good news, then. Let's get moving, I want to make as much progress as we can while the day is young." Nessar and Layton followed suit, gently kicking their heels into their horses' flanks and guiding them to catch up to Kiran.

Barely a quarter of an hour later, Layton commented, "I hear the water. We must be close."

Nessar looked up from his notebook and finally tucked it away in a saddlebag as he, too, noticed the distant sound of rushing water. "Well, let's get on with it. Gart already has a decent head start on us, and the sooner we can be on our way, the better." He reached down to touch his Jidaan, which he had rolled up in a cloth and lashed alongside his saddle. He preferred not to wear it on his back if he could avoid it, only because he felt it brought

35

attention. Of course, Kiran and Layton wore their Jidaan openly, but then they also knew how to fight with them. Although Nessar had been trained to use the weapon, his skills lay elsewhere.

The trio followed the tree-lined road until it curved to their right. The trees then opened up to reveal three small wooden buildings that lay between them and the rain-swollen river. The river hurtled past, bearing an occasional log or tree branch in its current. It was far too wide to cross without a boat, though Layton could Gate them all easily to the other side. A small barge and two smaller boats were pulled up on the rocky shore on the near side. The remains of a bridge foundation could be seen on either bank, the pilings partially swallowed by the rapidly flowing water.

Nessar whistled as he caught sight of the river. "Goddess, it's moving along, isn't it? I'm glad we won't have to swim that."

A rough voice answered him from behind. "You might just have to, old man. If you don't have the toll, I mean."

Kiran cursed under her breath and their heads turned to see that a half-dozen rough-looking men, armed to the teeth, had emerged from the trees behind them. One man whistled sharply, and another six men emerged from the larger of the three buildings, arrows already drawn in their longbows and aimed at the riders. They moved to surround the three Guardians, encircling them in moments.

Slowly, Kiran shook her head, suddenly feeling all of her forty-ish years. "We don't need this right now," she muttered under her breath. "I mean, I love a little exercise and a good scrap the same as anyone, but I'd happily pass on it just this once."

It was a dark-haired man who had whistled, standing just ahead of his peers. A shapeless brown highland hat covered most of his head, and a long mustache drooped on either side of a gap-toothed grin. He leered at Kiran and spat a wad of phlegm to one side. A broad-shouldered fellow, he wore a soiled shirt with the sleeves rolled up past his corded forearms, and a pair of trousers patched at both knees were tucked into a pair of worn boots. A broad-bladed knife was thrust into his belt, and he casually rested a hand on it, making sure it could be seen. "Whatcha say there, girlie?"

Easy, Kiran, Layton's voice sounded in Kiran's mind before she could respond in her usual inflammatory fashion. However, rather than comfort her, Layton's comment actually concerned her more than the armed men. It wasn't his words that stopped Kiran's customary outburst, it was the feeling mixed in with the words: Layton was angry. That surprised her. Layton never got angry. Ever. He fought in a dreamy world of calm, having mastered his emotions decades ago under the brutal tutelage of several Eastern masters. The discipline he had learned there was a part of him, just like his hands or his feet.

Don't worry, she replied firmly. *I'm good. Let's just get through this as easily as possible. We have bigger fish to fry. If need be, you can have us across the river before they could blink anyway, and their arrows couldn't breach my Wards on their best day.* His wordless reply was affirmative, and although still tinged with anger, Kiran could feel his usual calm returning. Relieved, she addressed the ruffian again, raising her voice so she could be heard over the rushing of the river. "I was asking if there's a boat that we could hire out?"

The man's eyebrows rose and his grin widened. "Well, well, lads! They want to hire a boat! That must mean they have gold on 'em!" To the Guardians, he said, "We'll happily take your money, but we'd just as soon not part with our boats. You'll end up down the river anyway, just not breathing!" A smattering of rough laughter assured the trio that these men had heard this play before and still found it amusing.

Kiran shook her head and turned her horse, moving it up between Layton and Nessar's mounts. The old man was eyeing the thugs warily. She could feel him gathering his energy for whatever might come. He was ready but not tense, as he had been taught to be.

"Is this the kind of thing you put in your stories, Vanessa Hills?" Kiran said, a sly grin on her face as she slowly reached back to loosen one of the straps that held her Jidaan in place.

37

Nessar shrugged and kept his voice low. "Maybe. Except there's more, um, dillydallying."

Just then, the gang leader spoke up, urgency in his voice rather than menace. "What's that? Vanessa Hills? Who said that?"

Kiran looked at him, suddenly perplexed. "I did. So what?"

The man's eyes widened and his mouth slowly dropped open. The men behind him started to whisper among themselves, but he turned and shushed them to silence. He looked Kiran up and down before he found his voice again. "Are you...Vanessa Hills?"

Kiran cast a quick glance at Nessar only to find that he was just as confused as she was. He answered her with a shrug, then she heard his voice in her mind. *Tell him yes!* She glared at him, but he grimaced at her and repeated himself. *Do it! Tell him you're Vanessa Hills!*

She sighed and turned her attention back to the man with the mustache, who was now looking at her with something akin to awe. "Maybe. Why do you want to know?"

The man gasped. "Sweet Goddess above! I'm so sorry, I had no idea! We never would have been so rude had we known it was you!" He turned to his men, who had started talking furiously amongst themselves. "It's her! The one that writes the stories that Old Lady Winifred reads us when she comes down the river!" Their angry muttering turned into an excited chatter as they looked on Kiran with new eyes. The leader turned back to face her, snatching off his shapeless hat to reveal a mostly bald head underneath. A huge grin showed even fewer teeth than before, and he crushed the hat nervously in his hands as he spoke. "I can read a little, but Winifred is better at doing the different voices. I-I'm Luther. It's such an honor to meet you! We're so sorry...please! Join us for a meal! Josuas is a fair cook, and you can tell us all about your next book!" He looked at the ground somewhat bashfully. "Ashes of Love is my favorite."

"Oi! Don't forget Thieves' Romance!" One of the men interjected.

"And Passion's Embrace!" A rousing cheer accompanied the mention of that particular tale and Luther's head started bobbing.

"Yes, yes! They're all wonderful! Please, I beg you, be our guests!" Luther crushed and recrushed his hat in his excitement, looking up at Kiran with adoration and then becoming embarrassed and looking away, then starting all over again. "And you can have any boat you want! The big one is called *Madalyn*!" He looked at her expectantly. Kiran just blinked at him like an owl.

She's the main character in 'The Captain and the Duchess,' Nessar explained, a hint of surprise and laughter bleeding into the words as they echoed in Kiran's mind. *Wow, that one wasn't even very popular.* He caught Kiran's eye and winked at her. *I guess he liked it though.* Kiran stared back at him, completely astonished. The old thief crossed his arms and allowed himself a gigantic smirk, thoroughly pleased with the turn of events. It had been a long time since he had seen Kiran rendered completely speechless.

Kiran turned back to the ruffian and found her voice at last. "Ah, yes. From the, ah, Captain and the Duchess...right."

Luther fairly burst with pleasure. "Exactly!"

Layton watched the exchange without saying a word, and his momentary anger slowly gave way to bewilderment. He looked from Nessar to Kiran to the gang of louts that now seemed far more likely to throw flowers at them than attack. Finally, he spoke through their mindspeech. *I'm sorry, but...what's all this? Who is Vanessa Hills? Would one of you tell me what's going on here?* Layton's voice was laden with confusion, and echoed urgently in Kiran and Nessar's minds. Both of them managed to keep a straight face, but just barely.

Kiran responded. *For now, just go with it. I write romance novels. But actually, they're Nessar's. He's Vanessa Hills. I mean I am. Oh, just hush up and let us do the talking!*

Layton looked at Kiran for a moment, then turned back to the excited, adoring group of men that were practically jumping up and down as they talked about their favorite Vanessa Hills stories. Layton shook his head slowly and thought to himself, *Romance novels? We've been saved by romance novels?*

Chapter 8

Melidia tried not to sneer openly as she watched Barovius enter the tent. He had rigged a makeshift leather sheath for Gart's Jidaan and strapped it to his back as the Guardians were wont to do. Unfortunately, he was thoroughly unused to the weapon, and it banged into everything as he passed by, no matter how he tried to arrange it. Finally, he sat down on one of the padded chairs that Melidia's servants had brought, muttering to himself all the while. Melidia had been concerned that Barovius would disappear with the Jidaan, leaving behind the promise of wealth and influence now that the weapon was his. Apparently, though, his inability to engage the Jidaan's power over the weather kept him focused on the original prize Melidia had promised. She smiled, thankful that the man's greed kept him in line.

Arkhan came in next, and Melidia noted with surprise that his left arm appeared to be whole and functional. The limb was wrapped in thick bandages from shoulder to fingertips, and looked misshapen and larger than his undamaged arm, but otherwise, he appeared as he always had. She had thought for sure he would lose the limb after Gart's damnable beast had mangled it so badly, but he moved as though it did not pain him at all. He came in and sat down on the opposite side of the table from Barovius, not bothering to look at him.

Melidia motioned for a servant to bring her more wine, and the man instantly complied, filling her glass with ruby red liquid. She sipped it and then sat down at the small table.

"What have you seen, Melidia?" Barovius' gravelly voice inquired. He knew that everything depended on her scrying ability, the visions that only she was able to see. "Why are we out here, this close to the Poravian Mire?"

Melidia sipped her wine again, happily making Barovius wait for her response. "The time has come for us to confront Gart. I know where he is going. We will meet him there, kill him, and take the Blood from him."

"You think it will be that easy, then?" Arkhan's voice was cold and quiet. "Even without his Jidaan, his magick is formidable." An ironic smile appeared on his youthful face. "And then there's his dog to consider."

"I killed that beast! Stabbed it to death, I did!" Barovius angrily interjected.

Melidia threw back her head and laughed, surprising both men. "It doesn't matter! We will win the day. I've already Seen it."

Arkhan and Barovius glanced at each other, then Barovius spoke first. "We know you've got powers of Sight, witch. Tell us how we're going to beat him!"

Melidia kept her smile plastered on her face. She had seen no such thing. Her visions stopped right at the moment Gart approached the steep cliffs that she knew only existed in the Mire. She saw him and his mangy beast walk towards a deep vertical cleft in the side of the bluff. The pair turned around in response to something she could not see, and at that point, all of her visions stopped. But even so, Arkhan and Barovius did not need to know that. She was confident in her plan. They could overwhelm Gart, take the Blood, and then she could dispose of her two annoying companions.

"Gentlemen, I've been working on a powerful spell, and the time is finally right for it to be put to use. The Mire is a very dangerous place, even for us, but I know a way to make that work in our favor." She eyed both men, and knew that she had their attention. She allowed a touch of her lustmagick to reach out and caress the two men, binding them to her plan with desire. She saw Barovius lean forward more eagerly, and Arkhan adjusted his spectacles, a nervous gesture of his. *Good*, she thought. *I have them.* "Certain things are buried in the mire, ancient and dreadful things. I can awaken one of them, and it will do my bidding."

Barovius gasped in horror. "Ye gods, woman! You don't mean..."

Melidia simply nodded, keeping the smile on her face.

Arkhan removed his glasses, this time placing them gently on the table so that he could pinch the bridge of his nose with his uninjured hand. "If you're talking about what I think you are, you had better know what you're doing. No one has tried to animate those..."Arkhan paused, searching for words, "beings, for centuries. They would just as soon kill all of us." He fixed her with a cold stare. "You are sure you can control it once awakened?"

Melidia leaned back in her chair, still smiling. "You think I would dare to call one of them if I wasn't? And besides, I will only awaken it if you two somehow botch the job!"

Barovius leaned back and cast a skeptical glance her way. "I thought you said you had already Seen our victory? Do we beat him ourselves or not?"

Melidia's mind raced at the unexpected question, but found her footing quickly. "Of course I have! Even so, the future is always shifting. I'm just making sure that nothing, and I mean nothing, is left to chance."

Barovius stared at her for a moment longer, but then nodded in reluctant agreement.

Melidia continued, "Just because I didn't See any of the others arrive doesn't mean they won't. So listen closely, loves, and we will emerge victorious!" She turned to Arkhan and pointed one finger at him. "You will use your powers to create enough of your creatures to overwhelm Gart. He's injured and tired, that much I know. You two did something right in that, at least. Get to work right away! And you, Barovius," she said as she turned her full attention on the older man, "I hope your elemental skills are stronger with earth and stone than air. You must be ready to hit Gart with everything you can muster. Together, we will put an end to Gart, and everything we've ever wanted will be ours at last!"

A heavy silence fell over the room, and Melidia forced herself to be patient. Melidia's eyes darted from Barovius to Arkhan. She sent another tiny hint of lustmagick at them, and saw them nod as their resolve solidified. She knew she had them.

Arkhan slowly put his spectacles back on his face; he had gone a touch pale around his eyes, but there was still the iron control Melidia had grown used to. Finally, he spoke. "All right, then. I will need men. Strong men. And others as well. I will create sufficient Joinings to achieve our goal." he said as calmly as he could. *And to keep me safe from Melidia's fiend,* he added to himself. He cast a glance over to Barovius, who had folded his arms and retreated into his usual scowl. *That idiot can fend for himself.*

"Certainly," Melidia nodded, pleased at Arkhan's enthusiasm, or at least, his lack of protest. She turned to the older man. "Barovius, is there anything you require before we head for the portal that will take us to the Mire?"

"A drink. Or ten." He stood up and left the tent, knocking over his chair with the sheathed blade of the Jidaan as he went. "Just let me know when we move out. I'll be ready." *She thinks I'm a fool!* he thought. *We'll see who's the fool once I have the Blood. She won't know what hit her!*

Melidia watched Barovius depart, followed more slowly by Arkhan. Her smile widened just the tiniest bit. They were playing right into her hands, just as she knew they would. Soon, she would have everything she needed, and no man alive could stop her.

Chapter 9

She felt the Mire long before she saw it. Drusilla had been speeding along a wide, lush plain, its flat surface bumped here and there with hills and swells of varying size. Trees were sparse, and the land as far as the eye could see was covered in thick, waist-high grasses that rolled and undulated as the wind caressed them. It was late afternoon, and they were chasing the sun as it made its way across the sky towards its nightly rendezvous with the horizon.

That same wind blew through Reyanna's long, raven-black tresses as Drusilla sped along. Unhindered by the long grass, her body rode high above its fronds and her slender legs worked ceaselessly to propel them both faster than a horse could gallop. Reyanna had managed to push aside her feelings of sadness and frustration over the men's attack back at the inn, exulting in the beauty of the land they passed through and the speed they maintained. *This must be what flying feels like!* Reyanna mused as they hurtled through the grass. Drusilla did not answer, choosing instead to simply continue on her westward trek.

Suddenly, as though they passed through an invisible barrier, a heavy sense of dread settled on Reyanna, and Drusilla hitched slightly in her gait before resuming her previous speed. Reyanna shuddered under the weight of an unseen oppression, and she quickly glanced in all directions before squinting her eyes westward again, attempting to find the source of her unease. She saw no immediate cause for her disquiet, but knew better than to discount her senses. Something had changed.

Far in the distance, a black line emerged on the horizon, ranging as far to Reyanna's left and right as she could see. A sick feeling began gnawing at the inside of her stomach as she finally caught sight of what she knew must be the Poravian Mire. She gently pulled on the reins so that Drusilla would slow, then brought her to a stop so she could collect her thoughts. The air was still now that Drusilla was at rest, and Reyanna listened to the quiet. Birds still sang, and there were other noises too, but something about the sounds bothered her. She shaded her eyes and looked skyward, searching for the cause. It took her a few moments to realize that the only birds she saw were behind her. Between her and the distant border of the Mire, she saw no living creature in the sky or near the ground. As she scanned the area, she noticed that the thick grass they had been traveling through had started to turn brown and thin out the farther west they had come. Where the ground had been firm and rich for miles, it now seemed to be more mud than solid earth. The wind shifted out of the west and Reyanna caught a foul stench.

She gagged and spat before she could help herself, but then recovered her composure. She had smelled worse. Just not lately.

"Come on, Dru," she said to the spider. "I think we're on the right track. Once we get to the trees, you can get on top of them and we'll see where we need to go from there."

Drusilla bobbed her body once, signaling to Reyanna to hang on, then she darted forward. Her long, slender legs squelched in the deepening mud but she kept her pace fast and even. Reyanna stared ahead, trying to shrug off the sense of dread that threatened to overwhelm her. The black line of trees came closer, and finally, details of the Mire began to emerge.

Although tall, the trees of the Mire were dark, their trunks twisted and bent. A fey mist hugged the soggy ground, revealing only vague, unsettling shapes from afar. The anxiety Reyanna felt only intensified as they approached, and she struggled to shield herself from it. The power inside her swelled and moved, answering her instinctive call, but that almost scared Reyanna more than the Mire. With an effort, she calmed herself and quelled her magick. Instead, she gritted her teeth and focused on ignoring the strong sense of oppression and hopelessness that seemed to be emanating from the Mire. She scanned the trees and thought how gnarled and sinister they looked compared to the thick and healthy timbers she knew from home. Somewhere in the distance, a long, low howl drifted over the swamp, rising, then falling into silence. Reyanna had never heard anything in the forest like that, and a chill ran up her spine at the mournful sound of it. Another beast somewhere in the mire shrieked, whether in fear or anger, she could not say.

Summoning all her determination, she leaned forward in Drusilla's saddle and urged the spider to go faster. Whatever fate awaited her, she wanted to face it head on.

Drusilla dodged the first few trees they encountered, then climbed up into the first stand of bent oaks that would bear her weight. The air was thick with the stench of rot and corruption, and the shadows seemed to cling to the trees, even under the bright light of the afternoon sun. Sharp cracks and pops punctuated Drusilla's movement as rotten branches gave way, shearing off from the main trunks and leaving greenish pus leaking from the wounds in the bark.

Reyanna's gaze jerked away from the horizon any time she detected movement, which was often. Misshapen things flew among the trees, too fast for Reyanna to identify. She was left only with impressions of sickly, twisted forms as they flitted from one shadow to the next. Drusilla suddenly shifted in her forward path, angling to the right for no reason Reyanna could see. Moments later, a burst of feline snarling and what could have been the roar of a bear exploded from the spot the spider had just avoided. A ferocious flurry of movement from within the Mire revealed a conflict that Drusilla's senses had detected, though Reyanna's had not. The leaves in the trees shook as some gargantuan predator and equally enormous prey played out their roles in the swamp below. The battle was fierce, but short, and the trees ceased their shaking in moments. The Mire fell silent once more as the unseen conflict ended.

"Thanks, Dru," Reyanna murmured, trusting her mount to hear her emotions rather than her words. "No sense getting involved in whatever that was down there." Then, she laughed in spite of herself. *I've got enough trouble these days without borrowing more.*

Reyanna refocused on navigating. She had to keep moving westward until she found the mountains from her vision. They were out there, somewhere. And so was the stranger they called Gart. *Hopefully, he'll have some answers,* Reyanna thought.

Chapter 10

Josuas was, indeed, a decent cook. Kiran belched behind a raised hand, then wiped her mouth with a napkin. "Nessar," she said quietly, "if this is how romance writers are treated, then sign me up and give me a quill."

Nessar chuckled. "I wouldn't know. Remember, you're the writer...*Vanessa*." He grinned wider than Kiran would have believed possible.

"Oh, you are loving this!" she said, smacking him lightly on the arm.

Nessar scanned the room around them. For the last two hours, they had been fed simple but tasty fare, and basically waited on hand and foot. The men absolutely adored Nessar's stories. Each had managed to recount their favorite scenes during the evening, some of which actually made Layton blush. The old thief had been deeply flattered to hear his own tales recounted with such enthusiasm, and he helped Kiran navigate the conversation by silently giving her the answers she needed as the occasion arose. Although she was finally almost comfortable playing the role of Vanessa Hills, it was Nessar who felt validated.

This is fun and all, but we should get moving, don't you think? Layton had long since pushed away his plate and leaned back in his chair. He was mightily amused when Nessar finally relayed the whole story to him, but he was feeling the pressure to get downriver. He knew Gart's level of determination; a man obsessed would have little use for dawdling.

I agree. This has been a nice diversion and we needed the food, but it's time to go. Kiran pushed her chair back and stood, causing all of the conversation to instantly still. Kiran stared at the men for a moment, then spoke. "We can't thank you enough for your hospitality, gentlemen. We haven't eaten like that in a long while. Unfortunately, we do have to be going, so if you could show us to a boat, we'll pay for it and be on our way."

Luther jumped to his feet, clutching his hat in his hands. "Miss Vanessa, before you go," he looked at his friends on either side who nodded frantically, urging him on.

Gathering his courage, he continued, "Would you be so kind as to tell us about your next book?" A chorus of hearty "Yes!" and "Hear, hear!" went up around the table.

Kiran's eyes widened and she glanced over at Nessar. She had yet to read the book of his she had brought from Guardians Keep. It was still in her saddlebags. "Ah," she began, waiting for Nessar to help her. He watched her squirm for a few seconds, then broke his silence.

Here, I have one you can give them. Nessar pulled a thin, leatherbound book from inside his coat and handed it to Kiran. *Tell them you only just finished it.*

Relieved, she took the book and held it up for the men to see. "You mean this?"

The men gasped, their eyes wide with excitement. Josuas, the cook, was first to speak. "Is...is that your newest book?"

Listening intently to Nessar's voice in her mind, Kiran replied, "It sure is. In fact, I only just finished it. It's called, um..." Kiran flipped it open to the title page and read. She instantly glared daggers at Nessar, which only made him grin. "Oh, I'm definitely going to kill you, Nessar, I swear it," she muttered just loud enough for him to hear. She grimaced as she forced herself to say the title out loud, much to Nessar's delight. "Kiran's First Kiss."

Layton nearly choked on a mouthful of ale while the men oohed and aahed. They immediately began chattering to each other about possible plots and other characters. Kiran cut her eyes at Nessar, only to see him slowly purpling as he struggled to hold in his laughter. *I'm going to shave off your eyebrows in your sleep, old man, you wait and see.* Kiran's mental voice seethed with fury.

Totally worth it, came his smug reply. *Hel, I'll shave them myself if you read some of that out loud to them. They'll love it.*

Layton finally managed to get through his mouthful of ale and set his mug down on the table. Wiping his mouth on his sleeve, he addressed Kiran. "As much as I am now dying to hear more about your book, Miss Hills, we really, really need to be going."

Kiran yanked her backpack off the floor and slipped her arms through the straps, adjusting her Jidaan so that it hung alongside it. "Layton, I could not agree more."

A short time later, they found themselves on the river aboard the *Madalyn*. Luther and his crew had only been too happy to trade the boat in return for Nessar's latest book and their horses. The Guardians had left the gang clustered around the book as one of them haltingly read Nessar's handwriting aloud to the others, and Kiran had hastened them into the boat so she would not have to hear it.

The trees and rocks on the shore moved past them in a blur as the river bore them downstream much faster than they could have ridden. When the river was straight and wide enough, Layton would create a Gate big enough for the entire boat to travel through, thus speeding their travel even more. Kiran passed the time by telling Nessar all the ways she was going to kill him, which only served to amuse him further. Layton kept his eyes focused on the water ahead.

The sun worked its way toward the western horizon, and Layton listened to Nessar and Kiran's banter as he worked the rudder of the flat-bottomed boat. For a change, he could not bring himself to join them in their playful bickering. Ever since he had awakened outside Corria, an odd feeling had gnawed at the edges of his consciousness. Even now, he still felt unsettled, on edge. It was a feeling that worried him deeply, which only served to unsettle him further. As his callused hands gripped the smooth wood of the boat's tiller, he tried to find that peaceful place within himself as he had been taught. He continued to stare straight ahead, but his spirit searched inward for the eye of his own personal storm, the stillness within the motion. It eluded him. As he prepared to send the boat through another pair of Gates, leapfrogging it a good half-mile upriver, he hoped he would be able to find it again.

51

Chapter 11

Deep within the Poravian Mire, enclosed by the swampy morass on all sides, a rough-edged mountain range split the black and green landscape from north to south. Its ruddy stone gave it the appearance of a jagged and bloody wound in the Mire. The crimson granite seemed to ward off the worst of the boggy land, and the more deviant creatures of the swamp tended to avoid it in favor of more sinister environs. There amid the rocky soil, the Mire held little sway and the ground was solid.

At the southern end of the range, the mountains faded into gentle slopes that would eventually be swallowed by the swamp. Many of the stones that lay about had a squarish look to them, resembling blocks strewn about by a giant child. Once, a wide, sprawling palace had stood there, huge and magnificent. Now, nothing was left but cracked jumbles of rock and dust.

Off to one side of the valley, three monolithic stones yet stood next to each other, the outer two tilted inward somewhat. Their faces formed nearly vertical slabs that looked man-wrought, though no mark from chisel or pick could be found upon them. The hollow they formed was quiet, as it had been for centuries. Once the inner corner of an immense chamber, it now stood open to the elements, broken and forlorn.

The flat face of the reddish stone suddenly flared brightly with ancient magick, and a high pitched whine of intense energy startled the misshapen birds from their perches in the trees nearby. A blinding scarlet light erupted from the rock, forming the rectangular outline of a door in the bare face of the central surface. Within the glowing lines of magick, the solid rock warped and wavered, like the reflection on a pool of still water that had been disturbed. The rough stone disappeared, revealing a corridor leading into an inky darkness.

In the next instant, Bessie clambered across the stone threshold, her eyes wild with fear and pain. Gart hunched over her neck, haggard and worn, barely keeping his sword in hand. Both were bleeding from wicked claw marks, Bessie on her left flank, Gart on left arm and leg. The wounds were not deep, but Gart was already dangerously weak. He could not afford to lose much more blood. He desperately clung to the saddle and reins, struggling to stay mounted as Bessie danced and shied. As soon as Gart was clear of the portal, Beauty shot through it, then turned and barked ferociously at something within its unnatural darkness. Blood welled in deep scratches on her right flank, though she paid them little attention, focused as she was on whatever pursued them.

Gart sheathed his sword, ignoring the greenish ichor that dripped from its ebony blade. As soon as his hand was free, he formed his shaking fingers into an arcane gesture and spoke a string of harsh, alien syllables to close the portal behind him. As he spoke, an arm covered in glistening scarlet scales reached through to swipe at Beauty. Its three fingers ended in wickedly sharp claws, still dripping blood from its last attack. Beauty dodged, and the deadly talons missed their mark. Gart ended his chant, simultaneously clenching his fist. The portal snapped shut at his command, severing the heavily muscled arm just above the elbow. It fell to the earth with a meaty thump, and the whine of ancient magick vanished, leaving behind a ringing silence.

Beauty barked at the arm, which twitched a few times before finally falling still. She stared at the limb, then cautiously moved forward for a closer examination. When she was satisfied that it was no longer a threat, she urinated on it, then kicked dust and dirt at it before looking for Gart.

"Atta girl," Gart mumbled. "You tell that scaly bastard that he...didn't scare..." Gart's world went dark for a moment, but he shook himself awake again. "Gotta rest. All of us, we have to rest." Gently, he reached into Bessie's mind with his magick and reassured her with images and feelings. She calmed immediately at his familiar touch, and then snorted loudly. "Yeah, me too, Bessie. Me too. They didn't write about what was inside of that particular gateway, did they?" He shook his head, too tired to be furious, though he desperately wanted to be. "No they didn't. Damned red lizard creatures...trying to kill us...bastards."

Gart eased himself out of the saddle and slid carefully to the ground, stumbling a little when his feet hit the rocky earth. There were flagstones visible in places, but mostly, the ancient floor was covered with windblown dirt and sand. Small shrubs had taken root in places, and Gart moved towards one of these. It took him a few moments to tie Bessie's reins to a sturdy bush, as his fingers kept refusing to do what he asked of them. Beauty whined softly, and edged closer to keep an eye on him.

"'S'all right, girl. Just let me get us set up here," Gart muttered. He dropped his backpack to the ground, then pulled the saddlebags off of Bessie and tossed them down near the pack. He touched the horse's wounds gently and winced as he saw the long slashes across her ribs. Ignoring his own wounds, he reached into his well of magick and concentrated. What magick he could call upon leapt to do his bidding, and he watched the long cuts knit themselves back together until they were no more than angry red welts. He knew they would still hurt like fire for a while, but Bessie had been through worse. Or was that another horse? Gart's mind wandered as he considered which Bessie was here with him.

Beauty whined again, bringing Gart's awareness back to the present. "Sorry, girl. Let me check you too." Gart knelt down beside his canine companion, only to stumble and fall heavily to his knees in his exhaustion. "Close enough," he muttered. Beauty's gashes were worse than Bessie's, only because she was the smaller of the two. Several of the terrifying, scaled creatures had attacked them all at once inside the portal, and their claws had been most effective weapons. Gart grimaced as he saw that Beauty's wounds were still bleeding heavily. "Can't have that. You're weak enough as it is." He carefully sealed up her cuts as well, using as much magick as he dared. Struggling to focus, he finally managed to close up his own wounds, at least enough to stop the bleeding.

His strength at an end, Gart collapsed against his backpack. He had a moment to feel grateful that it had landed close enough to serve as a rough pillow, and then

54

his eyes closed. Beauty whined, suddenly feeling a hitch in her chest. Gart opened his eyes again, guilt coursing through him in a flash. He had almost slept without seeing that the constant stream of magick was still flowing to Beauty's stricken heart. He would have wakened to find her dead. He doubted he could bear that. "I'm sorry...I'm sorry, girl," he mumbled, his bone-deep fatigue slurring his words. Urgently, he beckoned Beauty closer. She lumbered next to him and laid down alongside him, making sure her body was touching his.

"That's a good girl," Gart mumbled, resting a hand on her broad head and trying to scratch her ears. "Stay close. My magick will keep you safe. It's all right. We'll rest, and search for the shrine when we wake. It'll be all right. Everything will be all right." He continued murmuring to Beauty in a low, calming voice as he ordered his thoughts. The spell he had devised would continue the constant trickle of magick that she would need while he was sleeping. He knew it would continue to drain him, but there was no alternative.

Satisfied that Beauty would still be alive when he woke, Gart finally allowed himself to rest. His voice trailed into silence, and he slept. At his side, Beauty listened to the steady, slow beat of his heart. She stayed awake a while longer, just to be sure they were safe. Then she laid her big head on Gart's chest and closed her eyes as well.

Chapter 12

"I think we go that way," Kiran said, pointing to the smaller fork in the river ahead. The main flow of the river had been slowly curving southward, but the branch Kiran indicated flowed almost directly west.

Nessar already had his leather notebook in hand, checking notes he had made back at Elarin Glen. "That's right, Kiran. We're still a ways from the Mire proper, but from what I saw on Trian's map, that will take us right into the heart of it."

Layton gently moved the tiller, angling the *Madalyn* away from the wider river and towards the smaller, westward course. "That map was pretty old. Let's hope we're not wasting our time," he said sourly.

Surprised, Kiran raised an eyebrow at his tone. Layton had never been the cynical type. He had always been cheery and upbeat. Ever since Corria, though, he had been curt and impatient, even surly at times. She did not like this Layton, not at all, but instead of being angry at him, she was worried. Lowering her voice, she gently asked, "Layton, you OK, man?"

The warrior grimaced as he looked at Kiran for an instant, then looked away, embarrassed. He was silent for a long time before speaking. "I'm...I'm sorry, Kiran. I don't mean to be rude. I'm just..." He sighed, struggling to find the words to express the frustration he had been feeling. "You know I'm good at what I do. It's all I've ever been good at, honestly." He shook his head slowly. "Back there, I messed up. When you two were counting on me, I went and knocked myself unconscious. Useless." He looked into Kiran's eyes, sharing the despair that had been building within him. "That never should have happened. I left you unprotected, and it's been eating at me. I'm supposed to be better than that." He sighed. "I'm sorry."

Kiran looked at Layton for a while, her mind drifting back to the days when they had only just met, decades past. He had been a clean-shaven, wiry youth back then, barely older than she and neither of them on the far side of twenty. He had been faster than anyone she had ever seen,

56

and his acrobatic fighting style had been nearly impossible to emulate. His face always took on a dreamy half-smile as he fought, showing that no matter what kind of intense fight his body was engaged in, his mind was in a peaceful, calm state that allowed him to perform with unerring precision and timing.

Together, they had endured horrors the likes of which most people could never dream. They had faced ridiculous odds and survived to tell the almost unbelievable tales afterwards. And not one time had Layton ever exhibited a single shred of doubt, not one moment of reluctance. He flung himself into every battle as though he knew for a fact that he would survive, and had proven himself correct at every opportunity.

The bearded man at the tiller had wrinkles around his eyes that she only just noticed. He was at least thirty pounds heavier than the youth she remembered, broader through the shoulders and more solid in the torso and legs. He still moved with fluid grace that filled her with a kind of affectionate envy, but gone was the twitchy quickness that he used to have, the sense that he might burst into motion at any moment. He moved more efficiently now, with less wasted effort, the product of years of continued practice. And for the moment, his smile was gone, too. She realized that he looked far older without it. She thought about Layton's words for a few moments longer, then nodded to herself. She knew what needed to be done.

Without a word, she slapped him hard across the face, taking him completely by surprise and rocking his head to one side. Layton's eyes widened in shock as his cheek began to sting. Before he could speak, Kiran held up a finger to silence him.

"That was to snap you out of your self-pity, you knucklehead." Kiran folded her arms as she spoke. "Firstly, I am not a damsel in distress that needs protecting. I'm perfectly capable of protecting myself, and you, if necessary, as is Nessar. We, all three of us, are Chosen Guardians. We have different strengths, it's true, but we are equals. It's not solely your job to protect us, even if you are the Weaponsmaster. Nessar and I get by just fine, as we proved after your accident and many times over the years before we even met you." Kiran held up two fingers as she continued. "Secondly, we all make mistakes, and not for lack of skills or lack of effort. Sometimes, stupid things go wrong that we can't predict. You stumbled and conked out. Fine. We managed. We're family, we three, and we help each other, so you can just get over yourself." She folded her arms again and stared at Layton, her chin raised in challenge.

Layton blinked at her, his face still stinging from the slap. At first, his brows knit in anger, but only for a few moments. His face relaxed again as he sorted through his emotions, and then he sighed. A tiny grin appeared at one corner of his mouth. "Wow. When you say it like that, it makes me sound like an arrogant jackass."

"You said it, I didn't," Kiran retorted. "But if the boot fits, you can wear it."

Layton laughed and let out a breath that he felt he had been holding for days, ever since Corria. "All right, fine. That was arrogant of me, and I apologize. I hadn't thought of it like that."

"Obviously," Kiran said.

Layton laughed again, louder this time. When next he spoke, he was serious once more, though his smile remained. "Well now that we agree I've been an egotistical fool, the other thing that's bothering me is Gart. The way he uses his power is nothing like Mordak. Even without using the Jidaan of Storms, Gart snuffed us out as easily as blowing out a candle. We didn't have a chance to fight at all. I know we have to find a way to stop him, but I'm at a loss. We can't just kill him. He's our friend."

Kiran slid onto the wooden bench beside the tiller as she mulled over Layton's words. "Yeah, I know exactly what you mean. I've been thinking the same thing," she admitted. "I was looking right into his eyes when he knocked me out. Didn't have a chance to say a word."

Layton nodded in understanding, turning to focus on the water ahead.

Kiran continued, "You're right, though. We do have to do something to stop him. I'm hoping a solution will present itself. Otherwise, maybe we can knock some sense into him. You know I like a challenge." She elbowed him in the ribs and grinned. "And you do too. Don't lie! I'm sure you've got some flippity-flip crazy kick that you're just dying to try on someone, admit it!"

Layton accepted the ribbing stoically at first, but then a smile crept back onto his face as though he was powerless to stop it. "All right, you've got me there. Running the Academy is wonderful, and I love it, but it does lack a certain kind of excitement. We'll figure out something."

"There you go, I knew it!" Kiran crowed in triumph. "And besides, I'm positive that someone else is out there causing trouble. Remember those air daemons that attacked me? Gart wouldn't have sent those; he'd have just zapped me with lightning or something if he was that far gone. He had that opportunity back at Corria, but all he did was knock us out. There's got to be some logic left in him; he doesn't want to hurt us either. There's a chance we can still talk him out of this nonsense. And that means someone else deserves an arse-kicking for sending the air daemons."

Layton's eyes widened slightly as he rolled that over in his mind. "You're right! That kind of elemental magick takes a lifetime of study, not only summoning the daemons but forcing them to stick to a task like that. Someone else is trying to interfere!" His grin reappeared in full force, and he cast a sly glance over at Kiran. "And I do, indeed, have a special flippity-flip kick I've been dying to try."

Kiran laughed and the years fell away from her. Pounds had been gained, hair had grown lighter and longer, and wrinkles had appeared on all of them, but their spirits still burned brightly. They were Guardians, now and always.

Nessar's gravelly voice interrupted them. "Hey, look up there. We're definitely on the right track." Kiran and Layton both stood to get a better view, looking at where Nessar was pointing.

The difference was first noticeable in the trees that lined the river. Where they had been tall and strong before, there was a marked deterioration in their condition along the tributary they now traveled. Trees that might have been tall and majestic before now had a slumped, shadowy aspect to them, their limbs twisted and strained. Their leaves, too, were various shades of dirty brown, almost gray in places. The water that flowed past their boat gradually took on a murky green tinge, and the banks of the river turned muddy and slick where they could see them. A faint smell of rot reached them, slowly intensifying as they continued on their way. A sense of dread fell upon them all, and they knew the Mire was near.

Suddenly, Layton's right arm was a blur, and there was a *whissk* sound followed by a dull thumping and thrashing in the stern of the boat. Kiran turned to see an enormous snake writhing about at Layton's feet, its decapitated head a few feet away. Kiran jumped back and drew her dagger even as Layton put his away.

"Sorry," he apologized. "That thing was just about to strike you when I saw it. It was almost too fast for me."

Kiran stepped over and examined the snake's head, spearing it with her dagger and holding it up so she could see it better. Its fangs were as long as her little finger, and its eyes were wide and staring. Something about it looked wrong, though she could not put her finger on exactly how at first. Then she saw that there were several rows of teeth in the snake's mouth rather than just one, and the eyes looked almost human rather than serpentine. She grimaced and tossed the head out into the water. Instantly, the water boiled and frothed where the head had sunk, as something apparently enjoyed a snack. Layton quickly heaved the snake's body over the side as well, with a similar result.

"I can't say for sure, but I'm thinking we've entered the Poravian Mire." Nessar glanced skyward to gauge the position of the sun, then peered ahead again. "We'll follow this for a while, but then we'd best keep our eyes peeled for a safe place to camp. I don't want to be on the water after dark, though I somehow doubt that the land will be much safer."

Layton responded, his voice regaining some of his usual cheer. "Right. If you see a likely place, just sing out." He sat back on the wooden bench by the tiller, keeping his hand on the handle. Killing the snake before it could hurt Kiran had made him feel better. And he had a strong feeling that he'd soon have ample opportunity to keep his friends safe, whether or not they thought they needed him to do so.

60

Hours later, the boat ran aground in the middle of a swampy morass of mud, algae, and water. It slid to a stop, and it was apparent that it would go no farther.

"Well, that's just a fine how-do-you-do," Nessar complained. "Looks like the river petered out and now it's nothing but muck all around us."

Kiran stood and peered at the trees on either side of them. A hundred yards ahead, the trees closed in, signifying the definite end of the river, but there was still a long and muddy walk to either bank from where they had stopped. "I don't like the thought of slogging through that," she said cautiously. "We don't know how deep that mud actually is, and it's hard to fight if something attacks while our legs are bound up in muck like that. I could use my Wards for us to walk on, but I think that would attract attention after a while." The others mumbled agreement as they stared at the green-streaked, foul smelling gray ooze that surrounded the boat.

Layton spied what looked like a more solid spot off to one side under some larger trees. In a flash, he ignited the power of his Jidaan. Its pommelgem flared brightly as its magick awakened. Layton quickly created a pair of Gates, one in front of him, the other among the trees on the far bank. He stuck his head into the nearest portal and found himself looking down at the ground under the trees on the other side of the opposite Gate. Moving slowly, he reached through with his right foot and tested the ground. It was solid enough, and he stepped back through so that he stood in the boat once more.

"That seems like a good enough place to start," he said, sliding his arms through the straps in his backpack and settling it in place. "It's solid enough at least for us to regroup and figure out where we go from here."

Nessar squinted up at the sky behind them. It had slowly clouded over with iron gray thunderheads, as though the bad weather was chasing them, but was also in no hurry to catch up. A faint rumble sounded in the distance, hinting that rain might not be far behind. He sighed, grateful that if they were headed into the swamp, at least they were moving away from the rain instead of straight into it. Nodding at the spot Layton had indicated, Nessar said,

61

"Right, that's actually the direction I think we need to be headed. Let's go. And watch for snakes."

Layton created a Gate in the middle of the boat, and one by one they stepped through it onto the solid ground of the shore. Nessar pulled out his notebook again, and they gathered around him as he got their bearings and they discussed which way to go.

A sharp crack startled them all, and they snapped their heads up in time to see their boat jerk and shudder as something attacked it from below. The sound of splintering wood reached them as the boat shook and then fell still again, though now it listed to one side in the muddy water.

"Looks like we got out of there just in time," Kiran quipped. "No wonder the Mire has such an awful reputation. We're just entering the fringes and it's like it's already trying to eat us."

Nessar shook his head. "There's probably more truth to that than we'd really like to know. Let's just keep our wits about us and get moving, shall we? We're at least four days out from those mountains, and that's if Layton can Gate us a few times a day so that we cover more ground."

Kiran made a face. "Four days? In this?" She sighed theatrically. "Well, it could be worse. I'm not really sure how, but at least we're together. That counts for a lot. Let's move."

Nessar tucked his notebook away and set off in a vaguely westerly direction, Kiran and Layton close behind. Their boots made nasty squelching sounds as they walked, and every so often one of them would slip into a puddle or a deeper pocket of mud. As the hours passed, their trousers were soaked to the knees and their legs ached from picking up boots heavy with mud as they struggled to keep from falling down.

Twilight slowly descended upon them, and along with it, a bone deep weariness began to set in. Kiran was so tired she was not even irritated anymore. The foul smelling water had long since soaked through her boots and pants and even her usual habit of complaining just to pass the time ended up taking too much energy. She lapsed into an exhausted silence just as the others had.

"We should find a place to stop,' she finally muttered, "I'm beat, and you both are, too. The light will be gone soon, and I don't want to stumble into something out there in the dark."

Nessar's tired but relieved voice drifted over his shoulder to her ears. "Kiran, I could not agree more. I've marched over all kinds of terrain, but this sucking mud is absolutely awful." He stopped, and the others moved up to stand on either side of him. The light was dwindling rapidly, but they could still see enough to make out the twisted shrubs and drooping trees that surrounded them on all sides. A fey mist was slowly rising from the ground around them, only inches at a time, but soon it would obscure the marshy land beneath their boots completely. They needed to find a place to camp right away.

Layton suddenly crouched a few inches, instinctively going into a battle-ready stance as he pointed off to their right. His voice echoed clearly in Nessar and Kiran's minds. *Do you two see that light? It looks like someone carrying a lantern.*

You mean someone lives *out here?* Kiran's reply was thick with disbelief. *They've got to be crazy!*

Crazy or not, they might be able to help, Nessar voiced his optimism, then followed up with a more typical comment. *If they don't try to kill us instead. Let me get a closer look. I can sneak up on whoever it is and get some idea of what we're dealing with before they know we're here.*

Layton and Kiran looked at Nessar and each other, then nodded their agreement. Nessar willed his Jidaan to life, its pommel suddenly swirling an inky black as its power of Stealth was awakened, and then he vanished.

Kiran smiled and shook her head. *Aaaaand he's gone again. Poof! Just like that.*

An answering grin split Layton's beard and Kiran allowed herself to be comforted by the sight. She had been worried about her old friend after Corria, but even as exhausted as they all were, she now saw the same twinkle in his eyes that she had known back when they were two decades younger. Apparently, her slap had worked its own magick.

63

You know he loves that, he agreed. *Whenever he...hey, look over there.* He silently pointed off to his left, far from where Nessar had gone. Kiran followed his pointing finger with her eyes.

In the trees fairly close by was another bobbing light. It was steady and strong, though she had trouble seeing the man who held the lantern. It stopped for a moment, as though the lantern bearer was examining something, and then it began to move away again.

Is that the same one? Kiran was confused. She looked off to her right, where they had first seen the light, and saw nothing but the rising fog. Of Nessar, of course, there was no sign. *Nessar?* she called through their mental link. *Ness! Answer me, you old bastard!*

A wave of nausea suddenly roiled her guts, and she took a deep breath to steady herself. Her head swam for a moment, and she put out her hands to keep her balance as she stumbled a step. Something was wrong. She shook her head to clear it, and when she looked around, Layton was gone.

*   *   *   *   *   *

Layton pointed out the dancing lantern light to Kiran and saw her take a step towards it. He stared at the light for a moment, then another, following it as it danced through the trees, moving slowly. The light soothed him as he watched it, and he fastened his gaze on it, desperately trying to see what held it aloft. A sense of calm washed over him and he relaxed, suddenly feeling as though he had not a care in the world.

He found himself walking, though he had no recollection of why he had started or where he was going. He was content just to walk. He dimly remembered that he was supposed to be quiet, though he could not say why. Nevertheless, he trod as carefully as he could manage, watchfully placing his sodden boots on the driest patches of ground he could find. The fog rose around him and he felt happy and contented at the sight of it. Everything was all right. There was no reason to worry. In fact, he could just lie down and rest, he was so safe here. He stopped walking and stared at the soggy ground in front of him, thinking it would be nice to lie down, just for a moment. He was so tired; a nap would be nice.

Something splashed in the mud behind him, and Layton felt a surge of fear at the sound. He drew his Jidaan from the sheath at his back and turned to meet whatever approached, stumbling slightly as he did so. He felt slow, sluggish, and a part of him knew that was not how he was supposed to be.

Out of the mist, a shape emerged; it was dark, shadowy, and human-sized. It seemed to glide over the marshy ground. Layton crouched when he saw that it was a corpse, its flesh rotting and falling off as it moved towards him. Filthy matted hair hung down around a skeletal face, its lower jaw broken and hanging awkwardly to one side. Its long, shriveled arms reached for him, gangrenous flesh hanging from the thin bones in leprous strips. Layton stared at the oncoming lich for only a moment, then he raised his Jidaan high over his head and brought it down, preparing to cleave the creature right down the middle.

Just before the razor-sharp Jidaan made contact with the creature's skull, it slammed into something harder than any steel. The jarring impact rattled Layton's teeth and hurt his hands, and there was a brilliant flash of sapphirine blue where he had struck. The shockwave flung him on his back in the muddy earth, momentarily stunning him. The thickening fog disappeared in a widening circle, pushed away by the magickal blowback.

Layton! Kiran's frantic voice exploded in his head. *Layton, is that you? Goddess, I almost killed you!*

On the ground, Layton shook his head, driving off some of the grogginess that had overtaken him. When his eyes came back into focus, he saw the lich standing over him encircled in a blazing dome of blue energy. Within the dome, its hideous form suddenly hunched over and blurred. Its outline shifted and changed until the glamour finally fell away to reveal the familiar shape of his friend. Kiran stood with her Jidaan in hand as though she was ready to stab him with it, and her eyes were wide with excitement.

Sweet Rowann above, I thought you were this...this awful, undead thing! Kiran's mental voice dripped with disgust. *Are you all right?*

Yes, he replied, a bit of chagrin seeping into his words as he lay there in the mud. *I'm a complete mess, but I'm all right. To be fair, I should tell you that I thought you were the undead thing. I'm glad you Warded yourself; I tried to cut you in half.* He held out a muddy hand. *Help me up?*

After you just tried to kill me? No way, you get up your own self. Even as she said it, she reached out for his hand anyway, helping him get to his feet again. *We saw each other as monsters. How could that be?*

Layton shook his head as he wiped his hands on his trousers, then resheathed his Jidaan. *I'm not sure. I felt really odd there after the fog rose. I think there might be something about it that affects us. When my Jidaan struck your Ward, the blast of magick seemed to push the fog away enough for us to clear our heads.*

They looked around and saw the wispy fog was moving quickly to envelop them again. Kiran instinctively created another Ward around the two of them, a pale glowing sphere that kept the fog from getting too close. It rolled up against the outer surface of the energy shield as though searching for a way in.

As they looked at the fog, something struck the Ward behind them, the impact flashing brightly in the gloom. They turned to find one of Nessar's daggers lying in the mud a few yards away.

It's got Nessar, too, Kiran observed. *He probably sees us both as monsters right now.*

Layton frowned. *We've got to protect him from the fog.*

How? With his Stealth, he'll have a dagger in our guts before we can defend ourselves.

Layton was silent. He had no idea. Another flash lit up the night as a second dagger bounced off of Kiran's Ward from a different angle. *How many daggers does he have, anyway?*

Kiran laughed, and began speaking aloud. "More than you would think possible. I've seen that old man fill a bucket with knives while wearing only a pair of short trousers and sandals."

"Wonderful. He'll probably just skulk around out there throwing knives at us until we can find a way to wake him up." Layton looked around as he turned the problem over in his mind. "We either have to get the fog away from him, or get him away from the fog, at least long enough for him to clear his head."

"The fog is everywhere," Kiran observed. "It seems like it would be easier to move Nessar, but we can't hear or see him as long as he's using his Jidaan. How can we find him?"

Layton paused a moment more, then snapped his fingers as an idea came to him. "You can shape your Wards, right? Usually, they are spheres or walls, but I've seen you manipulate them into other shapes."

Kiran nodded. "I can, yes. Walls and spheres are easiest, but I'm pretty sure I can make them do whatever I like." She remembered decades past when she had made a Ward that acted like a sheet of cloth, which she wrapped around an Ogre's head so that it suffocated. She felt a pang of regret about that, knowing as she now did that the Ogre had been compelled by Mordak's magick and had not known any better. "What do you have in mind?" she asked. He told her.

A few minutes later, another dagger struck the Ward, giving them a rough idea of Nessar's location. Instantly, Kiran created six horizontal bars of blue energy parallel to the ground, each above the other to form a wall. The space between them was too small for Nessar to squeeze through, and she spaced them high enough that he could not jump over them even if he used his magick. The glowing bars stretched out into the darkness of the marsh at a slight angle from whence the dagger had flown, and Kiran swept the wall from right to left, towards the spot she guessed Nessar would be.

"He'll have already been moving the instant the dagger left his hand," Kiran muttered. She kept her focus on the Wards she had created, sweeping the bars carefully, but quickly enough that she knew he would not be able to escape. If his mind was addled enough by the fog, he might

67

not even see them. As she brought the wall around to her left, she felt something man-sized strike the lower bars in the Ward, and in that touch of magick, she recognized her old friend. "Got him!" With a flex of her will, she sent the bars forward to snare Nessar, who had been crouched low to the ground in an attempt to avoid them. She felt him struggle mightily as the bars joined together and flowed over his body, pinning his arms to his sides.

"I can't see anything," Layton murmured. "You sure you've got him?"

Kiran opened her eyes, not realizing that she had closed them to focus on the heightened sensations of touch through her extended magick. She peered out into the murk and realized that she could not see anything either, though she could feel exactly where Nessar was standing, encased neck to toes in her Ward.

"Yes, I've got him," she said, laying a hand on Layton's shoulder. "His Jidaan is still hiding him, but I can feel him. Let me guide you, and you can bring him in here with us."

Layton opened himself to Kiran, feeling the connection between their minds growing stronger. Soon, he could feel her magick exactly as she felt it, and was able to locate the struggling form of the old Guardian. "Wow," he whispered, awed at the sensation of Kiran's use of magick. He knew his own power intimately, but the feel of Kiran's use of her power of Warding was wildly different than the Jidaan of Gates. "Ok, there he is. Make some room and I'll get him in here where the air is safe."

Kiran expanded the sphere of her Ward, opening it at the top to let more fresh air inside. Layton ignited his Jidaan, and its opalescent glow shone brightly as it answered his call. A man-sized doorway appeared next to them inside the Ward and farther away, its twin burst into existence. Using Kiran's sense of touch through her magick, Layton swept the far Gate over Nessar's invisible form, moving the closer Gate simultaneously. The closer Gate moved only two feet from its original position, then vanished as Layton let it dissolve. They stood there for a moment, staring at the spot where they knew Nessar to be, but still seeing nothing. They waited.

"Ness. Hey look, it's us. We're not monsters, it's the swamp gas that's making us look like this." Kiran spoke loudly in the confined space of the Ward, but at first there was no response. "Come on, wake up."

Suddenly, Nessar winked into sight before them. Confusion and fatigue were written all over his face. He had finally stopped struggling to free his arms from his sides where Kiran's Ward had imprisoned them. In one hand, he still held a wicked looking dagger. He squinted at Kiran first, then at Layton as his eyes widened.

"It is you, isn't it?" he finally asked. "Really you?"

Kiran and Layton sighed with relief. Kiran answered, "Yes, you old fool, it's us."

"Hey, there are three fools in here right now," Layton laughed tiredly. "We were all ready to kill each other earlier." To Nessar, Layton said, "It's the fog. There's something in it that makes us see things. Kiran cleared the air inside this Ward, so we're all right for now."

Nessar eyed them both somewhat suspiciously, then completely relaxed at last. "All right then. Whew, that was awful. I tried to follow that light, but it disappeared almost as soon as I left you two. I got dizzy and then my head started to swim..." he paused to remember. "Then I saw you two, but you were the most horrible, ugly creatures." He cast a sideways glance at Kiran. "Well, *you* were a monster, Layton. Kiran looked pretty much the same as always."

"Ha ha, you're funny, old man," she grumbled, though she was relieved beyond words to have Nessar back in his right mind. She released him from the captivity of her Ward and he slipped his dagger into a hidden sheath inside his coat. Kiran sighed and continued, "We'll have to find someplace to rest that doesn't have this fog everywhere. I'm getting tired, and I can't keep this up all night, I have to sleep sometime."

"Agreed," Nessar muttered. He pulled out his notebook again and glanced up at the stars overhead to catch his bearings. After double-checking his directions, he pointed off to one side. "The mountains we're looking for should be in that direction. Let's keep moving until we reach a safer spot."

"I think that 'safe' is a very relative term in this place," Layton suggested. "But you're right, of course. Let's go." He nodded at the surrounding Ward as he turned to Kiran. "Can you keep this Ward up until we find a place to camp?"

"Looks like I'll have to," Kiran answered, both weariness and determination in her voice in equal measures. "Let's get moving then. And Nessar gets first watch for throwing knives at us."

They traveled deep into the night as they tried to escape the clutches of the mist. It seemed to be everywhere, and it slowed their progress even more by hiding the ground. Several times, they nearly walked into stagnant pools or wide stretches of deep mud before seeing the danger. As dawn approached, they finally found a spot where the ground rose in a gentle slope that plateaued well above the level of the fog. It was uncluttered by the stunted trees and shrubs that had hindered their passage through the Mire, and they made their way to it as quickly as they dared. They climbed to the top of the hillock, and once they were sure the mist had stayed down below, Kiran released her Ward with a sigh of relief. She curled up on one side, pillowed her head on her arm, and was asleep before Layton and Nessar could even sit down.

Nessar chuckled. "She was always able to do that, fall asleep in moments."

"It's a handy skill for a warrior," Layton replied. "We never know when we'll get an opportunity, so we take what we can get."

"I hear that. You go on ahead and rest, I'll keep watch."

"Dawn will be coming soon," Layton said, looking up at the starry sky overhead. No matter how alien and dangerous was the land on which he stood, the stars had always given him comfort.

"Yes, I know. We need the rest, though. I'll wake you in a couple of hours so I can sleep some, then we'll move out." He glanced at Kiran. "Just let her rest. That Ward took a lot out of her. She can take first watch tomorrow."

Layton agreed and adopted a pose similar to Kiran's. He had a bedroll stuffed in his pack, but the ground was relatively dry. He did not want to waste time unrolling it when he could be sleeping. In only slightly less time than it had taken Kiran to doze, Layton joined her in the land of dreams.

Nessar pulled a dagger from somewhere and set about digging mud from under his fingernails. He was tired as well, all the way to the bone. Even so, he found that he needed less sleep these days. Whether it was because of the magick the Jidaan had awakened in him or because he was just getting older, he did not know. At least it made things easier sometimes, and he would take what he could get.

He scanned the Mire around them. They were surrounded by shadows, dark and twisted trees, and shifting mists. The night sounds in the Mire were much different from the other forests he had been through, somehow more sinister for the fact that he could not readily identify what made them. Even the buzzing insects that droned in the distance sounded different. Nessar glared into the darkness a while longer, then turned his attention back to his knife.

Gart, he mused. *Why'd you have to do this, man? We've all lost loved ones; we all know that pain. Why risk it all for this? One mistake, and the world could become a Hel on earth. Why?*

The mist had no answers.

When morning arrived, Nessar had gone to sleep and left Layton on watch. The sun's light seemed dim and pale as it filtered through the shadowy trees. Layton grimaced as he looked at the sky overhead, overcast and gray.

Something tickled the edge of his awareness, and he went still. Mist still ringed the bottom of the hill where they had camped, thick enough that it could easily hide almost anything. Layton scanned the area but could not see anything amiss at first glance. Out of the corner of his eye, he caught another glimpse of movement, but when he casually turned to look, there was nothing to see. Finally, he relaxed and reached out with his magick as Brunar had once taught him, questing into the mist with his power in an attempt to find what lay hidden there. Suddenly, he touched a figure, something large, but then it vanished from his senses. Elsewhere, something else loomed, but it, too, escaped the faint touch of his magick. Again and again, he sensed figures in the mist, but could ascertain nothing other than the fact that they were there, and there were quite a few of them. Puzzled, he withdrew his power and decided to wake the others.

"Kiran," Layton's voice was quiet, but urgent. Kiran slept on. He poked her gently in the ribs with the toe of his boot, unwilling to chance anything more startling, lest she lash out in her sleep. He switched to the internal communication Brunar had long ago taught them. *Hey. Wake up. We have visitors.*

Finally, Kiran opened one eye and looked up at her friend, grimacing even in the dim morning light. The import of his words finally struck her and she tensed, one hand on the closest of her daggers. *Visitors?* Her eyes cut to the left and right, but she saw nothing except the stubbly grass of the hillock on which they sat and the thinning mist that still surrounded it.

Layton nodded once. *They're in the mist, just close enough to fill us with arrows if they like. I've caught only a couple of glimpses of them. They're humanoid, but I can't be sure exactly what they are. Taller than Gholans, at least. They've not advanced farther than that, so I haven't seen anything more.*

What about Nessar?

I wanted to wake you first in case they decided to use us for target practice. A half-smile appeared on Layton's face and the old twinkle resurfaced in his eyes. *You handle things like that better than I.*

Damn straight I do, Kiran replied proudly. Moving slowly so as to avoid startling any of their unseen watchers, Kiran sat up, making a show of stretching and looking thoroughly unconcerned. Carefully reaching out with her magick, she probed the mist, looking for the figures Layton had seen. Quickly enough, she found them, though it was surprisingly difficult to get a true bearing on their position. They were indistinct to her perception, only marginally more solid than the mist that hid them. *I can feel them out there, but not very well. Ten, maybe a dozen?*

That was my guess, too. I think the mist is hampering us somehow.

Figures, Kiran retorted. She then turned her attention to Nessar. *Hey, Vanessa. Wake up, you old coot. But move easy. We've got company.*

They turned to where Nessar had been sleeping, but he was gone. Both Kiran and Layton quickly turned back to each other so they would not call attention to their missing comrade.

I think he's already checking things out for us, Kiran grinned as she reached for her pack and began to pull out her rations, paying no attention to the mist or the figures hidden within it. *Let's just play it cool until we hear from him.* Layton knelt next to her and followed her example.

*   *   *   *   *   *

Nessar moved slowly so that the mists would not swirl around his invisible form, revealing him to the unseen denizens of the Mire. He had awakened as soon as Layton had 'spoken' to Kiran, and quickly cloaked himself with the Jidaan's power of Stealth. He knew he could assess the danger better than either of them. Wary at first of the fog, Nessar found that it had a different smell and feel than the sinister vapor of the night before. It felt like any ordinary morning mist, and Nessar let out a quiet sigh of relief.

Moving with a preternatural stealth borne of both magick and long practice, Nessar eased through the shifting fog, keeping a wary eye out for whatever had been watching them. He glimpsed a shadowy movement out of the corner of his eye and edged toward it, his senses on high alert for any other signs of movement.

Without warning, huge, strong hands grasped his arms tightly, binding them like iron. Something thick and strong whipped around his legs and jerked them together, completely immobilizing him. A slender cord was looped around his neck, then pulled just tight enough that he did not want to challenge it. He nearly fell, but the unseen hands easily kept him upright, his toes barely touching the

73

ground. Nessar looked right and left as best he could, but saw nothing but mist. *Uh oh,* he thought. *This is bad.*

A low, gruff voice came out of the mist in front of him, almost a growl. "We see thee, interloper. Our eyes see by a different light than thine own. Thou art our prisoner. Unwise it is to walk the Mire unescorted."

Nessar took a deep breath and let it out. He had been in far worse situations, though he was hard pressed to recall any of them just then. He thought for a moment about what he should say, then shrugged and decided on the truth.

"You have our apologies for the intrusion. We mean no harm. We are on a mission of great importance and are only passing through." He paused, thinking, and then continued. "Had we known that this territory was yours, we would have gladly asked for permission. Indeed, we didn't know anything of you or anyone living in the Mire. I apologize again for our trespassing."

Silence was the only response for a few moments. Nessar simply waited.

"Thou art at least polite," the voice finally responded. There was another silence before it continued. "How do we know thou art speaking truth? That thou mean no harm to my people?"

Nessar sighed. "I only have my word, and that of my companions. We carry the Jidaan, and are not given to harming innocents."

An odd-sounding chuckle, almost a gargling noise, answered him. "Yes, we saw thy magickal spears. Of them, we know little, but their power is plain to us." There was another pause, and then, "We are a people who value honor. Dost thou give thy word that thou will not attempt to harm us? If thou art deceitful, death will be thy reward and the same for thy companions, regardless of the magick they possess." There was a calm surety in the speaker's words, and Nessar believed wholeheartedly that the unseen figure spoke the truth.

"We will defend ourselves, but only if necessary," Nessar said, taking a chance. If they respected honor, then they might also respect his speaking plainly. "We only fight if we must. We have no quarrel with you or your people. We only wish to make our way to the mountains. Our friend is headed there to make a grave mistake, and we would stop him if possible."

There was a sudden tenseness in the air as Nessar's words were considered, and Nessar thought he had made a mistake. Then his legs and arms were released. He staggered a bit, but quickly regained his balance and rubbed his arms where they had been held. The voice came again.

"You interest me, old one," the low voice sounded as though on the verge of a chuckle again. "Although we could easily overwhelm you and your friends, I have no desire for unnecessary bloodshed. We have enough of that from others who enter the Mire, others who bring death with them. I offer you peace as long as you give the same in return."

Nessar let out the breath he did not know he was holding. Adopting the formal manner of speech his captors seemed to favor, he responded, "I offer you our good behavior, sir, and we thank you for your forbearance. May I introduce you to my friends?"

"Yes, indeed," the voice agreed. The mist suddenly began to disperse, rapidly thinning to reveal the owner of the voice as well as his companions.

"Great goddess above," Nessar could not stop himself from expressing his shock. "I mean, um..."

Standing before Nessar was a seven-foot tall crocodile, though its arms and legs were longer and more manlike. Its deep, olive green skin was roughly scaled, and its pointed snout boasted an impressive array of teeth, some as large as Nessar's thumb. Bits of armor decorated its upper arm and thigh, and there were brightly colored tattoos in intricate designs on its pale chest. Around its thick, muscular throat dangled a necklace of what looked like human teeth, and a simple leather loincloth was its only other clothing. It held a long, jagged spear in one scaled hand, and a short sword that hung from a plain leather belt at its waist, though the claws and teeth of the creature negated the need for such in Nessar's mind. The creature's other hand was raised in a magickal gesture, and a faint greenish glow shone from it as it dispersed the surrounding

75

fog. Stretching out behind it, Nessar could see its powerful tail resting on the ground, thick with muscle and sporting two rows of short, cruel metal spikes embedded along its natural ridges. Its eyes were bright and aware. It blinked once, a clear membrane flashing down over the creature's irises, then snapping back up again. It stared down at Nessar impassively, though the old man could swear the creature was grinning. Nessar glanced to either side and saw the two crocodile warriors that had held him captive. As the mist receded, Nessar saw dozens more of the strong, stealthy warriors standing nearby, all watching with great interest.

Nessar quickly regained his composure. "Well, this is definitely not something you see every day." He bowed low to the leader, exercising long-unused courtly manners. "I am Nessar of Rualtha, a Guardian. I carry the Jidaan of Stealth." He stood to his full height once more. "I'm very pleased to meet you."

The huge man-croc blinked again, then inclined its head slightly towards the old thief. "Well met, sir Nessar. I am Rulyeh, leader of the Dyles. We dwell here in the Mire, as we have for years untold. We have no love for outsiders, but then, they seldom trouble us. The Mire is without mercy, and protects us from all but the strongest."

"You can say that again," Nessar grumbled. "It nearly got us more than once." He gestured towards the low hill where Kiran and Layton waited, just out of sight of the hollow in which they stood. "With your permission, I'd like to introduce you to my friends. I'm sure they will be most interested to meet you. We had no idea that anyone lived in here as you do. Even the Weya made no mention of your kind, and they sent us here."

At the mention of the elfin race, a low growl went through the assembled warriors, and Nessar suddenly realized he might have just made a mistake. Rulyeh made a sharp coughing sound and gestured sharply with one muscled arm, and the noise was instantly silenced. Whatever misgivings the warriors might have had regarding the Weya, their desire to follow Rulyeh's orders was far stronger.

76

"My apologies for the behavior of my warriors," Rulyeh rumbled. "There is an ancient feud between our two peoples, and the mention of them apparently caused a momentary lapse of discipline. I will address that later." Rulyeh's gaze swept over his soldiers, and as one they bowed their heads in shame at the rebuke. The massive man-croc returned his focus to Nessar. "For now, I should like to meet thy friends."

Nessar made a mental note to tread carefully around the Dyles on the subject of the Weya. That the small, fair race would feud with anyone came as a complete surprise to Nessar, having always seen them as a wise and compassionate race. The only enmity they had ever shown was towards the steadfastly evil Gholans and Krell, who reveled in their own hatred of everything that was not their own. He would have to ask Rulyeh about the feud, but later. He gestured to the huge creature and began to walk back to where Layton and Kiran awaited.

I'm bringing some folks to meet you, Nessar silently sent word to his friends. *They are pretty fearsome, but we're on friendly terms, so do not attack them. Got it, Kiran? No stabbing. And don't mention the Weya, they don't like them.*

The resulting burst of mental communication from Kiran almost made him laugh due to the sheer amount of profanity it contained, but he kept a neutral expression as he escorted Rulyeh and a couple of his officers up the hill. He could not, however, stifle a grin at the shocked expression on both Kiran and Layton's faces when they saw what he had meant by 'fearsome.'

Chapter 13

"Dru, watch out!" Reyanna caught a glimpse of something quick and whiplike snaking up through the leaves of the trees. Instantly, Drusilla shifted direction, angling to their right, but that turned out to be exactly what the creature below had hoped for.

Suddenly, the twisted tree limbs Drusilla had been using to travel above the Mire came alive with darting, whipping vines as thick around as Reyanna's wrist. Each was tipped with a toothy maw filled with sharp, biting teeth. The big spider danced away from the nearest only to find more boiling up through the sickly leaves below, grasping and biting at her slender legs and wrapping themselves tightly around her limbs. Reyanna felt Drusilla's fear and pain in her mind, compounding her own feelings of rising terror. Clinging tightly to the saddle with her legs and clutching the pommel horn with her left hand, Reyanna drew her long dagger and looked for something to slash.

In a series of sharp jerks and yanks, Drusilla was pulled down into the swamp. She fought ferociously to remain above the trees, but the coiling vines were impossible to resist. As she fell toward the marshy ground below, more vines snapped out of the shadows to ensnare the struggling spider. Seeing that she could do nothing to help Drusilla where she was, Reyanna quickly threw her bow and quiver to the ground, then unbuckled the straps that held her tightly to the saddle. The instant she was free, she dove from the spider's back towards a relatively clear spot on the ground. Jostled by the spider's frantic thrashing, she hit harder than she anticipated, and the wind went whistling from her lungs as she rolled on the damp earth. Reyanna pushed herself up to her knees as she struggled to breathe.

Drusilla was hissing now, her legs flailing about as she tried to pull herself away from the ropy vines that held her. Her huge fangs ripped and tore at the greenish coils, but her teeth were made for puncturing her prey, not cutting it. Finally, she spat an intense, ropy burst of spider silk from her spinnerets, at the same time she spewed her deadly venom from a gland beneath her fangs. The silk sprayed out in front of her, fouling many of the nearest vines, welding them together so the venom could dissolve them when it hit. Somewhere in the shadows, something growled, a low and ominous sound that seemed to travel through the marshy earth as much as the humid air. Drusilla hissed again and sprayed another burst of silk and venom, catching more of the grasping, biting vines, yet suffering mightily from others that seemed to pour out of the darkness. The small mouths bit hard wherever they could, each becoming another burning spot of agony on the spider's body. Slowly, Drusilla was drawn down towards the ground, her strength fading as the thorny mouths drew her life's blood from a hundred small wounds.

"No!" Reyanna snatched up her bow and arrows and ran across the swampy soil towards the battle. She hunted for the source of the vines and saw that they all emerged from the hollow base of an enormous tree, long blackened and dead. The trunk was easily as big around as Reyanna's dwelling back in Allinshae, but from within the dark hole at its base came hundreds of the thick, biting tendrils. Surrounding the dead tree were a thousand loose bones. Reyanna's mouth dropped open as she saw skulls, femurs, and partial rib cages, gleaming white in the dull light. Many of the skulls were easily recognizable as animals she knew, but some were horrifically enormous and deformed. All had been picked clean and then strewn about like a child's discarded toys. The horrific boneyard let Reyanna know exactly what was in store for both herself and Drusilla if she did not do something quickly. As she approached, she heard and felt a deep-throated growl that vibrated the earth around her. No animal she had ever heard sounded like that. No, this sounded *wrong*.

Reyanna looked up and saw Drusilla's great body nearly immobile in the green strands as surely as the spider, herself, might have caught her prey with strands of her silk. Her eight legs still struggled, but she seemed to be fading.

Whipping an arrow from her quiver and nocking it to string, Reyanna sighted what she thought would be the center of the writhing mass of vines within the dark wooden cave and let the arrow fly. Another was already in the air as the first disappeared into the hollow, slamming into something with a wet-sounding *thukk*. The vines convulsed. A furious howl of rage and pain erupted from the hidden creature within as the second arrow found its mark. Reyanna smiled as she dropped to one knee, pulling another arrow to her cheek and sending it on its way. *Sounds like that hurt. Good. I've got more.*

Many of the tendrils began to detach themselves from the spider, whipping with purpose in Reyanna's direction. The huge body of Drusilla suddenly fell hard to the ground, no longer held aloft by the squirming mass of green vines as their attention was diverted. They knew that Reyanna was the threat. She had hurt it, and that had to stop. The leathery green tentacles squirmed frantically towards the young Ranger as she dodged and ducked their thorny maws.

She let fly another arrow, and another, each eliciting a louder roar of anger from the unseen creature. As she prepared to loose another, a vine whipped itself around her ankles and instantly cinched them together. Reyanna started to fall, but other creepers found her and quickly wrapped themselves around her arms, her legs, her torso, imprisoning her in a swaddling wrap of rough green stems and thorns. She cried out in pain and frustration as the vines lifted her off the ground, holding their prize aloft.

From within the dark hollow at the base of the dead tree, something moved. Another deep rumble accompanied the shadowy motion, and from within the writhing mass of slender stalks that held Reyanna, four other appendages emerged. They were each as thick as her leg, ending with wide, spade shaped leaves that gripped the edges of the hole in which the creature lived. She saw and felt the vines contract as the beast finally pulled itself into the light.

Its huge, bulbous head emerged first, and Reyanna saw that its neck was a much larger version of the stalks that imprisoned her. The enormous pod that served as its head split open, revealing a maw filled with rows upon rows of hard, rooty teeth. Its bulky body barely fit through the opening, its green, pulpy mass seething with anger. She could see no eyes on the thing but knew that it could sense its environment well enough, for it faced her immediately and opened its toothy mouth to let out another roar of anger. The thick neck slowly extended out of the hole, bringing the huge head closer to Reyanna, who struggled frantically against the capturing vines even as they lifted her higher into the air.

Her arms pinned to her sides by the vines, and bleeding in a score of places from their rough skin and biting thorns, Reyanna felt panic begin to rise. Along with it, she also felt her magick awaken. She felt it as a fiercely boiling warmth deep in her core, both familiar in its touch and alien in its incredible intensity. All her life, she had felt it, but never this strongly. If what she had known as a child had been a gentle breeze in her soul, this was a howling hurricane. It terrified her, but also gave her hope. Drusilla needed her. As the creature edged its head closer, its mouth opening wide in anticipation of a meal, Reyanna reached into her power, embracing it.

Instantly, Reyanna's entire body flooded with her magick. Her eyes opened, and their golden light pierced the gloom of the Mire as brightly as if the sun had come down from above. A wave of warmth and strength bathed her, and she reveled in it as her panic from a moment before ceased to exist. She became aware of the distant smell of green wood burning as the vines that held her were suddenly seared through by her power. The creature bellowed in pain, thrashing its many limbs in all directions as it reeled in agony. Reyanna gazed at it absently, as though it was barely worth her attention. It released Reyanna, but she stayed aloft, buoyed by her own power, glowing a bright orange-gold as she floated above the swampy ground.

She vaguely recalled that she had burned through her clothes before, and slowly brought her focus to the garments she wore. They were already damaged in places, so she pulled her power back, letting it coil and move inside her again without burning anything that touched her body. Without knowing quite how, she reached into the cloth and leather, binding the fibers that remained so that the garments became whole once more. That accomplished, she allowed herself to drift downward until her feet rested on the marshy soil beneath her. Her glowing eyes latched onto the injured plant creature, which seemed to be having trouble retreating into the dark hollow of the ancient tree. Its limbs thrashed and whipped through the air, many much shorter after having been burned through by her power. Reyanna allowed a smile to appear on her face, almost unseen through the intense glow that surrounded her. She took a step towards the creature's tree, then another. The creature squealed harshly and redoubled its efforts to push itself back into the shelter of the rotten stump.

Reyanna raised both hands and called upon her magick. *This creature tried to hurt me,* she thought loftily. A sense of outrage surfaced in her mind. *That is unacceptable. It must pay.* Her hands suddenly glowed like twin suns as she poured magick into them. The plant creature finally managed to retreat back into the dark hollow, pulling its many arms inside along with it. However, it did not matter what the creature did; it was already doomed.

Molten fire erupted from Reyanna's hands in fierce twin streams, scorching the air as it hurtled into the creature's abode. It screeched in agony for the last few seconds of its life and thrashed frantically as Reyanna's fire burned it to ashes. Reyanna continued blasting the plant beast's lair until the entire rotten tree was a blistering bonfire. When she was satisfied that no trace of the monster remained, Reyanna halted the flow of energy and lowered her hands. She walked imperiously toward the inferno. Upon seeing that the tree and everything inside it had been completely incinerated, a strong sense of satisfaction arose in her.

Well and good, she thought, still smirking. Then a thought occurred to her. There was a reason she had been so angry. What was it? Her power flowed through her, making her feel invincible and strong. It also made it difficult to think clearly. *I was protecting something. What was I doing?*

With an effort of will that left her dizzy, Reyanna gathered her magick and forced it to coil in upon itself, to reduce its intensity and allow her to think. It obeyed, though reluctantly. As the sensation of inner warmth and strength ebbed, exhaustion hit Reyanna all at once. She staggered as the intense fatigue threatened to drop her to the muddy ground, but she fought it. She managed to get her feet under herself, and though she was still reeling and shaky, she stayed up. The heat of the fire she had created hit her as the remains of the big tree burned brightly into hot coals. Stumbling, she turned away from the fire and tried to catch her breath, still disoriented from being overtaken by her own magick. She rubbed a hand over her eyes, and when they focused again, they fell on the enormous body of Drusilla. The great spider lay on her side several yards away, unmoving.

"Drusilla! No, oh no..." Reyanna rushed to the side of the silent creature, easing herself past the long, spindly legs and approaching the spider's face. At least half of Drusillas long legs were obviously broken, and there were several circular bite marks on her torso that seeped fluid. As she came close, Reyanna could see reflections of her own face in Drusilla's unblinking black eyes, and she gently laid her hands on what she thought of as Dru's head. "Can you move? Oh, no, Dru..."

The spider did not answer, did not move. She was silent. Reyanna carefully reached for her magick again, using it to gently probe for the mental link they had once shared, but there was no response there either. All was dark and silent.

Reyanna sat with Drusilla for a long time, hoping, praying that she could find some sign that her friend had survived. There was nothing but the fetid breeze and the unnerving sounds of the Mire's creatures in the distance. She was completely alone. Reyanna laid her head on Drusilla's furry cephalothorax and cried until there were no more tears.

Chapter 14

Gart groaned. He opened his eyes to find Beauty's scarred face only inches from his. Her soft brown eyes were wide and focused on his face. The magickal link between them conveyed her happiness to Gart even as her tail began to thump heavily against his leg.

"Ow," he mumbled, not unkindly. "Beauty, you're killing me with that tail of yours." He scratched her ears and experienced her sudden ecstasy as if it were his own. In spite of his exhaustion and many aches and pains, he managed a smile. If only he had learned to experience that kind of single-minded, unbridled joy. Beauty instantly gave herself over to her happiness when she found it, and that was its own kind of magick. Gart wrapped his arms around her and hugged her thick neck for a moment, then gently nudged her so she would get off of him. "I need to get up. Move over, girl." Beauty obliged, and Gart worked his way up to his feet.

Everything hurt. Gart tried to stretch, but only managed to aggravate all of his injuries at once. Wincing, he probed the gashes on his left arm and leg. He had taken some vicious wounds on his forearm and thigh, and although he had managed to stop the bleeding before passing out, they were only partially healed and threatened to open up if he moved too sharply. He gauged the well of magick he had remaining and decided that the wounds would keep well enough for now. Even after a full night's sleep, he still felt exhausted, and was loathe to use up more of his energy on himself. Beauty needed it more than he did, and he could handle the pain. Pain was an old friend.

Moving like a much older man, Gart unrolled a feed bag and filled it with grain for Bessie, then attached it so she could eat. Then he pulled some food from his pack and shared it with Beauty, who gobbled hers quickly. Gart chewed on the dried beef slowly, relishing the salty taste of it as he gathered his thoughts for what lay ahead.

He was close; he could feel it. Although the earth was dead and barren where he stood, somewhere in the distance he could feel a faint vibration, the hint of faraway power. It was like a river heard from a distance, though there was no sound to accompany the current of magick that coursed below the earth's surface. It was just at the far edge of his perception, but strong enough for him to follow it easily.

Somewhere in the barren mountains, the Shrine of Malmathas awaited. Gart cast a glance skyward and saw that he had two days to find it. The moon would catch up with the sun then, casting the world into darkness. The rite he had planned could only be conducted at such a time, an in between time, neither night nor day, but both and neither. He had been concerned that he would not make it in time, but he was relieved to find himself so near the site. Judging by the sensation of magick he felt in his bones, Gart knew he would make it by the time the sun turned black. He would see Gennie again.

Gart checked his pack and found that the flask containing the Blood of Nimshi was still sealed and intact. Satisfied, he pulled out a heavy, cloth-covered lump from another bag. Carefully, he unwrapped the folds of linen and caught his breath when the sun hit the Heart of Corria, making it sparkle like a rainbow on fire. He gazed on it for only a moment, then he wrapped the massive diamond once more and stowed it away. He had felt the gemstone's pull on his already weary soul almost immediately, and had no desire to fight it. Safer to have it tucked away until he needed it.

"All right, girl," he said to Beauty. "Let's get up and get moving. We're almost there."

It only took a few minutes for Gart to get Bessie's feed bag stowed again. Then he loaded his pack and saddlebags and pulled himself onto Bessie's back. He picked up the reins and guided her away from the stone ruins, leaving the portal behind. Looking back at the remains of the ancient castle, Gart recalled the dimensional corridor that connected that pile of stone with another edifice many miles to the east. Overland, it would have taken weeks of travel, but the magickal way had taken only hours to traverse. Gart did not relish the idea of going through that Hel again, but since it was a shortcut that completely bypassed the worst of the Poravian Mire and many miles beyond, he was willing to endure it again once his quest was done. Next time, he would be ready for the dwellers within. *If there is a next time,* he thought. He shrugged off the unexpected chill that rolled down his spine. *Stupid. I can do this. We're almost there.* He dug his heels into Bessie's flanks, urging her forward and putting the stones behind them.

Beauty moved happily alongside her master, her eyes and ears alert for anything amiss. She felt Gart's concern, but also a faint and quiet eagerness. They would reach their goal soon, and if that made Gart happy, then it made her happy, too. Every day was a new adventure for her, and she was eager to see what was around the corner.

Chapter 15

Kiran and Layton stood with eyes wide and mouths open at the sight of Nessar leading three enormous beings up the hill toward them. The central figure was the largest, though the two walking crocodiles on either side were also hugely intimidating. Had Nessar not let them know he was safe, they would have instantly sprung to the attack. Even so, their hands itched to be filled with dagger, sword, or Jidaan. They relaxed slightly at the sight of Nessar's face, grinning at their obvious discomfort. That, more than anything, told them that their companion was in no danger.

"Yes, yes," Nessar was already talking as he approached. "I know they're big and scary, but so far, they're treating me with respect, and we'll do the same in return." He eyed Kiran sharply, and although she frowned, she nodded once in agreement. Nessar turned to the tallest creature and gestured. "Kiran, Layton, this is Rulyeh, the leader of the Dyle people."

Layton immediately slapped a fist to his heart and bowed towards the creature. "Sir," he said crisply.

Kiran looked sidewise at him, then copied his movements, though without his extreme precision. "Thank you for not killing us," she said, unsure of what else to say.

Rulyeh gargled and coughed loudly, and it took a few seconds for them to realize the big creature was laughing. In his deep, rumbling voice, he replied, "Thou seem to be formidable warriors, and possess powerful magick. Although we would likely emerge victorious, I surmise that thou would be worthy opponents." Rulyeh glanced to his officers on either side. "I would ask thee of the Weya. They have been our sworn enemies for centuries, and yet thou speak of them with respect. We feel no evil in thee, so how can this be?"

Kiran and Layton looked at each other before Kiran blurted, "Evil? They've always seemed wise and good to us, and to everyone who has ever dealt with them, to my knowledge. They're a little snooty, perhaps, but not evil."

Rulyeh rumbled low in his throat. "Snooty?"

"Ah, arrogant, I mean. Just a bit. But very polite otherwise." Kiran nodded firmly. The first time she had ever seen a Weya was at Guardians Keep over twenty years before, when three of them had come to alert Brunar of Mordak's whereabouts. They had met, trained with, and fought beside many since then, and she could not imagine anyone thinking them evil.

Rulyeh snorted. "Arrogant, yes. We found them to be exceedingly so. They spoke not of us?"

Layton joined the conversation. "No, sir. I've trained with Weya extensively over the last twenty years, and there was never a word said about your people, nor of any enmity that might exist. Not doubting your word, but they have always seemed to me to be kind and loving folk." Suddenly he frowned. "Do you know of the Gholans who live in the mire?"

All three of the Dyles growled loudly and shook their heads before Rulyeh replied. "Those foul beasts! Their spirit is even viler than their meat! The Gholanai shun us, for we kill any we find in our territory, and rightfully so! They have a penchant for stealing and eating our young, so we kill them on sight." He paused for a moment. "They have been somewhat scarce of late, and for that, we are thankful."

Kiran nodded. "We killed thousands of them during the war with Mordak. He called them to his service, and many died at Laro and Alverton Falls, where Mordak finally fell."

Rulyeh's two officers looked at each other and grunted, nodding slightly at each other. They obviously approved. Rulyeh took in Kiran's words and thought for a moment before speaking again. "Our fight with the Weya is thousands of years old. We have not spoken to, nay, even seen one in centuries. The Gholans have always been evil, it is their nature." The Dyle leader reached up with one clawed hand and absently scratched the underside of his long, powerful jaw. "We feel no evil in thou, none at all. Thou count as enemies the Gholanai, and say that the Weya are kind folk, not the spiteful, treacherous scum we believe them to be." Then he sighed and looked at all three of the humans before him. "I am intrigued. This thing with the

Weya...it is something we have always known. But your words interest me. You must tell me more."

Just then, another Dyle warrior appeared at the bottom of the hill. "My lord! Thy daughter! She was snatched by the gargoleth! Come quickly!"

Without a word, Rulyeh exploded into motion, as did one of his lieutenants, sprinting down the hill toward the Mire at astonishing speed. They disappeared into the swamp without a single glance at the humans they left behind.

The Guardians exchanged a look, and Nessar asked the one remaining Dyle, who looked exceedingly uncomfortable to have been left to guard them, "Pardon me, but what's a gargoleth?"

The huge reptile grunted and growled, obviously agitated, but it responded. "It is a thing from elder times, made of vines, twigs, and muck. Invulnerable to our teeth and claws, even our weapons hurt it but little. I fear for Shurlyeh. None who have been taken have survived."

Kiran fairly exploded. "What are you waiting for? Take us there! We can help!"

The Dyle looked at the smaller woman in surprise. "Thou? Against a gargoleth?"

"Absolutely! We've killed worse, trust me on that one."

The Dyle looked into the swamp where his chief had vanished, then back at the three humans, weighing its options. Finally, it spoke to the three Guardians.

"Rulyeh holds thou in high regard, else he'd have killed thee on the spot. Canst thou truly help?"

Kiran took a step towards the towering reptile, her jaw thrust forward. "Oh yeah, just watch us. Lead the way, you big lizard."

If the Dyle was offended at being called a lizard, it did not show it. Instead, it loped down the hill, gesturing for the Guardians to follow.

Nessar grumbled loudly. "This is not what we're here for, you realize that?"

Kiran shot back, "Look, I'm tired, I'm frustrated, and I miss my Oswald. I'm ready to kill something, and I mean right now. This thing will do."

Layton chuckled as he ran along beside them. "That's our Kiran!"

"Besides," Kiran muttered, almost to herself. "It's his daughter." No one indicated that they had heard her, but merely picked up their pace.

The Dyle was amazingly fleet-footed for being so large. He raced through the swamp in pursuit of his fellows, keeping to the firmest surfaces that would support its clawed feet. Close behind, the Guardians followed the Dyle's lead and used its footprints as a guide, thus speeding their travel. They ran for what seemed a long time, but in truth, was likely only a few minutes.

"We are totally lost now, you know that," Nessar observed as he glanced at their surroundings.

"We'll worry about that later. I'm sure one of the Dyles can show us the way out," Kiran suggested.

"Listen!" Layton hissed. "Up ahead!"

They all heard it, a commotion of low Dyle roars of anger and pain, splashing, and an odd keening they had never heard before. Rulyeh's throaty rumble was the loudest of all, easily identified over the din as he bellowed orders and attacked with unbridled ferocity.

They emerged in a sheltered, watery glade, the site of a pitched battle. Twenty Dyle warriors were hacking away at a giant mass of squirming wooden tendrils, doing almost no damage that the Guardians could see. Their bone and metal weapons shattered on the hard wood of the gargoleth, and they were nearly defenseless against its lightning-fast whipping attacks.

"Sweet baby monkeys!" Kiran swore.

"There it is!" the Dyle pointed unnecessarily to a huge roiling mass that took up most of the center of the glade. It was enormous, at least twenty feet high and nearly that around. It looked like a giant, living shrub, a huge mass of brown and green vines, covered with leaves and branches, all moving, all twisting and thrashing about. It dripped with moss and algae, and parts of it were packed with foul-smelling mud. As they watched, a thick vine reached out and slashed through a nearby Dyle warrior, its rough bark nearly cutting the hapless creature in half. The Dyles were bravely attacking the thing, but their weapons did little damage, and their teeth and claws counted for nothing against the mostly wooden creature. Rulyeh was everywhere, attacking the beast with all his strength and dodging its lightning fast attacks as he attempted to save his child. It brushed aside his onslaught as though impervious to his rage, and paid him no notice.

Kiran heard a higher pitched cry, and her eyes were drawn toward the top of the gargoleth. Enmeshed in the grasping vines and tendrils was a Dyle no larger than a human child, frantically trying to escape the creature's grasp. The gargoleth quickly sensed her feeble struggling and sent vines to claim her. The squirming, insidious tentacles encircled her body, covering her completely, and then pulled her out of sight, deep into the creature's center. "Rulyeh's daughter," she said through clenched teeth. She turned furious eyes on Layton. "Get me right in front of that thing."

Layton nodded, and Kiran saw the opal in his Jidaan flare to life as he called to its power. Kiran drew her own and burst into a run directly toward the beast, unleashing a vicious battle cry as she charged. A swirling, multicolored panel of energy appeared in the air in front of her as Layton created a Gate for her, and she leaped headlong into the portal. In the next instant, she emerged from another Gate right in front of the giant creature. The first swing of her Jidaan cut through the gargoleth's vines easily, parting them as though they were naught but blades of summer grass. Instantly, she reversed her swing and cut another huge gash across several vines, then once again scything through its limbs on the next cut. The Dyles stepped away, shocked at Kiran's ferocity. They had never seen a human fight as she did, and for a moment, they were awed.

The gargoleth emitted a piercing shriek, then quickly surged toward Kiran. It slapped and slashed at her with its hard wooden tentacles, its vines slicing wickedly through the air at her from all directions. She dodged and ducked and twisted out of the way, never giving an inch, always driving forward. She yelled in defiance at the immense, heartless beast before her, determined that it should not gain ground on her. Pieces of the gargoleth fell in a steady rain around her feet, dying as they were separated from the whole.

She was in her element now. Her enemy surrounded her. It was everywhere; she did not even have to aim. All she had to do was keep slashing. Her blood sang in her veins and her magick flowed through her body, infusing her with strength. Vines reached out to encircle her, but she sliced through them with ease. Instantly, they were replaced by more, and she cut them as well. Her fatigue was gone, replaced by a feeling of exultation and power. Suddenly, she was twenty again, taking on all comers, emerging bloodied but victorious every time. This is what she was born to do. She was a warrior. She was a Guardian. She was Kiran, and nothing could stop her.

The creature shrieked again, finally feeling the many hurts Kiran had inflicted upon it, slowly weakening from so many dire wounds. In the long centuries of its existence, it had never felt such pain, never met such opposition. It was a completely alien sensation which in turn gave birth to another new emotion: fear.

The gargoleth tried to move away from the incessantly slashing human, desperate to escape, but the Guardian followed. No matter where the gargoleth tried to go, Kiran was there, cutting, riving, hacking it to bits.

Finally, the massive creature went back on the attack, abruptly rolling forward. Kiran's body disappeared within its thick branches as they swarmed over her, mercilessly crushing in upon her. She vanished among the many thick vines and the muck that made up the gargoleth's body. Once it had her in its clutches, it tightened in upon itself, completely hiding her from sight.

Layton drew his Jidaan, but Nessar put a hand on his arm to stop him.

"What? It's eating her or something! She needs help!" Layton was confused.

Nessar shook his head. "I've seen her like this before. You'll just piss her off, and you know it. Wait a bit, then help her if she asks."

Layton raised an eyebrow, but slowly relaxed his stance. He turned back to the roiling mass of branches, earth, and moss that comprised the gargoleth. It had begun to emit a long, mournful sound that grated on the senses. Some of the Dyles had moved in again to hack at it, but their efforts had even less effect now that it had closed so tightly upon itself. The creature trembled and vibrated, then shuddered violently.

Nessar tensed as if listening, then he started waving his arms overhead. His gravelly voice echoed within the glade as he yelled for all to hear, "Get back! Quickly now, move away from it! Run!"

The Dyles looked at him, then at Rulyeh, who grunted his assent and turned reluctantly to move away from the creature. He had not taken five steps when a brilliant flare of cobalt blue energy exploded from within the center of the gargoleth, sending bits and pieces of wood, earth, and moss in all directions and throwing the Dyles face-first into the mud as they tried to escape. The creature had disintegrated, its parts blasted into tiny pieces that fell harmlessly into the Mire. Where the gargoleth had been now sat an enormous glowing sphere of energy, bluer than the sky far above and humming with intense power. It was much larger than the creature had been. The solid Ward Kiran had created deep within the beast had instantly expanded far beyond the gargoleth's confines. It had been unable to accommodate such a powerful explosive force, and it had burst into thousands of pieces.

Floating in the center of the sphere was Kiran. Blood trickled down her arms and face, but she did not seem to mind. In one hand, she held her Jidaan, its sapphire blazing like a tiny blue star. Cradled in her other arm, she held the child, Shurlyeh. It rested its toothy head on her shoulder, apparently asleep. A faint smile was on Kiran's face as she looked down at the Dyle child.

Rulyeh pulled himself to his feet, his gaze fastened on the human woman who had saved his one and only daughter. For a moment, he simply stood there, overwhelmed with gratitude and relief at the sight of his child, safe and whole. He did not bother to wipe away the gigantic tears that rolled down his snout.

Chapter 16

Reyanna itched. She tried to ignore it, but the worrisome irritation had grown more intense over the last hour, and she had none of her usual salve to soothe it. Lost in the Mire, she had finally resorted to climbing the largest tree she could find. From within its high, twisted branches, she had spotted the irregular sawteeth of the reddish mountains she sought, jutting sharply above the swamp's foliage far to the northwest. On her way down, she had also managed to rub up against some sort of gray-green fungus that had released a cloud of stinging spores. She had tried to move away from the foul-smelling particles as quickly as she could, but some of them had stuck to her neck and forearms, and now the skin in those areas was raised and itchy.

As a Ranger, she knew of at least three kinds of forest fungi that could bring not only irritation, but death. Although she did not recognize the type of fungus that had infected her, it did not resemble any of the more dangerous ones she knew. She figured she would be all right, although she reminded herself that this was the Mire, not one of her comparatively clean and healthy forests. Everything here seemed corrupted and foul, and she resolved to remain hyperaware of her own condition in the event it started to deteriorate.

She continued towards the mountains she had seen in the distance, trying not to scratch the infection on her skin. There were patches of dry ground, but often, spots that looked firm were not, and Reyanna's legs were already burning from repeatedly pulling her boots free of the clutching muck. Nevertheless, she kept doggedly moving forward. *I've been through worse,* she thought to herself.

Years ago, she had been given a backpack that seemed to weigh more than she did, and was told by her teachers that she had until sundown to retrieve a crystalline stone from the river bed of the Linshae River and bring it back to them in the center of Allinshae. "There will be obstacles," Amarin had said, a sly grin on his face and a twinkle in his bright eyes. "You must wear the pack at all times. There will be those who try to take it from you, and the river stone as well. If they succeed, the exercise is over. Do you understand?"

The young girl Reyanna had been back then had nodded and smiled eagerly, having no idea of the trial to come. No sooner had she disappeared into the trees than a dark-clad figure tackled her and nearly stripped the backpack from her. She had managed to kick free of her assailant and escape, already scraped and bloodied not a few minutes into the exercise. That had begun a long, long day, punctuated with furious scuffles with several hooded attackers. Traps had also been laid, and although Reyanna had avoided them all, some had come close to snaring her. She had reached the river in the early afternoon, pocketed her prize, and then headed back, knowing that she had already taken too long in her quest. She had picked up her pace and focused on avoiding the attackers so she did not have to waste additional time fighting them. It had almost worked.

The sun had already touched the horizon when Reyanna had come within sight of the village, the tops of the simple dwellings visible through the few remaining trees. She remembered sighing in relief as she drew near the end of her test, and she had pulled a small stone from her pocket, noticing the crystalline sparkle that proved its origin as the Linshae riverbed. That was the moment the final attacker had chosen to strike, slamming into her from the side as her attention was diverted. The stone went flying into the dirt, and the hooded figure snatched it up and sprinted away, heading for the center of town where the elder Rangers waited.

Furious, Reyanna got to her feet and sprinted after him, right on his heels. Although his features were hidden by a hood and dark face paint, Reyanna recognized the brute as one of the older trainees, Roarke. He had never given her so much as a glance, never bothered to acknowledge the young human in their midst, and his haughty attitude had always rankled. In spite of her exhaustion, Reyanna charged after the larger lad and gained ground. She was not about to let him show her up. As her anger rose, she had felt a blossom of warmth in her core, a hot swell of energy that quickly spread through her whole body. It both scared her and thrilled her. With an astounding burst of speed, she suddenly caught up to Roarke and tackled him from behind. He fell, grunting in surprise as the wind was knocked out of him mere yards from the waiting Ranger instructors. The sparkling stone flew out of his hands to land at their feet.

Amarin looked down at the stone and then sighed. "I'm sorry, Reyanna, you have failed." His voice was thick with disappointment.

Reyanna rose to her feet, ignoring Roarke as he pushed himself to a seated position and laid back his hood to reveal a very tousled head of blond hair and a split lip. His face was stoic, as was only proper for a Ranger training assistant. Reyanna was showing the signs of a long day of flight and combat. Her clothes were dirty and torn, one of her eyes was nearly swollen shut, and blood trickled freely from one nostril. She hurt from head to toe and was wearier than she had ever been in her life. She cast a quick glance at the setting sun, noting that there was still a good bit of it above the horizon.

"The test is not over until the sun completely sets, yes?"

Amarin glanced at the other Rangers who stood alongside him, and they all nodded.

"That is correct. But you have only moments; there is no way you can possibly reach the riverbed for another stone."

Reyanna pulled a second stone from her pocket, slightly smaller than the first, but glittering with far more crystals than the larger stone. "Then I'm glad I grabbed another one while I was there." She handed it to Amarin. She had relished the grin that slowly spread across the elder Ranger's face.

Now, trudging through a place that certainly was far more dangerous than a forest full of elder trainees, the memory made her smile. She had been only ten years old, and her parents had been immensely proud of her.

She thought about the stone, a beautiful little thing. It had sparkled in the sunshine with a hundred tiny rainbows. She felt the weight of it in her fingers, and wondered distantly how she had come to hold it again. Looking down at it, she turned it over, admiring the way the light played on the many crystals that encrusted its surface. She felt a pinprick on her palm, but thought nothing of it as she continued to enjoy the beauty of the stone she held. Another pinprick, then a third, then a sharper pain struck Reyanna's hand, making her flinch.

"Ow!" she cried, confused. She stared at the beautiful stone in her hand and then her head swam. Disoriented, Reyanna squeezed her eyes shut for a moment, then opened them again. When her vision came back into focus, she expected to see the glittering stone in her palm, but was astonished to see instead the decaying head of what looked like a muskrat, lips pulled back from its pointed little teeth. Its empty eye-sockets were alive with tiny maggots and ants were crawling all over the foul-smelling skull. Her hand was erupting with white-hot pricks of pain where the ants were biting her. "Ugh!" she cried as she flung the disgusting mass as far as she could into the Mire. She clapped her hands together repeatedly to rid them of the stinging ants, frantically slapping them away. When they all seemed to be gone, she wiped both hands roughly on her trousers as she panted with fatigue. Sweat had beaded on her brow and now dripped into her eyes, stinging them.

What happened? she thought, wiping the cleaner of her sleeves across her face. *I must be seeing things.* She took a few more steps to put some distance between herself and the rotting head she had somehow picked up. *I don't even remember finding that nasty thing. When did I pick that up?* She staggered slightly and slowed down to catch her balance. Dizziness crept in, and she struggled to remain upright. Gauging her steps with exaggerated care, she made her way to a nearby tree whose bark was relatively clear of slime and moss. She leaned heavily on it and tried to catch her breath. She pulled back the sleeve on the arm that had been touched by the fungal spores. Her heart sank as she saw that the skin of her forearm had turned an angry red. "Oh, no," she said aloud. "No, this can't be. I'm too close. I'm almost there!" Reyanna moaned as her stomach clenched painfully, then released, then clenched again. The

97

Mire's poison was flowing through her body now, first from the fungus, then from the ants. "No, I'm almost there," she repeated, her tone desperate. "Got to fight this!"

Reyanna pushed herself to her feet and took two doddering steps before she tripped and fell face-first into the muck. Her energy was suddenly gone, replaced with nothing but pain. Her hands clenched in agony, squeezing the mud through her fingers. They clenched again, but this time in anger. Her head rose from the mud, and eyes that had been sapphire blue had gone fiery red and orange as Reyanna's power finally emerged.

She tried to stop it. With everything she had, she tried to crush it back down beneath the weight of her will. But she was exhausted, helpless against the venom that ravaged her body, and against the raging bonfire of magick that had suddenly burst to life within her. It flared, searing her from the inside out, burning away the venom and scouring her body of its hurts and ills. Her awareness fell farther and farther away, and although she struggled mightily, it was no use. Soon, Reyanna the Ranger was gone into a dark and quiet place, a prisoner of her own power.

The Reyanna that remained stood tall amid her own flames of magick, glowing brightly as she expressed her power freely and gleefully. Fragile and unnecessary fabrics burned away, revealing her lithe form in all its glory. Her raven-black hair billowed around her face, held aloft by the surges of energy that poured from her. Reyanna floated above the ground, gasping in ecstasy as the incandescent nimbus of magick cradled her and lifted her. Water evaporated and plants withered in a wide circle around her, leaves and stems bursting into flame before vaporizing completely in the intense heat. Trees began to steam as their moisture was eaten away and they, too, burst into flame.

Reveling in her power, Reyanna scanned the area with her brightly gleaming eyes. *West*, she thought. *I want to go west to see the mountains. That is where I will go. I am to meet someone there.*

With her naked toes hovering an arm's length above the now-dried earth, Reyanna's body slowly advanced through the Mire, scorching the ground around her as she went. The jagged, red mountains were not far away.

Chapter 17

The sun beat down on Gart from directly overhead, and he felt thankful for the old floppy hat he wore. He had bought it from a poor youth many years ago, and somehow it had stayed with him ever since. Gart tilted his head back and squinted up into the sky, noting that a huge mass of clouds was approaching. Soon, they would cover the sun, leaving him in shadow. He thought that would be perfectly fine, as the heat had only served to exhaust him further the last two days.

The jagged line of mountains traveled northward, and Gart kept them on his left. The canyon in which he walked was dusty and dry, and the cliffs he followed rose straight up from the barren earth. It was as if the mountains had been carved by the downward sweep of an immense sword, cleaving the rock into a long, flat wall of stone.

To Gart's right, the terrain rose more gently away from the valley floor, its slopes not nearly as tall as those on his left. The land rose, then sloped downward again, gradually becoming more green and lush against the scarlet dirt of the mountains as it approached the Mire. The plants and trees closest to the Mire almost resembled the distant elder forests unless one looked more closely. Then the warped branches and haunting calls of strange animals that had never been heard in those faraway majestic woods gave away the true nature of the swamp beyond. As the Mire reclaimed the land, the reddish hue of the earth disappeared, giving way to the browns, grays, and sickly green that dominated the vast surrounding morass.

Gart kept his eyes forward, though he was only partially aware of what he was seeing. He was focusing on the distant vibrations of magick that lay deep within the earth. Even at that distance, he could sense them quite clearly, and he followed the sensations the way he might follow the ringing of a distant bell. Each step that his faithful mount Bessie took was one step closer to his goal. Exhausted, Gart shook his head sharply to keep himself alert as he struggled to stay upright in the saddle.

Almost there, he thought. *And I've still got time.* He had seen the sliver of crescent moon rising in the east just before sunrise, and if his calculations were correct, it would pass before the sun in late afternoon. He smiled slightly, remembering the exhaustive research he had undertaken to understand all of the elements of the ritual he was about to conduct; the patterns of the sun and the stars and moon in relation to the world he stood upon. So much of magick appeared to be connected to the natural laws of science. When things were arranged a certain way, the stars in just such an alignment, and certain substances combined, magick happened. And yet, there was another element, an elusive and ethereal component that had to do with the will and intent of the individual attempting to manipulate the vast energy that existed in the world. If that was not right, then nothing worked. Eye of newt and toe of frog be damned, no matter what else was done properly, magick could not be performed or manipulated by an unskilled, undisciplined practitioner.

Gart shook his head in bemusement. *And then there are some who just can't help but use magick. They're born with it. Like me. I don't need trinkets or potions to do some things; it's just like breathing to me. The power is just...there.*

He continued to muse on this as he rode. Magick was a peculiar thing. It could achieve seemingly impossible wonders, and yet it had limitations. Gart looked down at Beauty, who instantly felt his scrutiny and looked back up at him. Her mouth was open and she was panting happily, not knowing that it made her countenance even more terrifying than usual to an unsuspecting onlooker. However frightful she looked, she was just happy to be with Gart.

Gart sighed, thinking about Beauty's injury. *Limitations,* he thought. By rights, Beauty should have been healed. He had sealed the cuts and repaired the tissues, but it had not been enough. Unless he continued to feed her heart with his own magick, it would simply stop, killing her within seconds. A frown crossed his face, feeling perfectly at home there. *When this is done, I want to figure that out. There's got to be some way to fix her heart so it pumps on*

101

its own again. Maybe the priestesses of Rowann can do something. Brunar could have done it, I'm sure.

The thought of the long-departed Mage took Gart's thoughts down a different road. He had barely known the man, but by all accounts, he had been an extraordinarily noble soul, powerful as well as skilled with magick. He had dedicated his entire life to learning about magick and using it to help mankind as best he could. Brunar had spent centuries traveling the world and then returning to Guardians Keep to fill its library with books, scrolls, and magickal objects, as well as his own research. Gart thought about Beauty's problem and how he was determined to find the answer. He wondered if this was how Brunar had started out, trying to solve problems through magick, delving into different topics with such drive and determination that he eventually became a master of the arcane, a Mage. Gart recognized the last years he had spent, doing all of those same things in search of a way to see Gennie. He had followed that same path.

Am I to be a Mage, then? he thought, shocked at the possibility. *A Guardian, yes, but...* he pondered that as the echoes of Bessie's hooves clip-clopped from the tall face of the nearby cliffs. Gart thought about the responsibility that Brunar had shouldered. Fighting evil, training the Guardians, watching over the entire realm at the cost of his own life. *Is that my destiny?*

Suddenly, a haze of resentment colored his thoughts. *No,* he thought angrily. *I never chose that. That's not me. I never wanted that job, I only wanted to be left alone with my family. With Gennie and Rheann. I've already done my part; no one can ask any more of me. To Hel with them!*

Beauty whined, sensing his rising anger. Gart cut his eyes toward his longtime companion, glaring at her for a moment. Then he sighed. "Sorry, girl. I'm just getting worked up about nothing, I guess. Lots on my mind."

Beauty looked at him a moment longer, then snapped her head forward, listening. A low growl emerged from her throat, thick with menace.

"What is it?" Gart asked, turning his own gaze forward to see what had arisen. "You hear something up there?"

Gart squinted into the distance, trying to see what had bothered Beauty. The valley floor continued straight ahead, still hugging the vertical cliff face on his left. He caught sight of movement ahead on the slope to his right, far enough away that he could not hear anything. Three indistinct shapes made their way down into the valley floor, riders by the look of them, though they were still too far away to make out much more than that. They appeared to be riding slowly towards Gart and Beauty, and Gart instantly had a bad feeling about them.

He turned to Beauty again. "Three riders in the lonely mountains in the center of the Poravian Mire...I'm thinking they are going to be trouble. What do you think?"

Beauty growled again and barked once, a deep and unnerving sound. Spending so much time with her, Gart had almost forgotten that she was a massive and enormously strong former fighting dog, and not one of the tiny dogs he had seen tending sheep near his village. Beauty was huge and thick with muscle. A grim smile crossed his scarred face and he directed his sharp blue gaze back across the valley towards the newcomers. He hoped there would not be trouble, but somehow could not muster very much optimism.

"Well, they're between us and the shrine, regardless. Let's get this over with, whatever 'this' may be." He kicked his heels into Bessie's ribs and she hustled into a trot while Beauty loped alongside.

The approaching riders continued on their course as Gart rode towards them, staying fairly close together. All three wore cloaks with their hoods up, hiding their faces from his intense gaze. The rightmost rider's left arm seemed peculiar to Gart, wrapped as it was in thick bandages. It seemed misshapen somehow, but Gart dismissed it for the time being. The central rider was the smallest, and something about the way the figure moved in the saddle implied femininity, while the others were most likely male.

The leftmost rider had something strapped across his back, a weapon. Although it appeared to be swathed in rags, Gart felt an icy shock of recognition. He knew what was under those coverings, and by extension, he could guess the identity of two of the riders. They were the ones who had beaten him senseless and stolen his Jidaan. They had stabbed Beauty. She should be dead now because of them, might still end up dead. They had left them both bleeding in the dirt.

The old rage pushed itself to the fore and claimed him.

It had been a long time since Gart had experienced that kind of anger, the all-consuming fury he had so often felt as a younger man. This time, he welcomed it as he might an old friend. It gave him strength. All of his hurts fell away, scoured clean by the boiling anger that grew inside him. Had the riders been close enough to see the slow smile that appeared on his wickedly scarred face, they might have thought better of their plans. Gart reined Bessie to a halt and Beauty followed suit. The riders kept their faces hooded as they rode, still approaching, but in no hurry.

"That's far enough!" Gart yelled. "Unless I am mistaken, you have something that belongs to me. Barovius? Arkhan?" Gart took pleasure in the fact that the riders on either side shifted in startlement as he called their names. Watching their reaction told him that Barovius carried his Jidaan, while Arkhan was on the opposite side of the center rider. That one remained unknown to him. "You can just lay it on the ground and ride away if you like. Otherwise, I'll have to take it from you. Believe me, I will enjoy that."

"I am Melidia," a cold female voice crossed the distance between them. "We offer you a trade: the Jidaan for the Blood of Nimshi. We only require the Blood, and mean you no harm."

At this, the one carrying the Jidaan of Storms threw his hood back and hissed, "The Hels you say! It's mine! I never agreed to this, Melidia!" His bald pate gleamed in the sun and his wrinkled face was screwed into a tight scowl.

"Shut your mouth, Barovius!" the woman's tone was ice and steel. In a lower voice, she said, "You think I would honor such a bargain? I'm trying to trick him, you idiot! If we can get the Blood from him without a fight, so much the better! We can kill him once it's in our hands, and we don't risk losing it!" Barovius reluctantly held his tongue, though he reached one hand over his shoulder to touch the cloth-wrapped shaft of the Jidaan as though reassuring himself that it was still there. Melidia turned back to Gart and lowered her hood, exposing her mane of coppery red hair in the hopes that seeing her might put him at ease. So many men underestimated a woman, and that might just give her an edge. She raised her voice again so that he might hear. "What do you say?"

Gart sat atop Bessie and stared at them, unmoving. His scarred face was shaded from the intermittent sunshine by the brim of his hat, but his piercing blue eyes missed nothing. He gathered his energy, and although he was suddenly alarmed at how low his store of magick had become, he felt more than strong enough to deal with the three that faced him. Beauty sensed the current of rage that flowed in Gart, and immediately issued a thick, rumbling growl that carried to the riders. Their horses shifted uneasily at the sound. Gart silently reassured her, telling her to wait. She quieted, and Gart focused on his next move. Rather than say anything more, Gart let his magick do the talking.

Melidia saw Gart's eyes flash gold from beneath the brim of his hat and heard Barovius grunt beside her. Before she even knew what Gart had done, she reflexively cast a spell that created a whirlwind between herself and Gart, shielding her and her companions from view with a rotating cloud of stinging dust, dirt, and rocks. She heard nothing from Gart, although his enormous dog now barked and growled loudly enough to hear over the howling wind. That dog frightened her far more than she cared to admit.

She reached out with her senses and quickly found the thread of Gart's power, a slender but strong cord of invisible energy that had reached for Barovius' neck, cutting off the blood flow there as quickly and easily as any noose. The abrasive wizard's eyes had already rolled up in his head, and he slid out of the saddle like a boneless scarecrow that had slipped from its stake. Barovius hit the ground hard, his arms flopping limply. The Jidaan at his back started moving, tugged this way and that by Gart's magick as its true owner sought to dislodge it.

"Arkhan!" Melidia yelled, dismounting and rushing to Barovius' side. "Bring your Joinings! Bring them now!" Arkhan struggled to control his horse, startled as it had been by the whirlwind, but he nodded, eager to have his creatures join the fray. He spurred his mount into a gallop and made for the slope to the east, riding as if daemons were on his heels.

Frantically, Melidia dug in her pouch and came out with a tiny stone, carefully carved with eldritch designs. She reached for the thread of Gart's magick and found it again, then yelled the arcane words that ignited the power of the enchanted stone. The pebble in her hand flared an ugly crimson, its light leaping for the unseen cord of Gart's power. Upon contact, the swirling scarlet energy raced back along its length towards Gart.

Gart saw the red glow a bare moment before it slammed into him. He tried to shy away from it, but he had seen it too late to dodge it completely. He had once been kicked by a mule; this was worse. The impact took him in the head and chest, nearly knocking him clear of his saddle. He grunted in agony, but managed to remain on Bessie's back. Beauty continued barking ferociously, just waiting for a chance to rip someone to shreds. She had finally recognized their smell, and was eager for a rematch.

The woman's dusty whirlwind was not dangerous, only bothersome, but it hid them effectively for the moment. Gart groaned as he wiped the blood from his nose and tried to get his eyes to focus on one thing at a time. He saw one of the riders, Arkhan, leave the cover provided by the whirling dust devil and gallop up the eastern slope towards the trees.

"Beauty. Get him."

The huge canine exploded into a run after the fleeing horseman. Gart saw that Arkhan would reach the trees before Beauty could intercept him. Mildly alarmed, he cautioned her as she ran, *If he has friends in there, come back to me!* She replied with only a feeling, a strong sense of reluctance that Gart knew meant she might not obey.

She did love a good fight, and her blood was up. Louder, he sent, *Come back to me, dammit! If there are too many, we'll fight them together!* In return, Gart felt a combination of ferocious bloodlust and pure joy as Beauty imagined fighting at her master's side. She agreed. If too many attacked, she would return to fight alongside him. She raced up the slope, growling fiercely the entire way. Gart watched her disappear into the trees at the top of the farthest hill, right on Arkhan's heels. Gart smiled as he imagined Beauty leaping up and pulling him from the saddle.

"I hope she rips your legs off," Gart whispered in Arkhan's direction. Then he turned his attention back to the whirling cloud of dust and debris that shielded the other two from him. He took a deep breath and called his magick again, this time sending it up and over the tiny maelstrom. He sent his sight up with it. When he closed his physical eyes, he was able to see through his magick from high in the air. From that vantage point, he saw that the fiery-haired woman had thrown the unconscious Barovius over his horse and was trying to get both mounts turned so they could escape the way they had come.

"Oh, Hels no, you don't," Gart muttered. He opened his true eyes and saw again the dust devil that hid his opponents. With a grin he sent a wide wave of magick, searching for the edges of the spell. He found them, grasped them, and then *pushed*. The spinning cloud of dirt and rocks moved away from him, following the two riders. He grunted and pushed harder, sending the tiny storm forward until it engulfed the fleeing pair. He heard the woman screaming in rage and frustration, heard the horses whinny in fear as they were pelted with windblown dust and grit.

He knew they would not last long inside such a whirlwind, but since she had cast it in the first place, Gart figured that she'd dispel it soon enough. Gart put his hand on his sword and then thought better of it, and left it in its scabbard. He hated the idea of killing a woman, but from what he could tell, she was the brains of the operation. She still had to be dealt with. He looked around and quickly found a fist-sized stone nearby. With a flick of his magick, he yanked it through the air and into his hand, where it smacked roughly into his callused palm. Loosing a growl more suited to Beauty than himself, he spurred Bessie into a gallop, heading straight for the compact storm.

The sound of her shrill chanting could be heard over the swirling wind as she canted the reversal of the spell. Gart honed in on the sound and angled Bessie slightly to compensate even as the storm began to die. As the dust settled, Gart caught sight of the pair of riders, the woman leading the still-unconscious Barovius, who was draped unceremoniously over his mount's back. The woman's face was contorted with hate, her odd violet eyes flashing with rage as she looked back over her shoulder at Gart.

Gart flung the stone with a whip of his arm, knowing instinctively that his throw was true. He touched the stone in flight with his magick, compelling it to fly faster. It would not kill her, but she'd be knocked out of her saddle rightly enough. The stone whistled through the air towards her, heading directly for the middle of her back. When it reached its target, however, it simply passed through her. The figure turned and looked over her shoulder again at Gart as though nothing had happened.

Frowning, Gart spent a precious few seconds trying to figure out what went wrong, and then it hit him: it was an illusion. They were not actually there. *But if not there, where did they go?*

He received his answer in no uncertain terms a moment later. From behind a pair of large boulders to his left, a flash of crimson magick flared, slamming into his side and knocking him from the saddle. Gart had a moment of shock, a brief instant of weightlessness during which he lost his senses. The impact with the rocky earth brought him back to the present in the most abrupt fashion. The air exploded from his lungs and a bright spot of agony erupted in his right shoulder. He tried to roll with the impact, but only managed to scrape and bruise nearly every part of his body before it came to rest. For a moment, he lay there, face-down in the dust, stunned. He had never been so tired. His head was ringing loudly, and the sound of Bessie's frightened neighing nearby made it feel as though his skull would split apart.

The woman's shrill laughter fluttered across the distance between them, harsh and arrogant. "Some Mage you are! Is that all you've got, *Guardian*?" She sneered the word, injecting as much contempt as she could. Melidia had pulled Barovius from the saddle and laid him against the cliff, where he had begun to stir feebly. She stepped away from the horses and Barovius, leaving them partially sheltered by a rock formation. "You should have just given me what I wanted! At least then, you'd have had a chance to walk away!"

The anger rose in him, boiling to the surface and giving him strength. Gart pushed himself up on his elbows and spat, blood from his lip mingling with his saliva as it hit the scarlet earth below. He raised his eyes toward the woman and Barovius, and the intensity of his glare cut off her laughter better than any knife. He spat again to clear the rest of the dust out of his bloody mouth. He got one foot underneath him and pushed himself to a kneeling position.

Gart saw that she was using a short wand of some kind with a tiny, blood-red gemstone affixed to its tip. She gestured sharply with it and sent another intense blast of energy toward him, intending to incinerate him. He focused his power into a small shield and deflected the bolt so that it struck the earth nearby, sending up a shower of dirt and debris. He got his other foot beneath him and stood. He took a deep breath, keeping his gaze on her. Furious, she blasted him again, and again he shunted the searing bolt of energy to the side.

A dangerous grin slowly appeared on the unscarred half of Gart's face. "That's funny," he said, his voice low and menacing. "I was going to say the same thing to you." A look of uncertainty crossed her face at last.

He lifted his hands, palms outward, and readied himself to attack. She crossed her wrists in front of her and a hazy, indistinct wall of energy suddenly appeared before her, a Ward of some kind. Gart smiled. He knew she would do something like that. His bright blue eyes flashed gold and he released a blinding blast of concussive force not directly at her, but above her at the stone cliff instead. The resulting explosion brought a hail of deadly rocks down on both of the sorcerers, and Gart took pleasure in the woman's screams of frustration and fear. Their horses bolted, terrified of the falling rocks, and Melidia shifted her Ward overhead to protect her and Barovius from the avalanche. The instant she did, Gart threw another blast at her, this time directly at her undefended torso.

Distracted by the falling stone and the horses, Melidia had no time to recover. She took the shot full in the chest, and it slammed her backwards into the cliff. Gart heard her grunt in pain as she hit, and then the rockslide he had created poured over her and Barovius, covering them both. Gart watched the mound of rocks and dirt pile high on top of them for a few moments, then waited until the rockfall slowed and finally stopped. When nothing else moved, Gart let out a breath and sagged, utterly exhausted. A wave of dizziness struck him and he stumbled a few steps before righting himself. The blasts of magick had cost him dearly. He wondered if he would be able to stay conscious even if he did manage to pull his Jidaan from under the rubble and use it. It extracted a heavy toll for the use of its Gifts. Nevertheless, he knew he needed it, and the idea of it being in their possession offended him deeply. He started toward the scree, intent on digging out the Jidaan with his bare hands if it came to that.

Just then, Gart heard an unsettling sound behind him, a raw, pained screech that he had never heard in nature. It was followed by many others, the awful sounds grating harshly in his ears. He turned as fast as his aching body would allow, and saw something out of a nightmare flying towards him.

From the east came a flock of enormous bats, but they were not bats like any Gart had ever seen. These were huge and malformed, and vaguely humanoid. Some had awful half-human faces that screamed in either fury or agony; Gart could not tell which. Their bodies were easily the size of young children, though no children ever oozed such malice and hatred as these. Their wide, flapping wings savagely beat the air, and light gleamed on fang and claw as the horrible batlings swarmed through the air towards Gart.

Beauty! he called through his magickal link. *Get back here, I need help!*

110

In response, she sent a vision. Gart caught a fleeting glimpse of shadowy, bestial figures that surrounded her as she ripped and tore at anything that came close. Arms covered in fur reached for her and came back missing parts. He heard animal grunts and growls and squeals of pain from the creatures as Beauty's flashing teeth repeatedly found their targets. Some of them held weapons, but Beauty's pure ferocity and unexpectedly quick movements held them at bay. Gart felt no substantial injuries in her body other than a few scratches. Her blood sang as she gave herself to the fight, knowing only the purity of combat. Always before, Beauty had fought because her former overseers demanded it. She had been young and afraid back then. Now, though, she fought with ferocious abandon, and a savage joy filled her. She fought for herself and for the love of her master, Gart. He was her everything. It was kill or be killed, and Beauty had no intention of dying today. Gart's magick flowed in her veins and she was still fast as lightning as she latched onto another leg and snapped its bones with a vicious wrench of her powerful neck muscles.

Hels, Gart thought as he pulled his ebony-bladed sword and matching black dagger from their scabbards at his belt. He had no time to see more, but he had a strong sense that no matter what Beauty was fighting, she was holding her own for now. He was worried for her, but there was nothing he could do. He would just have to trust that she would survive, much less come to his aid. *I'm on my own here.* Frustration welled up in him. Time was running out, and he was battered and weary to the bone. He knew he was close; he could feel the magick coursing through the earth not far away. The shrine was very near, but apparently, he had to cut through a flying horde of misbegotten, bloodthirsty beasts to get there.

So be it. For Gennie.

Gart slipped into a fighting crouch, a blade ready in each fist, and watched the swarm drawing near on hellish wings.

111

Chapter 18

The entire tribe of Dyles was assembled, and the Guardians stared wide-eyed at the hundreds of powerful creatures that surrounded them. Kiran sat on a stone, thankful for the chance to sit on something relatively dry for a change, and studied them. All were clothed only in tattoos, jewelry, and brief cloths around their loins. Some sported leather belts that held various weapons. She noticed that the only difference between the sexes was a certain graceful way of moving the females displayed, as well as the fact that they were slightly smaller than the males. She was pleased to see that the females carried weapons just as the males did. As she looked at them, Kiran was suddenly thankful the Dyle warriors were friendly. She would just as soon not have to fight even the smallest of them.

"We must thank thee for thy assistance," Rulyeh rumbled as he cradled his daughter in his brawny arms. Looking down at Shirlyeh, he continued, "She wouldst surely have perished if not for thee."

Kiran smiled and wiped her forearm across her forehead, mostly clearing it of blood and muck. "Anyone would have done the same, chief."

Rulyeh made the odd coughing sound that passed for laughter for a Dyle. "True, but likely with much less success. That gargoleth hath terrorized my people for centuries." His voice quieted then, and Kiran only just made out his words. "It took my mate as well, and Shirlyeh is now everything to me." Lifting his gaze once more, he raised his voice so all could hear. "Thanks to thee, the gargoleth will harry us no longer. We are forever in thy debt. Canst we offer thee anything?"

Nessar cleared his throat, and all eyes turned to him. "Sir," he began. "I mentioned earlier that we are trying to reach the mountains near here. There is a place of power, a shrine of some kind, somewhere in the range. Our friend is headed there as well, and we think he may be trying to do something dangerous."

There was a low growl of worry among the Dyles, but Rulyeh ignored it. "Hmm. I know of that place. It is, indeed, a place of power. Thou canst feel its magick from nearby. We have always shied away from it. Its history is ill, and in any event, the mountains and valleys are too dry for my people." He paused for a moment, considering. "I will show thee the way. Indeed, I canst get thee to within a few hours trek of the shrine before the ground dries out and I must turn back."

One of the others stepped forward and bowed its massive head as it spoke in a series of grunts and hisses. Rulyeh made a calming gesture with one hand and replied in the same language. The chief took a moment to nuzzle his daughter one more time, then carefully handed her to the officer before turning back to the Guardians.

"What is it?" Layton asked, curious.

"My lieutenant was volunteering to go in my place, but I speak thy language better than he. I will go." Rulyeh turned and addressed the assembled Dyles, who looked on with wide eyes. In a loud voice, he spoke at length to his people in their own language, gesturing at the Guardians from time to time. When he stopped, all of the Dyles bowed slowly in unison towards the Guardians, who bowed uncertainly in return, and then the reptilian warriors turned and headed into the Mire. Rulyeh turned back to the three humans. "I have spoken of thy bravery and courage. Thou art now counted as friends of the Dyles, of whom there are few. Even though thou art friends of the Weya, thou shalt have our trust. Shall we go?"

Before any of them could respond, the Dyle chief started through the Mire at an easy lope.

Kiran looked up at Nessar and Layton, then sighed and hauled herself to her feet. "Well, there's no time like the present, I guess. It's not like we just fought a huge swamp creature or anything. Let's get moving." She set off after Rulyeh, with Nessar and Layton following close behind. She was dog-tired after her battle with the gargoleth, but Kiran was nothing if not profoundly stubborn. She found a rhythm soon enough and settled into it. Rulyeh kept to solid ground as best he could to make it easier for them to follow.

Some time later, the sun had climbed overhead, filtering down through the dense limbs. Rulyeh slowed to a walk and halted next to a grassy slope that looked free of mud. A bright beam of sunshine warmed the tiny glade, and Rulyeh gestured to it.

"Thou canst rest here for now. If we keep moving until nightfall and continue as the sun rises, we shall arrive at the foothills east of the shrine near mid of day on the morrow."

Weary from their travels, the three humans wandered into the glade and sat down, groaning in relief as they took weight off their tired feet. Layton quickly began to dig in his pack for food, while Nessar sat and pulled out his leatherbound journal, checking his notes against the position of the sun. Then he set about adding some notations in the first blank page he found. Kiran immediately lay in the grass, rested her head on her pack, and went to sleep. She began snoring at once as she drifted into dreams of anything other than mud, slime, and swamp.

Layton thanked Rulyeh. "This is perfect, sir. We will rest and eat, then be ready to continue soon."

Rulyeh nodded and fixed his slitted pupils on the bearded warrior. "I must hunt. I shall return soon, and we will move on." The Dyle turned away and they heard him splash into the water nearby, then only an eerie silence remained. They could hear the wind in the leaves above and the sounds of the many creatures that lived in the Mire.

"You know, now that I've spent some time in here, it's not so bad," Nessar quipped, jotting something in his book. Chewing, Layton slowly turned to stare at his old friend in disbelief. Nessar finally noticed his scrutiny and shrugged. "What? I've been in worse places. And the trees are actually kind of pretty. It's not like anything's on fire, at least."

Layton swallowed. "It's muddy, it smells, and almost every living thing here is trying to kill us. Name one worse place than this."

Nessar frowned and went back to writing in his book. Layton took another bite of his dried beef and waited. Finally, Nessar answered. "Ever been in the sewers of Ghal Spir? The port city south of Rualtha?"

114

Layton shook his head. "I can't say that I've ever needed to actually enter the sewers anywhere, Nessar. I don't think the passages beneath Laro count."

"I see. Yes, you've always been an awfully clean-cut sort, haven't you?" Nessar mumbled, keeping his eyes on his book. "As a thief, I've been to a number of unsavory locales, my boy. This place is alien to us, yes, but to the things that grow and live here, like the Dyles, it's home. It's a natural habitat, just like a forest or an ocean, albeit a dangerous one for us. I can almost feel it breathing; a giant, sprawling being with a life of its own." Then he shook his head. "The Ghal Spir sewers, on the other hand, they were made by men a thousand years ago. By rights, they are supposed to be a utilitarian system of underground waterways built to remove waste from the city. It sounds simple. But over the centuries, it's turned into something much more sinister than that. Various factions have taken up residence down there for one reason or other, hiding their activities from those above. Other creatures found their way down there and have evolved into things I'd prefer not to think about. Those stone tunnels are far more dangerous than this, I kid you not. Life isn't worth a damn down there, and you're likely to get your throat cut or something bitten off before you've gone a dozen steps into that stinking dark. I may be more familiar with the darker side of city life, but after being out here for a while, I almost find this relaxing." Nessar never looked up from his scribbling, wanting to finish jotting down his thoughts before they scattered. "Almost," he added.

Layton let his gaze wander, taking in the tall trees that surrounded them, seeing their gnarled branches in a new light. Though twisted, many were strong. The leaves, though grey and brown and odd-looking, seemed solid enough, in their way. And although the air had a very thick aroma, there was a fertile undertone to it. Even though the Mire was most certainly dangerous to the unwary, he realized that what he had always perceived as sinister and foul was not necessarily so. Taking a sip from his waterskin, Layton thought on his friend's words for a while. Although he had to take Nessar's word for it in regards to the dangers of the Ghal Spir sewers, he finally had to agree that the

115

trees had a certain elegance to them in the sunlight. Although he doubted he would want to build a summer home among them, he decided that they were, indeed, quite lovely.

Chapter 19

Gart screamed in rage and frustration as he swung the sword again, and yet again. Blood and gore soaked his arms to the elbow, and his forearms were on fire from gripping his sword and dagger. His weariness was a heavy weight on his back, threatening to drag him to the earth at any moment. Surrounding him on all sides were the hideous remains of Arkhan's unholy joinings. Large bat-creatures flapped their torn wings spastically as they died. They fell to the dust, horrid mutations of human and bat that the sorcerer had fused together, separating horribly as they died. The sight of the writhing corpses turned Gart's stomach, but he had no time for revulsion. He kept his eyes on the score of murderous creatures that remained, howling and screeching for his blood.

He lashed out and cut another bat-thing out of the air. Another darted in close enough to leave a pair of gashes on his neck, deep enough to hurt like fire but not enough to kill. Gart swiped at it with his dagger, but it had already flown out of reach, his blood still dripping from its talons. Sweat dripped down into his eyes, and he tried to blink the sting away. His chest heaved as he sucked in lungfuls of the dry air, struggling to catch his breath. Deep in his core, his magick swelled and rolled, but he held it back. He knew that he had to maintain the flow to Beauty to keep her alive. Ordinarily, that would have been easy to do, but his fatigue was bone deep, and he feared that he might render himself unconscious if he threw too much of his magick into the fight. If he passed out, that might be the end of Beauty, and certainly the end of him. Gart speared another of the bat-creatures on the end of his sword and flicked it away. *I've just got to get through these things,* he thought. He looked up and noted the position of the sun. *But I'm running out of time.*

Suddenly, the earth rumbled beneath his boots, and Gart stumbled a step as he cut another bat-creature out of the air. He heard a loud scraping sound behind him, stone grating on stone, and he glanced over one shoulder to find the cause. "Oh, Hels..." he breathed.

117

The pile of rubble that had covered Melidia and Barovius was moving. At first Gart thought that one of the two sorcerers was pushing their way through the scree somehow, but it quickly became apparent that the stones were moving on their own. Pebbles and rocks of all sizes pushed and scraped against each other as they rose into the air. Slowly at first, then faster, the rubble began swirling around in a tight formation, the whole of it forming a rough sphere. A low, rumbling growl erupted from somewhere within the spinning mass of stone.

Orith, Gart thought. *Oh sweet Goddess above, an earth elemental.* He remembered the stone sentinel that stood watch on the path leading to Guardians Keep. He remembered thinking how fortunate he had been that Orith had recognized him as a Guardian in spite of the fact that he had not yet claimed his Jidaan. The small cyclone of living rock had been most polite, but Gart had been acutely aware of how easily it could have crushed him into a bloody pulp. And now, here was another one, certainly not as friendly as Orith.

Off to one side, Barovius stood with his arms raised. He chanted a summoning spell, calling the earth elemental into being with his magick. The older man was completely covered in reddish rock dust, and one of his eyes was nearly swelled shut. His clothes were ripped from where he had pulled himself from the pile of debris. Blood ran from a jagged cut on his bald scalp, but his eyes blazed through the crimson mess as he stared at Gart, the object of his wrath. Gart's Jidaan was still slung awkwardly across his back, and an evil, triumphant grin was plastered on his bloody face as he continued his incantation.

Gart's frustration boiled over as he laid eyes on the man and outrage filled him as he saw his Jidaan still in Barovius' possession. Magick swelled within him, renewing his strength, though a dull ache arose behind his eyes. He cut another pair of bat-things down and then roared at the coalescing whirl of stones and its master, "Come on then! Have at it, and see what you get!"

Barovius laughed and made a pushing gesture with both hands. The stone elemental surged forward, a whirling cyclone of deadly rock. Gart immediately pressed outward with his magick to shield himself, but the elemental slammed a small boulder into his rudimentary Ward and sent him flying backwards. He tumbled painfully to the ground several yards away, and instantly, one of the bat-things latched onto his back, screeching and tearing. Screaming in pain as the creature's claws dug into the flesh of his back, Gart rolled over and gutted it with his dagger, spilling thick, red ichor down his arms. He flung the carcass aside and scrambled to his feet, turning to face Barovius and the elemental. He was in agony in a hundred places, but his rage still burned brightly.

"You're beaten!" Barovius yelled in his scratchy voice. "You can't stand against me! The famous Gart," he sneered, "Hero of Alverton Falls! Ha! I'll crush you where you stand!" He called out commands in a guttural, harsh language, and the whirling stones tightened their pattern, becoming almost a solid sphere of moving rocks and gravel.

Gart stood facing the creature, sword and dagger at the ready, knowing that they would do nothing against the granite avalanche that would soon engulf him. The creature surged forward, and he threw what power he could into a makeshift wall. The stone elemental crashed against it, pushing Gart back. A hot pain erupted in Gart's head, and blood trickled out of one nostril. He ignored it, and struggled to maintain his shield.

Just then, a faint warning call from Beauty echoed in his mind, wordless, but urgent. There was no vision, no other information, and Gart could tell only that Beauty was still alive. But other than that, there was nothing. That alarmed Gart, however, he could only turn toward the ridge from whence the call had come. His heart sank as he saw fifty or so huge, brutish creatures crest the ridge and rush down the slope toward him. Each was well over six feet tall, and man-like, but they were anything but human. Thickly-muscled and covered in coarse black hair, the creatures had the heads of giant boars, with beady black eyes and huge tusks protruding from elongated jaws. They squealed and grunted as they traversed the slope, wielding large clubs and axes in their great fists. Some of them bore wounds, but not all. He had only moments before they would reach him.

Although he still felt Beauty's presence, Gart felt little else from her. He had no idea how she fared, and that worried him deeply. He sent as much of his energy as he dared, hoping it would aid her, before turning his attention back to his own attacker.

The elemental slammed once more against his wall of magick and the ache behind his eyes intensified. The handful of bat-things that remained gathered themselves overhead for another diving attack, and Gart sighed. For a single, dark moment that seemed to last forever, he wondered what it would be like to just lie down on the stony ground and close his eyes, to leave it all behind. He knew he could not. Gennie awaited him, one way or the other. But he'd be damned if he gave up and died like a coward. He steeled himself to take on the first of the newcomers, hoping that he could hold the elemental off long enough to die fighting.

Suddenly, something flashed on the hill off to one side of the onrushing boar-men, a colorful brightness that was gone as suddenly as it had appeared. Gart squinted and made out a man, small in the distance, running towards the oncoming creatures. He saw the figure reach up and unsheathe a weapon from his back, the glint of its steel shining brilliantly in the sun, and then the figure disappeared into the herd. The aggressive grunts and squeals of the boar-creatures became howls of pain as their unknown foe slashed and cut in a devastating attack. His weapon shone again and again in the sunlight, flashing as it stabbed, slashed, and cut. Gart saw the lone figure for only a moment at a time, but he recognized the fighting style of the man immediately.

"Layton," he breathed, sagging in relief.

"Yep," Kiran's voice came out of the air next to him, and Gart started in surprise. "We drew straws, and he won. Lucky bastard. You've got some explaining to do, Gart, and although I'm not entirely sure what's going on here, *nobody* tries to hurt one of us and gets away with it."

The air shimmered, and both Kiran and Nessar appeared a few yards away as the older Guardian allowed the concealing power of his Jidaan to lapse into quiescence. Nessar quickly unlimbered his bow and began loosing bolts

120

at the flying monstrosities, killing them as fast as he could nock arrow to string. They fell awkwardly to earth, thumping wetly on the stony ground.

"Yech!" Nessar grimaced as he feathered another of the bat-things. "What Hel did these creatures fly out of?"

Kiran glared at Gart pointedly before she turned to face the looming stone elemental. "Leave the Wards to someone who actually knows what she's doing," she growled. She left her Jidaan in its sheath at her back, and the sapphire in its pommel glowed brightly as she invoked its power. An intense blue sphere of crackling energy sprang to life around the whirling elemental, capturing it. It bounced against the walls of its prison, and although Kiran grunted with effort, her Ward remained solid.

"No!" Barovius yelled, his voice breaking in his rage. "No, you can't do that!" He began to chant again, gesturing at the remaining rubble at the base of the cliff. The scree began to tremble as it struggled to answer his call.

Nessar feathered the last of the flying creatures and stepped over to Gart. He laid a careful hand on the younger man's shoulder and looked into his bright blue eyes. He saw despair and confusion there.

"Son," Nessar began, his voice calm. "It's time to stop. We know what you're trying to do, and it's too dangerous. Please, let's walk away." Even as he said it, Nessar knew that Gart would never turn aside.

"No!" Angered, Gart yanked his shoulder away from Nessar, though he staggered a step in his exhaustion. "No, you don't understand! I must! It's..." he paused. Finally, the rage that had fueled him for most of his life ebbed away. He had utterly spent himself; he was battered, bleeding, and exhausted. Gart tried to summon the rage again, but it had abandoned him. He fell to his knees before his old friend. Looking up into Nessar's kind eyes, he just could not find that anger anymore. A sob escaped him before he could stop it. "It's my last chance to see her, Ness. I failed her and Rheann, but I can still see her this last time. I have to. I have to!" He repeated. Tears finally broke free and ran down his cheeks, making trails through the blood and dirt. He glanced to the sky and said, "The sun and moon won't align this way again for centuries. Time is short, I have to

121

do this now." He paused as his pain overtook him. "I've got nothing else, Ness. Nothing."

Nessar said nothing, and Kiran did not bother to acknowledge Gart's words, though she had heard every one. She grunted again as the elemental slammed against her Ward, but she was not about to let it budge. She kept an eye on Barovius, who seemed to be having trouble calling a second elemental, but was making progress. Annoyed, she reached out with her power and created a second Ward, a sphere only a foot across. She solidified it and then whipped it toward Barovius, striking him in the chest and sending him to the ground in agony. The rubble he had been trying to awaken dropped back into place, inanimate once more. Kiran grinned in satisfaction. "Take that, you ugly bunghole," Kiran muttered, relieved to only have one threat to deal with, even if it was a big one. The existing elemental suddenly expanded in all directions, stressing her Ward almost to the breaking point. With a grunt of effort, she held it, and the creature resumed its normal dimensions within its confines.

To Gart, she said, "Look, you know what could happen if you botch this. You're not exactly in the best of shape, man, and from what we hear, it takes some major know-how to do what you suggest. It's not just you we're worried about. If this thing goes bad, we're all dead. You know that?"

Gart turned to her, and Kiran was shocked at the look in his eyes. She had always known Gart was the most powerful of them all. She had seen what he could do at Alverton Falls, back when he was young and inexperienced. He had only grown stronger over the years. He had always been tightly controlled, intense, and stoic. She could count on the fingers of one hand how many times she had heard him laugh, and she had never, ever, seen the least sign of weakness in him. Now, he was absolutely distraught. He was in agony of a kind she could barely recognize.

"Kiran," he pleaded. "I know you love Oswald," he said simply. Kiran was so shocked to hear her husband's name from Gart, she simply nodded. "I saw the way you looked at him at your handfasting ceremony. You *saw* him, and by the Goddess, he *saw* you too. All of you, the good, the bad, everything. He saw the parts of you that you'd kept hidden so far away from the rest of the world that even you had almost forgotten them."

In spite of herself, Kiran felt a hitch in the next breath she took. She turned her attention back to the trapped elemental, but she knew full well what Gart meant. And her heart had suddenly opened up wide in remembrance of her love for her husband. Dear, sweet Oswald, who would not have hurt a fly, had nevertheless captured her heart not through incredible deeds of bravery and muscle, but through the simple fact that he *saw* her. The real Kiran. The one who was strong on the outside and gooey on the inside, the one who loved flowers and flute music and puppies, the one who loved babies so much but could never have any of her own, *that* Kiran. And he loved every bit of her roughness, too. Tears tracked down her face before she could stop them.

Gart continued, "I can do this, Kiran. I'm exhausted and beaten up, it's true, but I've trained for over a decade for this. And," he hesitated before continuing, "Goddess above, I'm so sorry for what I did to you three. I'd never have hurt you. But wouldn't you have done the same? For Oswald? For just a few heartbeats, for just enough time to finally say goodbye, wouldn't you move the heavens above?"

Kiran was silent. She had never been one who succumbed to persuasive talk. She was stubborn and cynical by nature, and appealing to her softer side had never been the best way to get her to agree to anything. Even so, something about this felt different. She grimaced and turned to Nessar. "Ness," she said, her voice firm once more. "Go with him. If anything goes wrong, you know what to do with the stuff Layton gave you."

Nessar stared at her, incredulous. "Do what now? We've traveled across the continent and risked our lives multiple times to *stop* him from doing this, and now you suddenly want to just...*let* him? Have you lost your damned mind?"

"Oh, hels no. But...I don't know, something just..." Kiran's voice trailed off as she struggled to put into words exactly what she was thinking. Even before Gart had begun talking, the very sight of him had turned something over in her heart. Something deep inside her was telling her to go against every shred of better judgement she could muster.

Kiran watched the whirling elemental try to bash its way through her Ward again. It failed. She was tiring, but far from her limits. She threw a glance over her shoulder and saw Layton weaving his way through the herd of boar-beasts. Through their magickal link, she faintly caught his dreamy sense of joy as he did what he was born to do. He danced, whirled, stabbed, slashed, and fought in a state of perfect calm. He had found the stillness within the motion once more, and his spirit, mind, and body were as one.

Satisfied that she and Layton could handle the enemies on the field, she cracked a half-smile at Nessar. "Nessar, I may regret saying this, but my gut tells me that we need to let him do it." She suddenly glared sharply at her old friend. "And don't make me explain it! I don't know why, it's just something I feel, deep down." She threw a nod in Layton's direction. "We've got this under control here. You just keep a close eye on him and if anything goes wrong, do what you have to do. And *you*," she turned her glare towards Gart, who met it evenly. "You owe us big. So big. Don't muck it up."

Chapter 20

"You should have just given me what I wanted! At least then, you'd have had a chance to walk away!"

Melidia laughed, secure in her grasp of the situation. Gart was down, and she knew he was done for. She had won.

And then he lifted his head.

Melidia was barely able to stifle a gasp as Gart's intense blue gaze locked with her own. She saw power there, and an iron will that suddenly set her on her heels. As she watched, he pushed himself up to one knee. Melidia awakened the power in her wand and loosed another intense blast of energy at him, hoping to catch him off balance. Her previous attacks had scored, and he was obviously hurt. Gart surprised her by deftly shunting her crimson bolt aside. She watched him slowly pull himself back to his feet, his blazing eyes never leaving hers. Infuriated, she growled in anger and sent another blast of crackling energy towards him, and again, he deflected it harmlessly into the ground.

The unmarked side of Gart's face suddenly turned up in a wicked half-smile. "That's funny," his low, threatening voice drifted across to her, sending a chill up her spine. "I was going to say the same thing to you." Her eyes widened as she realized that she might be in trouble.

She saw Gart lift his hands in preparation for an attack. Melidia quickly crossed her forearms in front of her and touched her slender silver wristbands together, creating a burst of energy that instantly resolved itself into a hazy wall of protection. Whatever he was likely to throw at her would bounce off her shield. She saw his blue eyes flash gold as a powerful burst of magick erupted from him. She tensed for the impact, but none came, and she realized too late that he had not been aiming at her.

The cliff overhead exploded when Gart's power hit it, sending a brutal avalanche of debris right down on top of her. She vaguely heard the horses burst into a gallop to save themselves, but she had to focus on keeping herself alive, horses be damned. She screamed in anger and frustration and raised her crossed wrists over her head, shifting her shield upwards to deflect the falling rocks. As she set her feet to accept the stress of the impact, she briefly wondered if her shield was large enough to protect Barovius as well. Then she dismissed him from her mind. *If he dies, so much the better.* She could steal the Jidaan of Storms from his corpse with no fuss whatsoever. As she focused the power of her bracelets into the protective Ward overhead, she suddenly realized her mistake. Gart now had a clear shot at her.

He took it.

His blast of concussive force hit her fully in the chest, impacting her from shoulders to knees. Her body slammed back into the unyielding wall of the cliff, knocking the wind out of her. Her shield wavered and vanished as the first of the stones came down around her. Rocks slammed into the hard ground with bone-crushing force. Melidia curled up into as tight a ball as she could even as she struggled to draw in a full breath. Struggling, she brought her wrists together again and reformed the shield only a few feet above her body. Boulders, rocks, and gravel slammed into it, completely entombing her among the scree, leaving her in darkness. Through her power, she felt the pressure increase as more rocks and dirt fell on top of the pile.

Melidia focused her entire being on keeping the Ward active, keeping the heavy stones from crushing her. The air within her shield was warm and dusty, and it irritated her lungs. She coughed weakly, then finally managed a deeper breath. That calmed her enough to take stock of her situation. Beneath the blanket of dirt and rock, she could hear nothing of what might be happening. Arkhan should have brought his winged monstrosities into play, and then the boar-men. She had to admit, the lad had really come through there at the end, somehow creating a veritable horde of deadly hybrid creatures in the short time she had given him. Balroth only knew where he found the unlucky humans he needed to make them, since he had been forbidden to use her servants. Hopefully, his Joinings would finish the job, or at least keep Gart busy enough to allow her to escape her rough tomb. Although she was burning with rage and frustration, Melidia calmed herself and began probing the pile of rubble that lay on top of her, searching for a way out.

She felt a tremor in the scree that surrounded her, and she cursed as she realized that Barovius must have escaped the worst of the rockfall. He was calling an earth elemental, using the rubble that had fallen on her to form its body. As the trembling continued, she felt a lessening of the pressure above her as many of the rocks were pulled away by Barovius' spell.

There! she thought, triumphantly. A weak spot had developed in the pile of debris. Narrowing her violet eyes, she concentrated on the area, testing it with the energy from her shield. The bracelets were not designed to be that versatile, but she found that she could change the shape of the shield slightly if she focused hard enough, and she pushed a section of her magickal wall into the spot. It gave way, rocks and dirt tumbling aside and allowing a shaft of sunlight to fall on her. She squinted in the sudden brightness and began to squirm her way up and out through the small tunnel. It was rough going. She was scratched and battered, her chest still aching and bruised from Gart's attack.

Suddenly, she heard voices outside and froze. Melidia listened intently, then felt the crackle of energy as someone added their power to the fray, followed by Barovius' shout of frustration. She cursed, knowing that the other Guardians must have somehow found their way into the conflict. She had seen the trio disappear into the Mire and since then had not bothered to scry for them again, thinking the Mire would do her work for her. She had focused too much on Gart and the girl, and that had apparently been a mistake. She recalled seeing the girl stumbling through the Mire in one of her scrying visions, dying from ant venom and spore sickness. *One less thing to worry about,* she thought.

She felt the rubble around her begin to tremble again as Barovius tried to summon another elemental. The new tremor enlarged the tunnel she was trying to escape through, and she scrambled upwards toward the light. Suddenly, she heard Barovius grunt in pain, and she stopped. Melidia could not help but smile. *Serves you right, you old coot! Didn't even bother to help me out of this mess!* Moving carefully, she pulled herself up until she could see the battlefield clearly, her eyes and nose poking up out of the hole like a groundhog.

What she saw made her blood boil.

The whirling stone elemental was held captive within a shining sphere of blue energy - a Ward. The Guardian who controlled the Ward stood a safe distance away, her arms upraised, the sapphire in the pommel of her sheathed Jidaan blazing brightly above her shoulder. Melidia sneered as she got a good look at the woman she knew as Kiran. Her curves were those of an innkeeper, not a warrior, and she was no longer young. Her long brown hair was lightening at the temples and braided into a thick plait that fell over one shoulder. Melidia could see the wrinkles at the corners of her eyes even at that distance. The woman's face was a confident mask of determination, and there was skill and experience in her stance. She had beaten Barovius' air elementals weeks ago, and now she held his stone elemental captive without much effort. As Melidia watched, Kiran turned and spoke to Gart and a much older man, also wearing a Jidaan slung blade downward across his back. Its pommelgem was black as midnight, and her eyes seemed to shy away from it.

Nessar, she thought, *I thought you were dead!* He had passed out of public view ages ago, and had never appeared in her scrying attempts. She was shocked to see him still alive, looking spry as ever in spite of his white hair and wrinkles. Not keeping a closer eye on the Guardians had apparently been a grave mistake. *Nothing for it now,* she thought. *I'll just have to kill them too.* She spotted Barovius laid out on the ground nearby, unconscious. Gart's Jidaan was still on his back, but she'd relieve him of that burden in moments. *It's time I finally rid myself of your nonsense, Barovius! My dagger will send you on your way to Hel where you belong.* Melidia carefully began to push away the dirt and rocks on the far side of the hole, away from the view of the Guardians. She needed to stay out of their sight for just a few minutes more. When she had cleared a path, she slowly crawled out of the hole, absently lamenting the scrapes and bruises that pained her in a hundred places. *They will pay dearly for each and every one, yes they will,* she thought. Once she was clear, she would awaken the DireLord, and those stupid Guardians would either yield up the Blood of Nimshi or be crushed under the ancient being's unimaginable strength. She hoped for the latter.

Chapter 21

Hope blossomed anew in Gart's heart. He glanced at the sky. There was still time. He looked at Nessar, who was shaking his head.

The old man sighed. "She's crazy for allowing this, and I'm crazier for going along with it. But although I truly hate to admit it, I...I agree with her." He looked hard at Gart then, deep into his cobalt blue eyes. Nessar's hazel eyes were still clear and sharp, belying his eighty-odd years. Magick had kept his body strong over the last two decades, but his mind had never been an issue. He was still a deeply intelligent man. He sighed again. "Something about all this keeps pinging me somewhere deep. It's like a memory that I can't quite put my finger on, but I know it's there; I feel that I'm supposed to help you." He saw the beginnings of a smile on Gart's face and quickly added, "But I don't have to like you while I do it. Nope. You have been insufferable for years, man. And you knocked us out back there without a second thought. I haven't forgotten that, boyo."

Gart looked at the ground and his tired voice was low and remorseful. "I am sorry about that, old friend. I'd never have hurt you."

"Yeah, yeah," Nessar waved off the apology. "Stow it for now. Let's get you to the shrine before something else happens. You know where it is?"

Gart inclined his head to his left. "It's north of here, and not far. I can feel it."

Nessar sighed and nodded tersely at Kiran before taking off at a jog in the direction Gart had indicated. Gart quickly followed him, throwing a quick wave at Kiran as they left. Kiran waved back dismissively, then turned her full attention to the stone elemental she held captive. It had stopped slamming itself against the walls of her Ward, and now simply stayed where it was. It looked exactly like Orith, the sentinel that kept watch on the mountain road leading to Guardians Keep; a mass of stones of all sizes, from pebbles to boulders, all constantly swirling in the air to form a vaguely spherical shape. It had no facial features, no eyes or ears, but it still had a voice. It was silent for the moment, though Kiran had heard it growl and rumble at her when it had first attacked. Now, it appeared to be thinking.

"Hey there!" she yelled, hoping it could hear her from inside the buzzing energy of her Ward. "Hey! I don't want to fight you!" The sphere of stones continued to rotate, giving no sign it had understood. "I know one of your kind. His name is Orith. We're friends. Does that count for anything?"

The rotating sphere suddenly sped up. The stones that made up its body moved faster than they had before, and it became smaller as its formation tightened up. It still did not reply.

Kiran frowned, desperately trying to think of something. She could hold the creature for a long while yet, but it took almost all of her focus to keep the Ward intact. If she could not figure out a way to deal with the creature, there would certainly be problems. She raised her voice again, "Orith guards the way to our home. We're Guardians...Brunar trained us."

The creature slowed its rotation. A deep bass rumble came from somewhere within its whirling mass. "Orith. Brunar. They are known to us. Who are you to wield the Jidaan of Warding?"

"I am Kiran of Rualtha!" she answered proudly. The elemental began to spin faster again, and something about the way it moved made Kiran nervous. She cast about for something else to say. "Uh," she stammered, "Wait, what was his name...Durok!" she yelled triumphantly. "Durok wielded my Jidaan before me! I hear he was quite the ladies' man, though that was centuries before my time."

The stones slowed their rotation once more, and the bass rumble returned. "Durok. He is...was...known to us. He is gone?"

Kiran lessened the amount of energy in her Ward. She liked where this conversation was going. "Yes, he died a couple thousand years ago. I'm new."

The sphere slowed even more. "By our reckoning, Durok was here but a short time ago. Time passes more slowly for us." The being silently spun in place for a few moments as if considering. It remained where it was, hovering a few feet above the ground, still surrounded by

Kiran's Ward. "You say you know of Orith and Brunar, with whom we are familiar. More importantly," the creature paused and Kiran held her breath, "the weapon you bear marks you as a Chosen Guardian. We hold no malice towards you. My name is Ordeth. I was summoned and compelled to attack you. That compulsion has been lifted." It was silent again, and when next it spoke, Kiran could swear she heard a hint of laughter in its gravelly voice. "As he is no longer alive, and now that I know who you are, he has no power over me."

Kiran relaxed and allowed the Ward to vanish. Freed from its prison, the elemental being slowly approached her, its stones spinning in a steady rhythm. "Farewell, Kiran of Rualtha. I will tell the others of the demise of those Guardians we knew. They will be saddened, but pleased that others have accepted their responsibility."

Kiran bowed at the waist towards the creature, and opened her mouth to speak, but before she could, the stony elemental launched itself high into the air. It soared up and up, toward the edge of the cliff above, where it flew out of sight.

"Well, that's not something you see every day," Kiran said to no one in particular. She sagged in relief and sighed before remembering that Layton was still fighting somewhere on the slope behind her. She turned in that direction and saw that only twenty or so of the hybrid creatures remained, and they were all still trying to kill Layton. Reaching out with her magick, she connected with Layton and found that, although he was still moving well, he was tiring. Through the link, she felt the bumps, bruises, and cuts he had already sustained, and knew that he was going to need some help to finish off the last of the boar-creatures. She pulled her sword from its scabbard and cracked her neck first one direction, then the other. "All right, let's get this over with."

Suddenly, agony erupted across her back as something struck her from behind. The world spun and the stony earth seemed to jump up and hit her in the face. There was a moment of silence during which Kiran tried to get both of her eyes to point in the same direction, and then the pain started to register. Dirt was in her mouth and in her eyes, stinging mercilessly. She blinked away the hot tears that arose and spat blood to clear her mouth. Feminine laughter echoed around her as she struggled to catch her breath. Kiran rolled herself up on her side and twisted her aching neck so she could see what had hit her. She was shocked to see a red-haired woman, bruised and dirty, standing not far away. She had something slung across her back that Kiran instantly knew was Gart's Jidaan, even though it was wrapped in rags.

"Stupid sow!" the woman yelled, her face a twisted mask of rage. There was a crazed light in her eyes that Kiran recognized. She had seen it before in many of her opponents in the past – the ones that had been more than willing to give their lives to get what they were after – and her heart sank. Then her natural stubbornness reasserted itself.

No way I'm letting that floozy take me out like this. No way in Hel. She hoped the woman would keep talking so that she could have the precious seconds she needed to recover. Towards that end, Kiran addressed her in a voice that shook with feigned fear. "Don't...don't hurt me!" Even through the haze of pain that colored her vision, Kiran still mentally rolled her eyes at the sound of weakness in her tone.

The red-haired woman laughed again and spat her next words. "Hurt you? If you knew what's coming, you'd roll over and die right now!" Rather than elaborate, she whirled and ran off to Kiran's left, racing southward with her crimson hair flying behind her. Gart's Jidaan bounced awkwardly on her back, but she managed to keep it from tripping her by keeping one hand on it.

Shocked, Kiran watched Melidia run away. She tried to summon a Ward, either to imprison the fleeing sorceress or strike a stunning blow, but Kiran never got that far. Her vision swam and her head threatened to split as her magick overloaded her battered body. She groaned and rolled over onto her back, frustrated at having to let Melidia escape. *That's gonna come back to bite me,* she thought as she squinted into the bright blue sky above. The sounds of Layton's battle with the boar-creatures drifted over to her. She knew she could either pursue Melidia to take back

133

Gart's Jidaan, or she could go help Layton, who was reaching his limits. She sighed, knowing that they would stand a better chance against Melidia together after they dispatched the rest of the boar things, but it did not sit well with her at all. Not only that, she was feeling every single one of the years that had passed since she was a lithe young warrior, relishing the challenge of battle. An exhausted chuckle escaped her then. She still enjoyed a good fight; it just felt more like work these days. She took as deep a breath as her aching back and ribs would allow, then she rolled over with a grunt and doggedly pushed herself to her feet. She could feel her energy returning, albeit slowly. She walked over to retrieve her sword, which had fallen from her hand when Melidia had hit her, and began walking briskly towards the fight. As the pain lessened, she accelerated to a trot, then found the strength to sprint the last several yards to join the fray.

Mustering a battle cry, Kiran hurled herself at the nearest boar-man, cleaving its spine in half with a two-handed swing of her sword. It went down with a pained howl, and she instantly turned to the next foe. Out of the corner of her eye, she saw Layton. Blood covered his face and beard from a nasty gash across the side of his head. He still moved with his usual fluid grace, but it was obvious he was flagging badly. Kiran could see rents in his clothing and deep dents in the minimal leather armor he habitually wore, but he managed a glance at her in between slashes and winked. There were only a dozen of the creatures left. The two Guardians could handle that many in their sleep. Kiran grinned and thrust her sword into the nearest boar-beast.

Then it all went very, very wrong.

Chapter 22

Gart and Nessar left the battle behind them. Nessar's wrinkled face was set in a hard frown. He was not happy to leave Kiran and Layton to deal with those creatures, not happy at all. And yet, his gut told him he was on the right track. He glanced over at Gart, who ran beside him somewhat awkwardly. The man was haggard and worn, much thinner than he had been when last he had been in Guardians Keep. The intervening weeks had been rough on him, though it was not as if the three of them had been on holiday either.

"You know those bungholes?" Nessar asked.

Gart wheezed a bit before answering. He was struggling to stay on his feet to keep up with the old man. His magick was powerful, far more so than Nessar's on a good day, but the recent days had taken their toll. He was able to use his magick to bolster his stamina, but only barely. He still had to send enough to Beauty to keep her alive, and the distance between them made that difficult. "I know their names, but that's all. You saw all three of them?"

Nessar said that he had.

"All of them are sorcerers, though not like Mordak. He was worse; much more powerful than any of them. But three of them together are..."

"Troublesome," Nessar finished for him.

Gart almost grinned. "Yes, that. They want something I have, though I don't know why. Nearly killed Beauty and me trying to get their hands on it."

Nessar shook his head. "No mean feat, that. That dog of yours would make a lion think twice."

Gart tried to chuckle, but was too out of breath. "She would, yes." A sharp pang of guilt stabbed into his heart at the thought of Beauty, somewhere behind them, fighting for her life. He could not feel her very well, but the link they shared reassured him that, for the moment at least, she was still alive. He prayed she would survive. "She was fighting those things in the hills just before you came."

"We got there just after that, I think. Right before all those pig-headed brutes came out of the woods."

They jogged in silence for a few moments, then Gart started talking. "I think the woman, Melidia, is the leader. Barovius is the bald one. He's got my Jidaan, though it won't work for him. He seems to be skilled with elemental magick. There's another one, Arkhan. He seems to be able to create and control those hybrid things."

"Ah," Nessar said. "Kiran told me about some air daemons that attacked her before they reached Guardians Keep. I bet Barovius was behind it."

"Likely so. They want the Blood of Nimshi."

"Why?" Nessar asked. "What are they going to do with it?"

"I have no idea, but I'm willing to bet it won't be good," Gart replied grimly. "It's powerful stuff. I only know one use for it, but I'm sure there are others." Suddenly, Gart's eyes widened. "Wait, can you feel that?" Gart slowed to a walk and Nessar followed suit.

Nessar was silent for a bit, then replied. "The Weya said this was a place of power. If I concentrate, I *can* feel something." He pointed a gnarled finger at a spot on the cliff wall up ahead. Nessar's eyes were old, but still quite sharp, and he had spotted a vertical shadow in the rock that seemed to run from the ground all the way up the wall to the top of the cliff. "And I think I see something over there."

Gart opened his hands and held them out in front of him as he reached out with his magick. "The Weya knew what they were talking about. This whole area is thick with magick. It feels almost as though there are rivers of it beneath the surface that converge near here. They run deep, and are unbelievably strong. I don't even begin to understand how that could be, but it makes sense that someone put a shrine here. Whatever they originally used it for, it must have taken some serious power."

Nessar frowned. "I sure hope you know what you're doing, man. I feel like this is going to be like lighting a torch in the middle of a hay barn. If you're not careful..." he left the rest unspoken.

Gart sighed. "I know, Ness. I know. I've thought of nothing else for the last several years. The risks, the chances I'm taking. The consequences. All of it." He turned to his old friend and stared into his eyes. His piercing blue gaze showed no trace of insanity, only determination. "I know what I'm doing sounds crazy and selfish, and maybe it is. But even so, I'd gladly die to keep this world safe. I have to do this, but I'll be careful."

Nessar shook his head and picked up his pace, heading for the shadow up ahead. "I hope you're right, Gart. I hope you're right."

It took less than a minute for them to reach the spot Nessar had indicated, and it turned out to be a narrow vertical cleft in the stone that ran all the way to the top of the cliff. It was barely large enough for the two of them to walk shoulder to shoulder through it, and it led deep into the rock at a right angle to the cliff face. Without hesitation, they turned and walked into the cleft.

The high walls of the cleft were rough and close, but Gart and Nessar paid little attention, keeping their eyes forward as they searched for the shrine. The sun shone down from almost straight overhead, illuminating most of the narrow defile. The sound of the two men's boots scuffing on the stone was loud in their ears as they pushed onward. Soon, the passage opened up into a large, roughly square chamber that was open to the sky high above. They scanned the bare walls on all sides for anything resembling a shrine or altar, but there was nothing except flat, reddish stone staring back at them.

Gart let his eyes roam over the back wall of the dead end, scanning it slowly from left to right. No matter what his eyes were telling him, his magick told him the truth. "Here," he said. "It's right here."

Nessar looked at the spot Gart seemed to indicate, and saw nothing but an empty wall, barren of decoration. He could feel the power now, buzzing all around them. It was strongest beneath his boots, but still faint enough that he had to pay attention to recognize it. Gart, however, seemed to sense it far more easily. "I don't want to be a pessimist," Nessar began, "but I don't see anything but a wall. We followed the fissure, but where's the shrine?"

"It's here. Hold on." Gart raised his hands and his eyes flashed a dim gold as he reached out with his magick, using it to probe the cliff face for what he knew was hidden there. He was beyond weary, but his magick still responded, tingling through his body as it did his bidding. He explored the surface of the rock wall and quickly found what he was looking for. "Look at the wall, there, right in front of us. Engage your magick while you do it, and let yourself see what's really there."

Nessar grumbled, but did as he was told. He stared at the barren rock face and then called his own magick to life. Usually, he barely noticed his power. It moved through him the way his blood coursed through his veins, without conscious direction. However, like all of the Guardians, he had been made aware of the well of magick that resided within him. If he concentrated, he could awaken it and use it for more extreme activities. Nessar took a breath, then looked inside himself for his power. It answered his call immediately and flared to life. Nessar gasped as the wall before him wavered in front of his eyes and then fell away.

"Oh," he breathed. "Oh, my..."

In Rualtha, he had seen roadside shrines that were little more than small, waist-high platforms, enclosed on three sides and adorned with a tiny statue or two to depict the god to whom the structure was dedicated. For some reason, that was what he had expected to find at the end of the fissure. Instead, the collapse of the illusion had revealed an enormous façade carved directly into the stone. The Shrine of Malmathas appeared to be nothing short of a massive temple. It stood at least thirty feet high, and spread out to either side at least twice that far. Tall, fluted columns supported the upper levels and a wide, flat series of stairs led up toward a rectangular entrance that lacked doors. There was only a huge, shadowy rectangle of emptiness so dark that it might have been a solid block of midnight. Strange sigils were carved into the columns and the walls surrounding the opening, and they were alien to Nessar's eye.

With his magick awakened, Nessar could suddenly feel the innate power in the earth around them far more

138

readily, and its enormity awed him. "Sweet goddess," he murmured.

"Come on," Gart urged. "There's not much time."

"Wait, let me get a light going," Nessar was about to unsling his pack and dig for his candle lantern when Gart stopped him.

"No need," Gart informed him. Gart wearily raised his right hand as though he were waving at someone and a warm, golden glow surrounded it. Gart knew that another expenditure of magick was only tiring him further, but time was of the essence.

"Wow, that's a handy trick," Nessar quipped. "You'll have to teach us how to do that, those lanterns and torches are a pain."

Gart did not reply, but was already starting up the flat stone steps on his way to the passage. Nessar quickly fell in step beside him, drawing two of his daggers and holding them at the ready. The two men moved down the tunnel without incident.

The passage was square, easily wide enough for a half-dozen people to walk down side by side. Its walls, floor, and ceiling were all smooth as glass, with no hint of a chisel, no tool marks anywhere, and all the same scarlet stone of the mountain. The thrum of power was even more concentrated here, and with each step, Nessar could feel it intensifying. Up ahead of the pair, a light appeared, bright and welcoming. They both picked up their pace as they approached it.

Soon, the passageway ended in a vast, domed chamber, its curved ceiling supported by a circular array of huge, fluted pillars of the same reddish stone. Colorful mosaics covered the walls, depicting scenes from a bygone age. Humans were predominant, their dress archaic and odd to Nessar's eyes, but there were also the slight and fair Weya, their jewel-like eyes and pointed ears clearly visible. There were also strangely shaped beings that he did not recognize. Some were holding weapons while others seemed to be performing feats of magick. The pictures were eerily lifelike, and Nessar resolved to examine them more closely when he had the chance. His eyes were drawn to the far wall, which was occupied by a rectangular platform

139

supporting a blocky stone altar in its center. The altar's sides were chased in gold and jewels that glinted in the light. An enormous and ornate stone circle was carved in the wall behind the altar, the top arc at least fifteen feet from the bottom.

A bright stream of sunlight illuminated the room from above, coming through a glass lens which was housed in a metal contraption that poked through a hole in the ceiling. The light landed on a perfectly circular spot on the floor that was the size of a warrior's shield. Nessar glanced at it, then looked more closely. Something within the bright circle appeared to be moving.

"Be careful," Gart whispered, but there was no need. Nessar had been born careful and trained to be even more so. Gart set down his backpack, and Nessar winked out of existence as his Jidaan of Stealth worked its magick. He wanted to see what had moved, and there was no point in taking chances. Gart rummaged around in his pack for the few things he needed while Nessar moved silently out onto the floor.

Laid out on the floor in beautiful colored tiles was a large, elongated figure-eight. Various spots were marked and the accompanying text was unknown to Nessar. It was a beautiful, flowing script that was unlike anything he had ever seen. The glowing spot of sunlight drew Nessar's attention, and he crept toward it.

It was a clear image of the surface of the sun, but somehow, it did not hurt his eyes to view it. Nessar glanced at the lens overhead and saw that it was darkened to filter out the worst of the light. He turned his gaze back to the image and stared in wonder at the way it moved. He had never given the sun any thought, but now he could see that it was like a thing alive. Flares burst on its surface, reaching out hungrily only to die, then fall back into the flames so that others would emerge moments later. He saw for the first time black spots here and there, singly and in clusters, on the fiery surface. As he watched, a crescent of darkness slowly entered from one side, hiding the sun's brightness. The ebony disc's progress was visible, but only just. *The eclipse!* Nessar thought.

"It's starting!" Gart confirmed as he gathered the items from his backpack into his arms and started moving toward the altar. "I only have a few minutes. Just stay back, I don't want anything to happen to you."

"That makes two of us," Nessar answered wryly. Nessar moved away from the blazing image on the floor and walked to the pillar nearest the altar. He situated himself so that he had a clear view of Gart and the altar. "All right, I'm good. Have at it."

Gart mounted the steps and walked up to the altar. His heart was racing. Sweat dripped into his eyes, stinging them, but he barely noticed. He had spent years training for this ritual, and had even practiced with props to prepare himself. The ancient incantation was burned into his memory, but now that the time had come to use it, his mouth was dry and his throat was threatening to constrict with emotion. He took a deep breath and focused on the actions he needed to perform.

First, he hefted the Heart of Corria in one hand, and it sparkled invitingly in the dim light. The fist-sized gemstone pulled at his sight, wanting him to lose himself within it, but Gart was ready. His will was iron, and he ignored the call of the Heart and placed it in the center of the altar. As he did, he was astonished to see the hard flat stone suddenly come to life, undulating as though its solid granite surface had turned to water. It rippled outward toward the edges of the thick table, then the ripples reversed themselves. They converged in the center, where they suddenly joined to form a small pillar beneath the huge diamond. The diamond rose a few inches from the surface, supported by the animated stone. Before Gart's eyes, a circular ridge pushed its way up from the table's surface, just wide enough to surround the Heart. It stretched upward until the ridge was just above the middle of the diamond, and the Heart sat in a perfect bowl of stone.

Gart placed the rough vessel that contained the Blood of Nimshi in front of him. This would be more challenging than avoiding the gentle, persuasive whispers of the Heart of Corria. If the gemstone whispered, the Blood of Nimshi shouted with a thousand voices. As the jug met the surface of the table, it again rippled, though this time, the ripples bounced back and forth across the horizontal surface, gradually dying away. He took a deep breath and then let it out, clearing his mind as he did so. Years of painstaking effort and hours of solitary practice served him well. Everything else ceased to exist for him except the task at hand and the thought of his beloved.

"Anat su kaven, Gennie mi konen, anata si…" Gart began the ancient chant that would channel the power of both Heart and Blood into his spell. He would take their power and add it to his own, amplifying his will a thousandfold and bridging the gap between himself and Gennie.

Gart raised his hands and engaged his magick, creating a nimbus of protective energy around the stone jug, limiting its influence. His voice rose and fell as he chanted the ancient words, and the incantation echoed throughout the huge chamber. Moving carefully, he reached into the small glowing sphere of power and uncorked the jug. With both hands, he picked up the jug and carefully poured half of its contents over the Heart of Corria. The gemstone flared brilliantly and buzzed with energy as it sent a rainbow of intense colors sparkling all around the room. Its vibrations shook dust from the ceiling and there was a deep and ominous rumbling from deep in the earth. Gart felt the tremors beneath his boots as the power there seemed to waken in response to his ritual. He had known that was coming, and stood firm. He carefully replaced the stopper in the little stone jug and set it safely down on the floor at his feet. That accomplished, he focused entirely on the Heart. He raised his hands and guided his power into the flare of energy as he shaped his intent. Behind him, the dark crescent on the floor had covered roughly half of the sun's bright disk, but the light from the Heart was dazzling.

Imposing his will again, he began to channel the blazing energy from the Heart, focusing it and sending it toward the carved stone circle on the wall behind the altar. A part of him was screaming, terrified that all of his effort, all the risks, would be for nothing. Or worse, that he was calling down ruin on the world. Maybe he had forgotten something, maybe his words were mispronounced, maybe the scrolls had been wrong. Fortunately, he had long since sent all those doubts to a prison in his mind. He could not afford them right now. He had to believe he would succeed. His will had to be unbreakable, unstoppable, in spite of his pain and fatigue. He could not break. And he did not.

The stone circle in the wall opposite Gart erupted in golden light that should have blinded him. There was a sense of something ripping, a giving way, and a cool wind struck his face. A shadow appeared within the brightness. It was small at first, but slowly approached until it was roughly as tall as a man. It seemed to walk towards Gart from the far side, but then it stopped before it passed the plane of energy Gart had created. Its appearance was still indistinct and vague. It moved slightly, somehow giving an impression of grace and femininity. It stood there, as if watching. Waiting.

Gart burst into motion, dodging around the huge, square altar and lunging into the golden portal.

"Gart!" Surprised, Nessar yelled from behind the pillar. "Wait, Gart, no!"

Even as Nessar's words echoed from the domed ceiling, the old thief knew that there was no one else to hear them. He was suddenly alone in the chamber.

Chapter 23

A cold wind picked up from the south, howling through the valley and chilling Layton and Kiran as they hacked and cleaved at the remaining boar-creatures. At first, it was just a cool breeze, but within a minute, it had increased to the point that all of them, Guardians and Joinings alike, had to struggle to stay upright.

"Layton!" Kiran called out, hoping he would hear her over the moaning of the wind. "To me! Come here, now!"

At first, he made no sign that he had heard her, but once he dispatched the boar-beast that was closest to him, an opalescent Gate appeared an arm's length away and its twin appeared next to Kiran. With practiced ease, he took a single step through one Gate and came through at Kiran's side, then he allowed the Gates to vanish. It had taken less than a second.

Kiran put a hand on his shoulder and called on the power of her Jidaan once more, and a rectangular sapphire blue Ward appeared at their backs. About the size of a barn door, it created an instant shelter from the gale. The boar-beasts enjoyed no such protection, and they fell over each other as they scrambled to keep their footing and reach the pair of humans that had caused them such pain and suffering.

"Kiran, look." Layton stared through the translucent blue sheet of energy toward the valley floor that lay beyond. His gaze was fixed on two moving objects.

Kiran turned and looked to see what he had seen, and her jaw dropped slowly open.

"Oh, Hels," she cursed. "Just when I thought we were gaining some ground here."

Even a hundred yards away, they could see that one of the approaching figures was enormous, easily dwarfing the Ogres they had fought in the distant past. This creature was at least thirty feet tall, and moved with a rough grace seemingly impossible for something that big. Its skin was gray, though there was not much of it. Muscle was exposed in many places across its enormous chest, legs, arms, and torso, the pebbly hide gaping to reveal the ugly crimson

144

ropes of muscle fibers beneath. To say that it wore armor would have been untrue, for the thick iron plates appeared to be bolted directly to its body somehow, and the pitted and scarred metal had obviously seen brutal use. A horned helmet of black iron completely encased its head. Where eyes should have been, there was only a smooth expanse of metal entirely covering the face above the skeletal nose. The creature had no lips at all, and its huge, pointed teeth and bony jaw lay exposed to the elements. In one powerful fist it held a huge, rectangular sword blade, viciously chipped and jagged from use and stained with ancient blood. A relatively small black iron shield was bolted to its left forearm, a buckler of sorts. It had no left hand, the thick, muscular forearm ending in a cap of the same scarred, black metal. Sprouting from the end of the cap was a chain that dragged behind it, its links easily big enough to tow a ship. The thick chain ended in a great spiked ball that plowed a furrow in the dirt as it trailed along. The creature faced them, seeing them despite its lack of eyes, and it bellowed a challenge. The earth trembled at its might.

Flying near its right shoulder was Melidia, on the back of a creature Kiran had only seen a few times in the years following the war with Mordak: a red wyvern. It had huge, bat-like wings, and at first, Kiran thought it was one of the stone gargoyles, like the ones she had seen at Laro. But this was no noble creature of protection; instead, the creature she rode upon was ill-tempered and cunning, rather than intelligent. Its lizard-like head revealed sharp teeth as it squawked and screeched, and its slitted amber eyes were bright with malice. Claws at the end of each wing served as hands, and its muscular legs were tucked up beneath it in flying position as it glided on the currents, bearing the scarlet-haired sorceress on its back. With a wave of her ruby-tipped wand, Melidia ended the spell that had sent the chill wind down the valley, heralding her arrival. Her face was bright with triumph, and her magickly augmented voice reached the two Guardians clearly. "The DireLord is bound to me. I am its master! Prepare to meet your doom!"

In the next moment, the DireLord yanked on the chain and swung the enormous spiked morning star over its shoulder, whipping it towards Kiran and Layton. Kiran knew her Ward would not withstand the power of the behemoth's weapon, but even as she began to channel more energy into it, Layton ignited a Gate and moved it over them both, transporting them elsewhere. The enormous macehead slammed into the earth where they had been but an instant before, sending cracks in every direction in the dry, stony earth. The few remaining boar-men ran for the safety of the trees.

Kiran's stomach flipped, and she felt queasy for a moment until she oriented herself again. Layton's hand steadied her so that she did not fall from their new vantage point. His Gate had put them on a high ledge in the cliffs above and behind the attacking DireLord. Kiran caught her balance and mumbled, "Oh, I hate when you do that, but I'll thank you for getting us out of the way of that thing. I doubt my Ward would have survived unless I had been better prepared for the blow."

Layton wiped blood from his face with his sleeve. His green eyes twinkled with mischief, making him look much younger than his years despite his bloody countenance. "I thought this might confuse them for a bit. Be ready to move, though, they'll see us soon enough."

"How do we kill that thing? Hels, *what* is that thing?"

Layton shrugged his shoulders. "She called it a DireLord. I'd only heard of those in old legends, something about a war between Mages in ancient times. They used them to fight each other, I think."

Kiran grimaced. "That must have been something to see," she said. "I'd much rather have been a spectator than a participant, though. Hey, is it getting darker?"

Layton looked around and nodded. "Indeed, it is." He cast a quick glance skyward, then grimaced and looked away. "I think we got here just in time. The eclipse is starting. We have a handful of minutes, and then Gart's chance to perform the ritual will be over." He drew breath to say more, but was interrupted.

"Look out!" Kiran yelled.

The DireLord had spotted them. It turned with unnatural speed and aimed a horizontal swipe at them, its immense, squared blade whistling through the air on its way

146

to cut them in half. It slammed into the side of the cliff, cleaving a huge gash in the stone and sending an explosion of rubble and debris in all directions, but they were already gone.

Layton had moved them again, this time putting them back on the ground below, a good distance away from Melidia and the DireLord and closer to the trees on the east side of the valley. They took a few steps to hide themselves behind a cluster of oaks, where they both relaxed. Kiran breathed a sigh of relief as she saw how far away they were from the creature, but her relief turned to concern when she saw Layton waver on his feet.

"What's wrong?" she asked, her voice betraying her sudden worry.

Layton grunted in pain. "Wounded during the fight with the boar-men," he said. "Nothing broken and nothing's too deep, but I've lost enough blood that I'm woozy, and the Gates are taking their toll." He grinned and shook his head. "Not as young as I used to be."

Kiran swore in frustration and concern for her friend. "What do we do? We can't just leave that hussy out there! She's got Gart's Jidaan! And she's in control of that...that thing. Imagine the trouble she could cause if she got it back to one of the cities!"

Layton grinned. "Oh, I had no plans to escape. I'm just complaining. If I'm going to die, what a way to go, fighting that monster. Now *that's* a challenge!" He gestured with his Jidaan at the creature, who had yet to spot them. It was turning its iron-covered face this way and that in search of them. Melidia was flying above it on her wyvern, chanting something in an alien language as she strove to maintain control over the enormous being.

Kiran punched him lightly on what she hoped was his uninjured arm. "Don't talk like that, you arseling. We're both going to get out of here, but only after we take those two out. You want the big one? Fine. Then I get the barmaid with delusions of grandeur. I bet that's not even her real hair." Kiran glared across the space that separated her from Melidia. "She's got Gart's Jidaan, and I want it back. That belongs to *us*. To the Guardians." Aside from Nessar, and now Oswald, the Guardians were the only family that Kiran had ever known. Over the years, that kinship had meant more and more to her, and to see someone hurt one of them galled her. Someone trying to steal something from one of them was downright insulting, and not only that, it was the very symbol of their unity and power. She was not about to let that go unchallenged. Gart may have been a surly bastard, but he was *their* surly bastard, and that made him family. She pointed at a cluster of rocks in the valley, a maze of stone that was easily large enough to shelter her. "Can you put me over there among those rocks? If you're going to attack big and ugly, I know Melidia will be watching. That's when I'll hit her."

Layton nodded. He had been channeling his internal energy, the magick he still thought of as his ki, into his hurts to ease them. He had nothing so versatile as the healing power that the Guardian Alyssa used to wield, but his masters had taught him ways of maintaining his strength by focusing his internal energies to the task. Once his magick had been awakened by the Jidaan, that task had become markedly easier. Although he was still hurting and exhausted, Layton was feeling marginally better. "All right, just hunker down and I'll move the Gate over you. You'll come up just behind that big rock there. Ready?"

Kiran nodded, and Layton engaged the power of his Jidaan, sending her across the valley to her hiding place. That done, he wiped his bloody hands on his pants to clean them, then picked up his Jidaan. He looked again at the towering, unholy creature and thought about the best way to attack it. The great, scarred plates riveted to its body protected most of its chest and torso, and a ridge of metal had even been embedded in each shoulder to protect the neck on each side. Layton noticed a few weak spots though. The joints could not be well-protected lest they become immobile. He decided on a plan of attack. *This could prove to be interesting,* he thought.

Chapter 24

Gart passed through the thin membrane of energy that separated the Shrine of Malmathas from a place beyond that seemed to be filled with nothing but a warm, golden light. All of the hurts and aches he had been suffering were instantly washed away, leaving him feeling fit, healthy, and strong. The sudden change shocked him, and he gasped at the vitality he felt. The shape he had seen from the other side of the rift was clearly visible now, and the sight froze him in place. He hardly dared to breathe.

Standing before him was a beautiful woman, the one he had loved with all his heart. Her long, black hair flowed down past her shoulders, and her eyes twinkled with a knowing smile. She wore her favorite blue dress, the one she had made herself from cloth he brought back from one of his trips to market. She took a tentative step closer, and he saw that she moved with the same easy grace he remembered.

"Hey, Sunshine," she said. Tears had already tracked their way down her face even as she spoke.

That broke Gart. He had never told anyone that she had called him that, and she only did it when he was in a particularly foul mood. It had been her way of snapping him out of it, and it had always worked. A sob crawled out of his aching chest before he could stop it.

"Gennie," he began. "It's you. It's really you." Tears gathered in his eyes, making his bright blue irises shine. "I don't...I mean...I wanted to..." he struggled with his words. He had painstakingly crafted everything he had ever wanted to say, and practiced it incessantly, but the closeness of her drove all the words away like leaves in a strong breeze.

"Yes, it's me, love. In the flesh...just for a while." She opened her arms to him.

Gart stared at her for only a heartbeat before closing the distance between them and wrapping her in his arms. She was warm and felt just as she always had. She was both strong and soft, and his hands fell into the same places on her body they always had, a perfect fit. For the first time in decades, Gart cried for all he was worth, finally letting

149

out all of the guilt and shame he felt at not being able to save her. All of the pain and anguish that had built up over the years poured out of him as he cried on her shoulder and she held him tightly. Nothing had ever felt as good to him as holding her now.

"Hush, love," she whispered. "It's all right. I know what you're going through. I understand."

Gart stifled his sobs and pulled away to see his wife at arm's length. She was looking up at him, smiling, tears still on her face as well, and he had never seen anything so beautiful. "I'm sorry. I should have saved you, should have done something. I should have..."

She cocked an eyebrow at him. "You did all you could do and then some, you dummy." Gart flinched at the jibe, but remained silent. Gennie laid her right hand on his unscarred cheek, letting him lean into it. "You were not at fault. I'd have died anyway. Had you gone with Brunar when he first asked, I'd have died at Jor Dayne's hands just as I did. As it was, you stayed behind, and I still died. That's just how it goes, love. But in the end, you saved far more than just me. I saw it all. Well, most of it."

Gart's eyes widened. "You did?"

Gennie nodded and smiled brightly through her tears. "I did! I saw you ride in there at Alverton Falls and rip into that army with everything you had! You were so brave!" Her smile quirked to one side and she raised an eyebrow. "Well, knowing you, it was more like you were thoroughly pissed off."

Gart laughed and the sound startled him. There was no doubt it was Gennie. Tears continued to course down his face, making tracks in the ruddy dirt and grime that covered it. Suddenly, his eyes widened in alarm as he remembered Ishabel.

Gennie laughed at his discomfort. "It's all right, love, I know about Ishabel, too." Gart tried to look away, but she gently took his chin in her hand and turned his face back to hers. He met her eyes again, uncertainty in his. She smiled and her voice was soft and sincere. "I like her, Gart. She was good for you. I had been dead for years when your feelings for her finally started to show, and then you shoved them away because...well, because you're you."

Gart did not know whether to be embarrassed because he had feelings for Ishabel or because he stifled them, or because Gennie knew about it all. It had always been like that with Gennie. She had always been unusually insightful, especially where his emotions were concerned.

Gennie's voice became mock-stern. "You were a fool to let her go, you've got to know that. She still loves you. You should go to her. When this is over."

"I..." Gart's words had almost completely deserted him. Gennie's love and acceptance threatened to completely overwhelm him, and he had been wholly unprepared for it. He swallowed the lump in his throat, and finally found his voice. "I love you, Gennie. I've always loved you. And I'm sorry, so sorry. After I lost you and Rheann..."

Her finger suddenly alighted on his lips, hushing him. Gennie leaned in, her voice suddenly urgent. "She's not here, Gart. She's alive."

Gart's eyes widened again and he could do nothing but stare in disbelief.

"I can see lots of things from here, my love. I can't affect anything, and it takes a lot of energy for me even to watch, but I've kept an eye on her as best I could." She paused, as if considering how much to tell him. "She's coming here, right now, but she's not the little girl you remember. She's a grown woman, and the power she has..." she shook her head gently. "She's more powerful than you, more than Brunar, and she doesn't understand any of it. It's consumed her, and she doesn't know what she's doing."

The warm glow that surrounded them suddenly darkened, and thin streaks of murky scarlet ran through the golden light. Gennie glanced around, assessing, then turned back to Gart, her pretty eyes narrowed. "You've got to stop her from hurting anyone else, including herself. Only you have the power to do that. She doesn't know you, love, but her heart does remember. Find a way to reach her. Help her control her gift before she becomes something horrible."

Gart's mind reeled. His little girl, alive? After all these years, he did not know what to think. Then his lips compressed into a thin line that Gennie knew well. "I will. I'll help her. How will I find her?"

The swirling clouds of black and crimson were getting thicker around them. A crackle of power leapt from one cloud to another, scarlet lightning flashing in the growing darkness.

Gennie pulled him close and he returned her fierce embrace. He relished the feel of her, the smell of her, everything he had ever wanted, right there in his arms. Then she pulled away only enough to kiss him. Gart thought he would die right then and there and be happy about it. And then she pushed him away, holding his rough hands in hers. Thunder rolled as more lightning began to play in the gathering, ominous clouds.

"She's coming to you, to these mountains; she's not far away, and you'll know her when you see her." She let go of his hands and took a few steps backward. "I have to go. I'm needed elsewhere, and so are you. You can't stay here. Even now, others are coming and you must not let them pass. Go now, go and help her." A rising wind blew her hair across her face and she swiped at it with one hand. "Be the Gart I know, love. Let the world see that version of you. Not the one you've shown them all these years. Do that for me."

Gart took a halting step toward her, reaching for her, almost unable to bear her sudden absence. "Gennie, wait! Just a moment more..." Lightning struck again, the thunder close and dangerous. Gart became aware of other sounds, a low murmuring, as if from many voices. He looked around and saw distant shadows approaching. Thousands of them. Drawn to the light, other souls were coming.

Gennie yelled over the howl of the quickening wind, "No, there's no more time!" she said, urgency thick in her voice. "I love you, Gart! I always have! Now go and save our daughter!" She turned and ran away from him, her form quickly disappearing in the swirling mists.

"No!" Gart screamed, his voice breaking in anguish and rage. "No, Gennie, come back!" He took a step to follow her, ignoring the approach of the oncoming spirits. Their shadows were getting closer. The ominous rumbling grew more insistent by the moment. Before Gart could move any farther, something unseen grabbed him by the collar and yanked him nearly off his feet, pulling him back toward the portal he had created. He was caught off guard, and he flailed uselessly as he was dragged away from his love. His bootheels scrabbled and slipped on the surface beneath him and he could not get his feet under him. "No! Wait...let me go!" But the invisible grip that held him was iron, and would not be denied. It pulled Gart kicking and screaming back towards the circular portal.

A mighty heave threw Gart back into the ordinary world, over the altar and onto the stone floor of the Shrine of Malmathas. He landed awkwardly on his shoulder but managed to roll out of it without injury. He pressed himself up to a knee, glaring at the portal, which had gone blood red in his absence. It crackled and buzzed with power drawn from the depths of the earth beneath it. Streaks of crimson lightning lanced out from the portal to strike the ceiling nearby, sending shards of rock flying in all directions. The room was vibrating with frantic energy.

Nessar blinked back into view a few feet away from Gart, his fear plain on his wrinkled face. The inky black gem of his Jidaan swirled with ebony energy for a moment and then slept again, having fulfilled its job of hiding the old man while he had gone in after Gart. Nessar was breathing heavily, as he slipped his Jidaan back into its scabbard over his shoulder. He detached a leather bag from his belt and began fumbling with it, his eyes on the unstable portal at the far end of the room. He struggled briefly with the waxed string around the top of the bag, then pulled it open. With a quick shuffling step toward the glowing portal, he drew back his arm to throw.

"No!" Gart yelled as he scrambled to his feet. He tried to reach Nessar before he threw the bag, but Gart was too late. It sailed toward the glowing scarlet circle, trailing a thin line of blue dust from the opened end. Gart tried to check his rush but still ended up slamming roughly into Nessar, sending them both to the stone floor in a heap.

The bag sailed over the altar and burst upon meeting the thin membrane that separated two worlds, exploding into a cloud of blue dust. The powdery blue mist instantly spread over the entire opening, tinting the crimson light within a dark purple. When the swirl of dust had covered the whole of the circular portal, it fused together into a solid, translucent mass. Indistinct, roughly human shapes appeared on the far side, and both men could see them slamming fists on the barrier, clawing and scratching frantically to get through. The barrier held firm. The buzzing rose in intensity until both Gart and Nessar had to cover their ears or go deaf from the sound. Suddenly there was a bright flash and a wave of force exploded outward from the portal, knocking Gart and Nessar to the ground, their ears ringing and their heads aching. Silence descended on the room and the scarlet and purple radiance was gone. Gart and Nessar's eyes were drawn to the wall within the stone circle, but there was nothing there but the same dry stone as the rest of the chamber. Gart's eyes flashed to the glowing disk on the floor, the image of the sun above. The dark circle that had minutes ago covered the entire surface of the sun had already shrunk down to a slender crescent as the eclipse passed. It grew smaller, then smaller still, until it was gone as if it had never existed as all.

Chapter 25

The moon slid slowly across the face of the sun and the world gradually fell into a thick twilight. The glow from Melidia's ruby wand was like a bloody firefly next to the huge form of the DireLord, who looked perfectly at home in the growing darkness. His massively muscled chest expanded and contracted as he breathed, impressively displaying his grotesque armor and exposed muscle fibers.

Layton controlled his own breathing as he watched the DireLord in the valley. The thing was unbelievably fast for something of its size, and its weapons extended its reach to a dangerous degree. The morning star at the end of the thick chain was almost as wide as Layton was tall, each spike sticking out a foot or more. The enormous sword blade in its right hand should have been unwieldy, but the creature whipped it about like a willow switch. It would catch sight of him any moment, Layton knew, especially when he used his Gates. They would shine brightly in the dimming light. He cracked his neck first to one side to loosen it, and closed his eyes to prepare.

Layton took a deep breath and slowly let it out, finding his stillness. He inhaled again, then exhaled even more slowly, humming a note as he had been taught ages ago, a tone handed down from teacher to student for centuries. It was the first of three, and although he had not needed to use the ancient method of centering for years, he found it necessary now. The first tone focused on his body. As the sound vibrated through him, he became aware of everything; every bruise, cut, and scrape, but also the strength of sinew and muscle, the blood that coursed strongly through his veins. He was not young, but neither was he old, and his foundations were strong as bedrock. As he breathed, his body came alive and fortified itself for battle. When the tone ended, his body was prepared.

Again he breathed and hummed, the tone lower than the first, and with it, he focused on his mind. As the tone rumbled through his head, he imagined himself in a room of all white, with no ceiling or floor, no corners or edges anywhere, just a warm, calming glow that surrounded him.

He cleared out the jumbled thoughts that had gathered to distract him. Past, future, regrets, hopes, and worries, all were gently put away so that his mind was completely unburdened. Even the room itself disappeared as his mind stilled. When the tone ended, his mind was clear and alert.

The final tone was the lowest, a deep bass rumble that seemed to drop down into his chest. He reached deeply within himself, to the center of his being. What his teachers had called ki and chi, and Brunar had named magick, was the energy that empowered his entire being. He found it, concentrated upon it and willed it to fully awaken. He coiled it upon itself once, then again, letting it grow. When he was satisfied, he released it to flow throughout his body, bringing it to its full potential. At last, his mind, body, and spirit were joined as one, and Layton drew himself slowly to his full height. His chin came up and his shoulders dropped back as strength flowed through him. He was ready.

His eyes opened and an easy smile appeared on his face. He hefted his Jidaan in both hands, twirled it once, and then jogged out of the trees to meet the DireLord.

Melidia immediately spotted him and pointed. "There he is! Smash him!"

With a gargling cry of anger, the DireLord whipped the huge mace through the air at the oncoming warrior. It slammed into the earth where Layton had been, but the Guardian expertly dodged the blow and picked up speed. The DireLord bellowed again and swung its sword down at the little man, but again, it struck nothing but dirt as Layton easily skipped away from the impact.

There was a burst of bright color, and suddenly Layton escaped through a Gate, only to appear right in front of the creature's armored sternum. Layton stepped through his Gate into empty air, and as he fell, he jammed the blade of his Jidaan into the DireLord's vulnerable belly, just below the armored chest plate. Holding to the weapon's shaft with both hands, Layton let his weight do his work for him. As he fell towards the DireLord's feet, the Jidaan carved a neat vertical gash down its torso. Even as he fell, Layton created a horizontal portal below himself, and he disappeared feet-first into the glowing Gate.

156

The creature screamed in agony as the wound opened up in its belly. It immediately hunched around its pain, slamming its right arm across its body in an attempt to smash Layton, but the warrior was already gone. There was a flash next to the creature's ear, and Layton dropped lightly down onto its massive shoulder. Without hesitation, Layton stabbed his Jidaan deeply into the DireLord's thick neck, then pushed the blade forward so that it opened another massive wound as it exited the dense muscle. The creature screamed in pain and anger again, and Layton Gated elsewhere.

Pawing at its wounded neck with its fist, sword still clutched in hand, the DireLord howled in rage. Neither wound would kill it, but the pain was infuriating. When it failed to find and squash the worrisome little man on its shoulder, the beast growled in confusion and turned its steel-covered face left and right, trying to find its prey.

"He's beneath you, you idiot!" Melidia yelled as she yanked her wyvern to her left, flying around behind the DireLord so she had a clear view of Layton below.

Her warning came too late. Layton slashed at the back of the DireLord's ankle with his Jidaan, and the immensely thick tendon above its heel parted easily. The Creature roared in agony and lifted its injured foot to stomp on the source of its pain. The huge, misshapen foot came down hard enough to make the earth shake, but Layton had already Gated safely away. As bright, searing pain shot up the DireLord's leg, the beast stumbled. Melidia screamed in rage at the sight.

Melidia used her knees to guide the wyvern around again as she searched for the nimble warrior. Without warning, a blue sphere of intense energy appeared around her, surrounding both Melidia and her mount. The wyvern squawked as it slammed into the Ward and flapped awkwardly within its spherical prison. Melidia screamed again, furious at being caught. She looked around and spotted Kiran off to one side behind a cluster of rocks. Her Jidaan's sapphire was glowing brightly at her back, and her hands were raised in front of her as she controlled the Ward. Kiran threw an obscene gesture as soon as she knew

Melidia was looking, which made the sorceress even angrier.

"You think you can hold me?" Melidia flung her hands outward as she cast a spell. On the ground, an explosion of sparks, fire, and smoke erupted right at Kiran's feet. With her concentration broken, the Ward vanished, and Melidia urged her wyvern forward again, making it twist and swoop in its flight so that they were harder to catch. She raised her ruby-tipped wand and loosed a blast at the Guardian below, who was still disoriented from Melidia's spell. The scarlet bolt of power slammed into Kiran's left shoulder, and the impact spun her around and sent her to her knees. Clenching her teeth to keep from shouting in pain, Kiran clutched at her injured shoulder and fell heavily on her side. In spite of the agony, she scrambled as quickly as she could to put the nearest stone formation between her and the airborne sorceress. Blood slipped through her fingers and her left arm went numb.

"Hah!" Melidia yelled in triumph. She whirled her wyvern around for another pass, the ruby wand glowing in anticipation of another burst of power.

The DireLord had gone down to one knee, howling in pain. Layton appeared in front of it and simply stood, waiting. In an instant, the enormous creature swung its sword down at Layton, but he sidestepped it as he had before, allowing the beast to embed the blade in the ground again. This time, Layton darted forward and slashed at the creature's hand with his Jidaan. The enchanted blade laid the skin open to the bone, though no blood came from the wound. The DireLord reflexively yanked his hand away from his sword, leaving the huge blade stuck in the earth. Layton Gated forward again, intending to strike at the other ankle, but somehow, the creature anticipated the move.

As Layton passed through the glowing magickal portal and swung his Jidaan towards the exposed tendon above the creature's other heel, the DireLord reached down with the dark iron cap on its left arm and swatted him across the valley with a meaty thud. Layton tumbled across the stony ground in a whirl of limbs until he finally came to rest in the dust. His left leg was twisted at an awkward angle, and his Jidaan lay out of his reach a few yards away. He lay there, still and silent.

"NO!" Kiran yelled. "Layton!" Another blast from Melidia's wand sent a shower of dirt and rubble over her, and Kiran crawled farther into the jumble of rocks. The pain in her shoulder was intense, making it hard to concentrate on holding a Ward. She told herself that she had been hurt worse plenty of times, but that had been a long time ago. Angry tears squeezed out of her eyes despite her disdain for them. She tried to remember what Alyssa had once told her about using her magick to ease the pain, but her shoulder felt like it was on fire. Kiran grimaced as she heard the wyvern squawk nearby and realized that Melidia had landed.

"Come out, *Guardian*!" the sorceress sneered as she stalked towards Kiran's hiding place. She threw another blast of power into the rocks and was rewarded with a cry of pain from within. "You should never have gotten in my way! You could have just given us the Blood, and we'd have let you go. Now you'll all die!"

The DireLord bellowed in triumph, then reached down to grasp its sword once more. Its gargantuan weight shook the earth as it limped towards the fallen Layton, who still had not moved. It towered over him, staring down with its blank, metal-covered face, its shadow falling over Layton's inert body. It cocked its head to one side and examined the tiny being that had managed to injure it. Most weapons barely marked its thick skin. The humans that wielded them were slow and easy to kill, and it had killed thousands of them in its day. But this one was different; it had hurt him. A hideous, low chuckle rumbled from deep within its guts as it stared down at the broken man below. It would enjoy smashing him to a pulp.

As the enormous creature prepared to squash the life out of its adversary, it felt a wave of heat on the left side of its body. It paused and looked in that direction, seeking the source of the sudden warmth. Yards away, Melidia felt the burst of heat as well, and turned away from the rocks and the injured Guardian that lay within. What she saw made her gasp in surprise.

The sky to the east was glowing as though a bonfire raged underneath it, and a bright yellow-orange glow illuminated the trees from within the forest. Soon, the crackling of burning wood reached their ears as the heat intensified. Through the trees, Melidia saw the brightness approaching, although it was not a widespread fire as she had initially thought. The blaze seemed more localized, and it was moving fast. The bark on the nearest trees suddenly burst into flames, and the thick trunks quickly melted away under the intense heat, leaving a flaming gap in the forest about sixty feet wide. Floating in the center of the blaze was the figure of a woman, the source of the light and scorching heat.

The woman was young and lithe, her naked skin unharmed by the blistering flames that surrounded her and held her aloft. Her eyes, too, blazed with power. Behind her was a straight, clear path through the forest, all of the foliage completely incinerated down to the bare earth. She emerged like a goddess of flame, her toes hovering several feet above the ground, her raven hair flying behind her on the superheated air.

Melidia knew her instantly: the girl from her scrying visions. She knew not how she had survived the Mire or what power had possessed her, but she now knew why she had been so prominent in her visions. Even so, she was amazed at the astounding amount of pure power that radiated from the girl. It dwarfed that which had caused Melidia to flee the inn where she had last tried to kill her. *That* she had not foreseen. Melidia turned back and threw another burst of destructive magick into the rocks where Kiran lay, showering the unseen Guardian with debris, then she ran and jumped on her wyvern's back and took to the air. She had to divine the girl's purpose. Mayhap she could persuade her to her own cause.

Pressed up against one of the larger rocks, and bleeding in several places from Melidia's blind attacks, Kiran waited a few seconds, then peeked around the sheltering rocks. The hulking shape of the DireLord still loomed over Layton's unmoving form, but its attention was riveted on the newcomer.

Seeing her opportunity, Kiran gathered what power she could and awakened her Jidaan's gem of Warding, gritting her teeth under the strain. She lay on her side and stretched out her uninjured arm, focusing her power around Layton's still form as well as his nearby Jidaan. A tight, close Ward appeared around him, a second skin of blue power that cradled his broken body. Grunting with effort, Kiran began to slowly drag him from under the distracted DireLord's feet, careful not to make any drastic movements that might catch its attention. Gradually, Layton's body and his Jidaan slid across the ground, drawing nearer to Kiran and the rocks that sheltered her, and she winced as she got a better view of his broken leg.

"Hold!" Melidia yelled as she flew as near to the blazing figure as she dared. Her wyvern tried to shy away from the heat, but she harshly wrenched it back on course. "What do you seek? Do you wish to join us?" she called. She could hear the heavy footsteps of the DireLord as it took a few ponderous steps forward, moving closer to her as it assessed the threat. Melidia brought the wyvern down and alighted on the ground at the DireLord's feet. The heat was nearly unbearable, but Melidia crossed her wrists and engaged her bracelets, creating a hazy shield of energy between herself and the approaching girl of fire. She stared through the translucent shield at the girl's face. In spite of the growing heat, a chill ran down her spine at the imperious look in the girl's eyes. They blazed with power that far surpassed Melidia's own. Suddenly, Melidia felt an emotion she thought she had put behind her as fear sank its icy claws into her. She had been about to speak again, about to ask the girl her name, but the words died in the dryness of her throat. The blazing girl fixed her haughty gaze on the sorceress, and a sly smile crept across her face.

Kiran watched the meeting out of the corner of her eye, paying more attention to moving Layton as carefully as she could with the power of her Jidaan. Unconscious, he slid across the rough ground without complaint, in spite of his shattered leg. The moment he was close enough, Kiran grasped his hand and pulled him alongside her behind the rocks. His breathing was labored and wheezy, but steady, at least. She touched his neck with her fingers and sighed with relief when she found his pulse to be slow, but strong.

"Thank the Goddess," she breathed. She looked at his leg, badly broken below the knee, and grimaced. "That's

161

gonna leave a mark, Laytie dear." She knew he'd probably never walk with the same easy grace, but first, she had to get them both out of harm's way. "I don't know who that girl is, but this whole thing looks bad. Got to get us a bit farther away. Stay asleep, man, you don't need to feel any of this." Her shoulder still burned with agony, but she did her best to ignore it as she dragged Layton farther into the rocks, taking as much care of his broken leg as she could. The terrain was more open on the far side of the cluster of stones. She wanted to get clear enough that whatever might happen between Melidia, the DireLord, and the newcomer would not kill them both. Absently, Kiran noticed that the ambient light had begun to brighten again as the eclipse neared its end. *Gart, I hope you're not screwing us all right now, you sullen bastard.*

Near the edge of the valley, Melidia shrugged her shoulders, trying to settle the cloth-wrapped Jidaan better in its harness. It had never sat well on her, impeding her movements and generally hampering everything she did. Keeping her eyes on the girl, she shrugged again, then called, "I am Melidia. I have no wish to hurt you. Have you a name?"

The girl continued smiling as she cocked her head at Melidia. She looked at her as though the battered, scarlet-haired woman was, at best, mildly entertaining. Then, she tilted her chin up and looked at the DireLord, taking in the enormous horns that jutted out of its blank-faced helmet, its skeletal jaw and ghastly physique, all with that same vaguely curious expression. Then she lowered her gaze back to Melidia and spoke with a voice that reverberated louder than Melidia had thought possible.

"YOU STAND IN MY PATH. MOVE ASIDE."

The power of her voice was a physical force that sent a shock wave throughout the valley. Even the DireLord visibly flinched. Angered, he growled and adjusted his grip on his sword. Had Melidia not engaged her energy shield, she'd have been thrown backward with tremendous force. As it was, her shield nearly failed.

"Wait!" Melidia yelled frantically. Feeling the enormous magnitude of the girl's power, she knew she had to think of something, and fast. "I have gold and jewels aplenty! Join me, and it's yours! You'll be rich beyond your wildest dreams! Together, we can rule the Realm!"

The girl looked at Melidia as she might an insect, though the enigmatic smile remained. She did not seem to understand why they would not move. She wanted to continue on her way, and they were impeding her. They should step aside. Or she would have to make them.

"MOVE," she said again, but with even more power than the first time. The DireLord took a step back from the force of the single word, and Melidia's shield barely held together enough to save her and her mount from being shattered by the power in the girl's voice.

"Kill her!" Melidia shouted to the DireLord, knowing that she, herself, was no match for this being of fire and magick. "Kill her now!" Her only hope was to have the DireLord destroy her, or at least distract her so that she could get away. The huge creature was one step ahead of her. Its sword was already raised for a titanic strike. With a savage cry, the unholy being struck downward with all its might, intending to slam the jagged edge of its sword right down on top of the girl. Melidia struggled to get the wyvern under control so she could get it in the air, but in its terror, it had decided to rid itself of its burden. The wyvern shook and whirled, trying to knock Melidia off its back. The sorceress clung to the beast for dear life, but at the last, she lost her grip on the reins and tumbled to the stony earth below.

The giant sword blade came down, and before it could strike, the girl suddenly glowed white hot, her power creating a sphere of molten energy around her body. The instant the rectangular length of steel touched it, the sphere melted the ancient metal straight through. The tip of the sword blade flew away into the forest, and the DireLord stumbled forward as the power of its swing threw it off balance. The gargantuan creature tried to keep itself upright, but it tripped over Melidia's wyvern, smashing it and killing it instantly. The DireLord unleashed a bellow of rage as it lost its balance and began to fall, but the rage turned to fear and pain as it came down on top of the raging inferno that the girl had become. Its body slammed into the earth with an enormous crash, completely covering her, but the immense heat began burning through the DireLord's chest even before the impact. The sizzling of incinerated flesh and iron flash-forged into molten metal mingled with the creature's howls of agony as it died, burned completely through by the girl's incandescent power. Melidia screamed in outrage. All of her plans were ruined.

Kiran peeked over the rocks that sheltered her and Layton, mindful of the waves of heat that buffeted her even at that distance. She struggled to believe her eyes. The DireLord was down, and a glowing sphere of fire was burning its way through its back, rising slowly through its twitching body with the strange girl at its center. Movement caught her eye and she saw a rider on horseback burst from the trees to one side. The man was cloaked and hooded, his left arm bandaged to the shoulder. Even at that distance, she could see that he was bloodied from battle. He galloped his horse between them and angled towards Melidia as she struggled unsteadily to her feet. The shadows had finally fled and the sun shone down brightly, catching glints of Melidia's crimson hair as the rider slowed only enough to roughly haul her up on the saddle behind him. The rider whipped his horse into a desperate gallop, racing away to the north, hugging the tree line until they disappeared into the forest. Kiran grunted in frustration as she saw her escape.

"Damn, Arkhan and Melidia are still alive," Nessar's gravelly voice near her shoulder startled her almost out of her skin, and he popped into view, kneeling next to her.

"Nessar, you scared me half to death, you moron!" Kiran was overjoyed that her friend had survived, but not so much that she could not punch him smartly in the face with her good arm.

"Ow!" Nessar rubbed his chin and made sure his nose wasn't broken. "Well, I missed you too, baby girl. Is Layton going to make it?"

Kiran sighed, "Yes, but his leg is a mess. He's still out, so that's good, I guess. But hey, we've got to get out of here. There's a magickal being out there, a girl, and she's more powerful than anything I've seen since Mordak."

"That's Gart's daughter."

164

Kiran stared at Nessar, who looked back at her with no hint of joking in his eyes. "You're kidding."

"Nope. And I hope he can stop her, or she's going to kill us all." The old man pointed a finger back across the valley. "There he is now."

In the valley to the north, a lone figure had appeared. His long coat flapped in the wind created by the girl's power. He reached up and cinched the drawstring of his floppy hat under his chin so that it would stay on. A faint nimbus of energy surrounded him, keeping him safe from the worst of the heat. He walked purposefully towards the body of the DireLord, then stopped to look at something on the ground. He stared at it for a moment, then bent unhurriedly to pick it up. It was wrapped in cloth and leather, but he sent a jolt of magick through his arm and the wrappings burst apart. They fluttered to the ground, revealing the Jidaan of Storms. Its emerald pommel came to life at his touch with a bright viridian gleam. Gart hefted the short spear in his hand, enjoying the feel of it. With it, he felt almost complete again. Almost. Sliding it into the empty scabbard at his back, he turned to face the girl that floated in a sphere of molten fire only a stone's throw away.

"Rheann!" he called, managing to keep his voice steady. "Rheann, baby, it's me! It's Gart!" He caught his breath before continuing. "I'm your father!"

Floating above the body of the DireLord, the girl eyed the man below. She cocked her head to one side, then the other as she examined him.

Without uttering a word, she raised her hands and blasted him with fire.

Chapter 26

Gart had emerged from his visit with Gennie whole and strong. His body was healed, his magick was stronger than ever, and something inside him had settled. He had regretted tackling Nessar at the last and told him so repeatedly. Nessar had merely looked him in the eyes for a long time and then nodded. He had stuck out a hand and Gart took it, then the old man surprised him by pulling him in for a hug. Gart surprised himself even more by returning it. He counted Nessar as a friend, and he suddenly realized that he had precious few of those. Not only that, these few had apparently tracked him across the continent not only to stop harm from coming to the world, but because they cared about him. They had initially thought to save him from himself. Rather than stopping him from reaching his goal, they had aided him in the end. By letting him go through the portal, they had allowed Gart the catharsis he had so desperately needed, regardless of the risk. In truth, they truly had saved him. Gart was humbled by their sacrifice and trust.

And now, he faced something he had not expected, and he knew that it was a far worse danger than he had just survived. Through his enhanced senses, he saw not just the flames the newcomer emitted, but the vast depth of magick that fueled them. He knew he could not match it on his best day.

The moment he saw the fiery girl's face, he knew she was his daughter, just as Gennie had said. His heart skipped a beat or two as he looked at her. A lacework of thin scars glowed white with power on her side, drawn in fire along her right arm, shoulder, and outside of her neck, ending in a delicate web that traced along her jawline on that side. The shape of her face was almost a twin to Gennie's, as was her long, raven hair. The shape of her eyes, too, was familiar, though he would not quite recognize them as his own without a mirror.

It's her, he thought. *It's really her.*

He had tried to talk to her, but she had not been terribly receptive. The blast of fire did not catch him completely unaware, though. It was what he might have done in her place, especially if her power was clouding her judgement. The instant her hands came up, he raised his own left hand, palm out, as he prepared to deflect her attack. Gart delved deeply into his magick and formed a wedge of energy that shunted her power away from him. The intensity of it took his breath away, and he knew that he would have been vaporized had he used any less of his own strength to protect himself.

"Please, listen to me!" he called when the blast ebbed at last. "I'm so sorry. I didn't know you were alive! Rheann, I'd have come for you sooner, but I didn't know!"

Still within her sphere of blazing power, the girl floated closer, and Gart stepped back to keep some distance between them. She moved past the smoldering body of the dead DireLord and drifted lower until her feet were just a few inches above the ground. The sparse grass was scorched away in an instant, and bright spots of glass appeared in the sandy earth as she passed by. When she was still a few yards away from Gart, she stopped. Her expression had not changed from one of vague curiosity, and her eyes blazed with power.

"FATHER." It was neither question nor confirmation. She said the word as though testing it, then fell silent again.

Gart answered quickly. "Yes, I am your father. I lost you when you were little, only a few years old. There were..." he paused, trying to figure out how to describe the massacre in a way that she might remember, "scary men with red eyes. And monsters! They hurt everyone, and set fire to the barn where you were hiding! I thought you had died, but you didn't. Someone took you in."

She frowned at that. A look of anger flitted briefly across her face, and she threw another blast of power at him so intense that he thought it would end him. Gart curled his fingers into a claw as he poured more of his power into the shield he had created. He almost miscalculated, and smoke arose in wisps from his clothes. When the blast ended, an enormous crescent had been burned into the edge of the forest, instantly incinerated by her power, and most of the DireLord's body had been eaten away behind her. When she lowered her hands, she looked somewhat surprised to see him still alive.

"I'm sorry, Rheann," Gart said, his heart aching in his chest. He kept his left hand raised, just in case. "I'm so sorry. I spent my life thinking you were dead, but here you are, and your power is like mine. Like mine, but much greater! I can help you control it, baby. I can help. Let me help you!"

"HELP ME." Again, not a question or a plea, just repeating the words. She raised her hands again and erupted in a blast of such magnitude that Gart thought he was going to die. Nevertheless, he leaned into his shield with everything he had, pouring power into it, but he knew it would not be enough. She was too strong.

Just as he felt his shield start to give way, a blue haze appeared in front of it and thickened into another barrier, further protecting him from the white hot river of flame that poured over him.

Kiran! Gart thought. His heart flooded with gratitude as he saw her Ward appear and solidify, adding its strength to his own. He squinted into the flames and saw that the flow of power from the girl was not dying; it was increasing. Even with Kiran reinforcing his own shield, he knew he could not hold it forever. He had to do something. With his right hand, he reached over his shoulder and unsheathed his Jidaan. It came free easily, and its emerald blazed as if eager to do Gart's bidding.

Throwing as much power into his shield as he could, Gart called on the Jidaan of Storms. It answered. The sky overhead rumbled as an enormous gray thunderhead suddenly coalesced out of the clear blue. It quickly became a towering mass that stretched high into the sky. It blotted out the sun and again cast the world in shadow, making Reyanna's fire seem brighter in the dimming light.

With a crash of thunder that shook the ground upon which Gart stood, a torrent of rain suddenly slammed into the dry earth, Reyanna at the center of the deluge. The water came down with the force of a mountain waterfall pummeling everything in its path. Gart squinted into the flames that Reyanna kept trained on him. He peered through his shields, and saw that she remained unaffected.

The rain simply evaporated the instant it touched her fire, creating huge clouds of deadly steam. She did, however, turn her attention away from him for a moment, seemingly confused at the sudden downpour. Seeing that the rain had no effect, Gart called it off, and it ceased as quickly as it had begun. Reyanna's flames decreased as well, and she looked around as she tried to understand what had happened.

When the fire died down, Gart sagged and caught his breath. His Jidaan was in his hands now, its emerald glowing brightly. He was awed to see that the corpse of the DireLord had been completely vaporized behind the girl, and an even bigger chunk of forest had been laid waste. When she saw Gart was still standing, a huge smile of delight crossed her face. Gart realized that it might have become a game to her.

Gart saw her smile and his heart stuttered and flipped within him; she looked so much like Gennie. But there was still a hardness in her face. *That's got to be from me,* he thought absently. "Rheann, baby, please. I mean you no harm. I just want to know you. I want to help you. Please."

She stared at him, her smile still there, but Gart was dismayed to see no recognition in her fiery eyes. She did not know him. Her next attack might be so intense that nothing could stop it.

A dozen plans of attack flitted through his mind, and the clouds overhead rumbled in response, ready and willing to shower enormous hailstones, spawn a vicious tornado, or even send down a blast of lightning that would crack a mountain in half. Gart's magick was boiling inside him, aching for release, and his Jidaan stood ready to answer any summons.

But she is my daughter, Gart thought as he looked at her. And his choice was made. All of his rage, the anger that had fueled him for most of his life, was useless now. Maybe it had been useless all along and he had never known it. He drew a deep breath, and let it all go. Never again would he allow the rage to be his guide. It had no place in him anymore. He would never reach his daughter with it. It was time for him to find a new source of power, the power he knew was inside of him the whole time, but one he had always been afraid to embrace - love.

Just then, a flash of movement caught his attention in the trees to the south. Gart glanced in that direction, praying his daughter would not incinerate him in that moment.

Oh, Goddess...it's Beauty.

Limping out of the trees was the battered and bloody mastiff, her head hanging low. As Gart watched, she lifted her head and caught sight of him, and he felt her burst of joy.

No! he cried, sending his thoughts towards her. *No, Beauty, run away! It's not safe!* She ignored his words and made her way toward him in a lopsided run that nearly broke Gart's heart. She was badly injured, but the magick he had been feeding her had kept her alive. He had gotten so used to maintaining it, he had not even noticed it when his powers had returned. It had become something he did without thinking, like breathing. Now, he fed her a healthy dose of his renewed magick, strengthening her and easing her pain. Again he tried to dissuade her. *It's too dangerous! She may kill me before she understands! Run away!*

Beauty only increased her speed. *You die, I die. Together. Beauty loves Gart.* She was at his side in moments.

Gart knew he risked much in taking his attention from Rheann, but he knelt and hugged Beauty to him, mindful of her dreadful wounds.

Gart was afraid that Rheann would kill her on sight, deeming her just another threat, but Rheann simply watched the huge dog approach with the same level of curiosity she had displayed at everything else she saw. When Beauty had had her fill of Gart's attention, she settled on her haunches right next to him, her eyes on the glowing young woman that floated before them.

Gart sighed as he turned to face his daughter once more. Slowly and deliberately, he turned his Jidaan so that the blade pointed downwards and then stabbed it into the earth so that it would stand on its own. He slowly removed his hand from it and held both hands up so that she could see them.

"Rheann, this is Beauty...my friend." His voice broke at that. He realized that Beauty had done more than simply become his friend; she had kept him alive in more ways than one. She had given him purpose, especially after he pushed Ishabel away. Taking care of Beauty had kept him going for years before his quest to see Gennie had taken over his life, and even then, she had been steadfastly loyal. She had been with him every day, loving him without conditions, as only dogs can do. He looked down at her and stroked her huge head and scratched her ears. "She's been with me a very long time. Please don't hurt her."

The girl looked at Beauty for several moments. Beauty looked back at her, staying close to Gart's side, her long tongue hanging out as she panted in the heat. Rheann stayed silent, but shifted her fiery gaze to Gart, who met her eyes with his own of icy blue. She looked at him for several heartbeats, then her eyes narrowed as though she was considering. The heat began to rise again. The next blast would end it.

Get away! he silently sent the message to his friends. *You can't stop her, but if you can get to the LoreMages, they may be able to do something! Run!* Kiran and Nessar talked over each other in frantic refusal, but Gart ignored them. He silenced their words in his mind and focused everything on the girl.

Rheann, he thought, projecting his words towards her with all his might. He saw her fiery eyes widen, and the tiniest hope blossomed in his heart. She might have heard him. *Please, just...just listen.*

Gart closed his eyes and cleared his throat. He began to sing, uncertainly at first, then gaining confidence as the song progressed. He had not sung in well over twenty years, and had not been good at it even then, but this song was burned into his heart. It was a lullaby, and his voice shook with emotion.

Pretty little baby, my sweet Rheann,
You are my lovely, you are my lamb,
The sun is low, dark is on the land,
And you should be sleeping, my sweet Rheann.

171

As he sang, Gart thought of his daughter as he remembered her. In his mind, he saw her as a baby, cooing and crying and laughing. As a toddler, he remembered her walking unsteadily and singing nonsense to herself. As a young child, he remembered her learning to swim in the river, sputtering and laughing as she splashed. And he remembered holding her, feeling her warmth and the soft skin of her cheek as he stroked her face, soothing her to sleep with his song. All this he remembered with painful clarity, and sent it towards her on the invisible arms of his magick.

Reyanna gasped as Gart's memories struck her. She was still for a moment, then she squeezed her eyes shut and shook her head once. Her fists found their way to her temples as she struggled with the visions in her mind. Gart continued the song. Her song. Her fire slowly began to weaken.

> Pretty little baby, my sweet Rheann,
> I love you so, I'm your daddy-man
> But it's getting late, love, you know you can
> Play in your dreamland, my dear Rheann.

Reyanna's body floated down until her bare feet rested on the ground. She dropped to her knees still thrusting her fists against the sides of her head. She made no sound. The heat around her dwindled until it finally dissipated completely, and long black hair fell loose down her back. There was a sense of pressure released, and all was silent as the young woman found a world of old memories that had been locked away, finally unleashed by Gart's own.

Beauty whined and before Gart could stop her, she limped over to his daughter and began licking her face and arms. Gart held his breath as he watched them together. At any moment the girl could erupt again and incinerate them all. Suddenly, she laughed and wrapped her arms around Beauty's thick neck. There were tears mixed in with the laughter, and Gart choked back a sob. When her eyes opened again, they were bright blue, just like Gart's. She looked up at him as she tried to avoid Beauty's repeated licks.

"Daddy?"

Chapter 27

Melidia held tightly to Arkhan's waist as he guided his horse away from the battle. She was furious beyond words, and disgusted at the fact that she had ended up depending on Arkhan to save her from that flaming little wench.

Who in the name of Balroth is she to be that powerful? She thought, her mind already running at top speed as she tried to figure out a new plan. Gart was out there somewhere, and he might still have the Blood with him. But she was in no shape to confront him now, even if he did not have...*The Jidaan!* she thought frantically. She reached back with one arm to confirm her suspicion, then quickly replaced it around Arkhan's waist. *Damn! It's gone!* The fall from her stupid wyvern must have dislodged it from her back somehow. *No matter. Whatever that girl might have been, she'll probably kill the Guardians and keep right on moving. I'll go back to find it later. If Gart finds it again, he'll be that much harder to subdue. I must have the Blood!*

Arkhan rode through the forest until they were well away from the site of the DireLord's demise, and then he reined the horse to a halt. Preoccupied with her planning, Melidia was surprised when rough hands covered with short, coarse fur grabbed her from the horse's back and yanked her violently to the ground. She banged her head on the hard earth and everything spun crazily before it all went dark.

A time later, she awoke to a pounding headache. She found herself seated on the ground with her back against a tree. There was nothing but the forest in her line of sight. She could hear sounds of activity behind her, as well as various animal grunts and growls. Her ankles were manacled, the dark iron cuffs connected by a short length of sturdy chain. Her wrists, also, were chained together behind her back with fingers wrapped and secured into tight fists. A wad of cloth was stuffed in her mouth and a gag tied securely around her head. She could breathe, but could only mumble and not form words at all. Her fury knew no bounds. She tried to scream behind the gag, and then she heard Arkhan order someone to bring her. Within moments, two of the burly boar-men came, their musky stench making her retch. They picked her up by the arms and dragged her, kicking and mumbling, around the tree. Melidia's eyes widened at the sight that confronted her.

A half-dozen of the powerful boar-men Arkhan had created were breaking camp, loading things onto a wagon. Arkhan came around the front of the wagon to greet her.

"Ah, you're awake. Splendid. We will be moving out of here soon."

Melidia tried to shout at him, but her words were lost in the gag.

"What's that? Oh, my apologies for the gag and the restraints. But I couldn't have you casting spells that might be bothersome, now could I, hmm?" He reached up with his bandaged hand and removed his gold-rimmed spectacles, then began cleaning them. Melidia saw that the wrappings had come off in places, revealing tufts of black fur underneath. Arkhan saw her looking and chuckled. "Yes, my old arm was nearly bitten off by that huge mutt. Hurt like Hel. I had to replace it. Want to see?" Arkhan did not wait for an answer, but instead simply replaced his glasses on his nose and began unwrapping his left arm, exposing the leanly muscled and furry arm of an ape. He clenched the fingers of the powerful hand and held it up for Melidia to see. "The longer palm took some getting used to, but it's wonderfully strong. The ape I took it from was none too happy about the trade, though. I almost felt sorry for the poor creature." Then he turned his eyes towards Melidia, whose anger was starting to give way to fear. "You're wondering why I've bound you?"

Melidia nodded, keeping her eyes on his. She had always known that Arkhan, despite his apparent youth, had been the more dangerous of her two reluctant allies. Barovius' motivations had been simple greed, but Arkhan's had always been a mystery to her. He had accepted the promise of gold and jewels just as Barovius had, but she had always felt that they meant little to him. As she looked behind his easy smile and into his eyes, she saw deeper than she ever had before. And finally, she was afraid.

"I'm terribly sorry to tell you this, but you are going to pay a debt on my behalf." Melidia started mumbling frantically, but he cut her off. "I know, I know, you've got plenty of money, and I'll certainly be going back to your estate to help myself to even more of it, but that's not what I mean. No, what I did for you wasn't easy. It cost me, and that's the debt I'm talking about." Melidia's confusion was plainly written on her face, and Arkhan continued. "All those Joinings…do you think I had the power to create scores of them on my own? My arts are powerful, but to make fifty boar-men and an entire flock of those bat-hybrids, and in the short time frame you required, that was beyond me. I had to make a deal with a greater daemon in order to get that done."

Melidia stared at him, uncomprehending for a moment. Then her eyes widened and she saw Arkhan smile.

"Yes, I had to promise myself to the daemon for a year. This particular being gives great power, but the price is…high. It likes to inflict pain, you see. The greatest agony you might have ever felt is as nothing compared to what the daemon will do to you. It is quite inventive in its methods, and can keep you alive no matter what happens to your body. When you have been burned, strangled, broken, and cut over every inch of your flesh, when he has skinned you alive and broken all of your bones, the daemon will heal you and start over, this time hurting you in a thousand entirely different ways."

Fear shone in Melidia's eyes as she stared at him. He laughed, almost sadly, before continuing. "I've dealt with this daemon once before. I spent a single day with it in return for the beginnings of my power." He went silent and his eyes behind the spectacles suddenly went somewhere far away. "It was many years ago, but I remember every single second of it. It's part of the deal. You can't forget any of it, even if you try." He shuddered once and then looked at her again, smiling faintly. "When you emerge, you will be whole and healed, just as you are now." He smiled knowingly and shook his head. "But it's going to be a long, long year for you. And the nightmares afterward will take some getting used to."

176

Her gag muffling the noise, Melidia screamed in rage as the two boar-men grabbed her arms and tossed her unceremoniously in the wagon, where she landed hard on the unyielding wood. She kept screaming until her voice was gone. Arkhan mounted his horse and gave the command to move out. One of the boar-men climbed into the wagon and cracked the reins at the horses. The wheels began their steady rumble as the group made their way north to wherever Arkhan's plans would take them.

When Melidia's voice gave out, she simply stared at the sky. *Mighty Balroth!* she prayed, reaching out with every fiber of her being to the Daemon-God that had been her patron, her mentor, the very light of her life. *Help me! Help me escape so that I may bring you back as I promised!*

There was no answer. All was quiet save the grunts of the boar-men, the sound of the horses' hoofbeats in the soft earth, and the gentle sounds of the forest that edged the Poravian Mire. She pleaded, begged, and cried, praying Balroth would come, but the only reply was a mocking silence.

Chapter 28

"Look!" Kiran pointed, excited. "They're hugging! You think it's safe?"

Nessar peered across the valley and saw the two figures embrace, Gart and his daughter, with Beauty wagging her tail and leaning against their legs so she could be a part of the hug. The former thief rubbed his grizzled chin. "I could be wrong, but that looks to me like they've reached an understanding." The old man stood, wincing as his back cracked with the motion. He waved his arms and bellowed, "Hey! Everything all right?" Both figures turned in their direction and they saw Gart point to them as he spoke to his daughter. She nodded and replied, though they were too far away to hear. Gart took off his coat and put it around her bare shoulders as they began to walk towards his friends, Beauty panting happily at their side. Not wanting to leave Layton, Kiran and Nessar simply stayed where they were, watching with a certain amount of anxiety as the pair approached. When they were close enough, both Guardians were shocked to see two pairs of identical blue eyes staring back at them.

"Well, look at that," Nessar breathed as he took in the uncanny resemblance. While the girl was the spitting image of the lovely woman Nessar had seen Gart talking to on the other side of the barrier, she definitely had her father's eyes. She also had his power, though she had somehow inherited far more even than Gart appeared to possess. Before Nessar could dwell on that thought, Beauty nearly bowled him over in her quest for more petting and ear scratches. She remembered Nessar quite fondly from their days together at Guardians Keep. He laughed and obliged.

"Nessar, Kiran," Gart began, "This is Rheann. My daughter. I thought she died along with Gennie all those years ago." The wide grin he wore felt strange, tugging as it did on his facial scars, but the expression stayed there despite any attempt of Gart's to remove it.

"I've been Reyanna for almost as long as I can remember," she volunteered. "My adoptive parents call me that. But I remember being called Rheann, especially when you sang it like that." Her voice hitched and tears fell, but they were happy tears, and she did not mind them in the least.

Introductions were made, then Gart's eyes fell on Layton's still body and his frown returned. "Oh, no. Is he dead?"

Even as Kiran went to answer, Gart extended a hand towards the fallen warrior. His eyes flashed golden as he reached out with his magick, delving into Layton's body.

"That leg's bad..." he mumbled. "Ribs are broken...cracked skull...he's lucky to be alive. Then again, he always was a tough fellow."

As they watched, a warm, golden glow enveloped Layton's broken body and lifted him a few inches from the ground. His shattered leg suddenly cracked and popped as it moved back into place. Cuts knit themselves closed and bruises faded away before their eyes. Layton's body shuddered as other, unseen injuries were put aright. Gart held him aloft for a moment longer, checking his handiwork, then he gently set the fighter back down on the ground. He sighed.

"I'm not Alyssa," Gart said, apology in his voice. "I never even met her, but I heard of what she could do with the Jidaan of Healing. I've put him back together, but his leg is going to ache like Hel when it rains, I bet."

Kiran broke out laughing, surprising everyone. After all of the stress and fighting, a laugh always helped ease her tension. "I'm pretty sure he'll survive an achy leg, Gart. Thank you."

"I'm just glad I'm strong enough to help him," he replied, looking at his daughter again. *My daughter*. He could hardly believe the sound of the words. He looked into her eyes and saw her looking back at him, her emotions awhirl and each one plain on her face. Joy, uncertainty, relief, and even a little fear, all were rolling around in her. He understood those feelings well, for they matched his own.

"What will you two do now?" Nessar asked.

Gart sighed and looked down at Beauty, who looked back up at him with unbridled joy. With Gart's magick renewed, she felt positively spry. The people around her were all happy and seemed to care about each other, which in turn made her happy too. She had not a care in the world.

"I need to take Beauty to see the Priestesses of Rowann. She almost gave her life for me many times, and now she needs a kind of healing that I can't quite figure out. And then," Gart looked at his daughter again, "I want to meet your parents. The ones who took you in. I want to thank them and let them know that I'm not trying to take their place. They raised you, not me. But if you allow it, I would like to be a part of your life now. I want to help you understand your powers. Together, we can learn a lot."

Reyanna's eyes filled with tears as she looked up at the man she only knew from distant, but powerful memories. She could sense the truth of it all; his power was like hers, and she could feel that it was the same. Where hers was the unbridled heat of a raging bonfire, his was the focused power of a smithy's forge, and he used it as such. She knew she needed his help to become whatever she might be.

"Yes," she said, laughing and crying at the same time. "Yes, I'd like that very much." She sniffed and continued. "I want to see my parents again; I'm sure they are worried sick. I want them to know I'm all right." Her brow furrowed as she thought, and again, Nessar and Kiran were both struck by her resemblance to their old friend. "I've known that I had power ever since I was a child, but I hid it. I tried to ignore it because I was afraid that the Weya would make me leave if they knew I could use magick."

Gart's eyes widened. "You were taken in by the Weya?"

She nodded. "Yes, I've lived with Rask and Shrya in the village of Allinshae since I was little. I love them dearly." Her eyes glimmered with tears as she thought of them. "I should have told them about my powers, but I was just afraid they wouldn't want me."

"Judging from my experience," Nessar said, "the Weya are well-acquainted with magick. I'd think they'd have embraced yours."

180

Reyanna wiped her eyes and nodded. "I've heard that more than once since the elders sent me to find out about the vision." The she laughed a little sadly. "It seems that I got that notion in my head as a little girl and never thought to look beyond it. I was just afraid of losing what I had."

Gart hugged her with one arm and she let him. "I know that feeling, all too well. Um...should I call you Reyanna?"

She thought for only a moment, then said, "That's been my name for as long as I could remember until today. Yes, call me that. I'll still be your daughter, but although I was born Rheann, I've had many years to become Reyanna." She looked up into his eyes, hoping she was not hurting him. "I hope you can understand that."

Gart laughed out loud, a sound of pure joy that none of the Guardians had ever heard from him. He surprised Reyanna by hugging her tightly, but only for a moment, then he let her go. With tears in his eyes, he explained. "Reyanna, I'm so happy you're alive, so happy that I've found you after all these years. I don't care if you called yourself Bob, Myrtle, or Rutabega. Reyanna is just fine with me."

Reyanna beamed. "Thank you. I did not want to hurt your feelings." She looked at Nessar and finally answered his comment, "I think you're right, sir. The LorMage came to see me after the vision, and I think she will be very helpful in teaching me to control my...my powers."

Kiran leaned forward. "Wait, you saw the vision, too?"

"Yes, as did the LorMage." She raised an eyebrow. "Did you see it? What did you see?"

Kiran relayed what she had seen, followed by Nessar. Reyanna frowned in thought. "What does it mean, do you think?"

Nessar was the first to respond. "I think it represents exactly what happened here. We all saw Gart here in these mountains with Beauty. He turned around to face an enormous and powerful...something." Nessar pointed one gnarled finger at Reyanna. "That something was you, Reyanna."

Reyanna shook her head. "But I was there, and he didn't see me. He was looking at something above me, something much bigger."

Nessar grinned. "Exactly! What's inside you, that enormous power, that *is* much bigger than you! At least, bigger than what you appear to be."

"It looked like he was ready to fight, though," Kiran interjected. "We all saw that. He drew his Jidaan and yelled at whatever it was, remember?"

Nessar nodded as he spoke. "That's true, yes. It didn't happen that way, though." He thought for a moment and said, "Maybe it didn't have to happen exactly that way. What we saw, all of us, pulled us together and set us on a quest that led us here. And make no mistake, we needed to be here." He shook his head and sighed. "Whatever sent that vision sent us exactly what we needed to see. There are forces and beings out there that are far more powerful than we understand, the Goddess Rowann being only one of them. Hel, we know such beings exist because we saw one: Balroth. Since we know he exists, I think it's a good bet that Rowann does too. Maybe Rowann sent the vision."

Kiran stared at her old friend for a few seconds before asking, "When did you get all philosophical, Ness?"

Nessar chuckled. "That happens when you get old, Kir."

Gart looked embarrassed. "Wow, I had no idea that even happened. You all saw me in a vision that brought you together here, I..." he searched for words, "I don't even know how to feel about that."

"Hey, you're worth the trouble, apparently." Nessar replied. "You may be a complete arse, but you're one of the most powerful people in the Realm, maybe the world, Gart." Nessar winked at Reyanna, "Well...maybe more like second most powerful."

Their laughter was music to their ears, and they enjoyed every moment of it.

Nessar scratched his chin. "Now that things have settled down, we need to get out of the Mire and start heading for home. I think we'll have a much easier time getting out of it than we did getting in, at least. We have some friends in there now, I'm sure they can get us through."

Gart spoke up. "I know a way that will cut weeks off that trip, and only take a day or so." His brow furrowed as he continued. "It's not exactly an easy passage, but if Kiran is willing to Ward us as we pass through, it'll be a piece of cake."

Kiran sat down on a rock and groaned as she took the weight off her aching feet. She winced as her injured shoulder sent another jolt of pain through her. "Hey, I'm all for a shorter trip, handsome. I'm pretty banged up, but I can still hold a Ward for as long as you need."

Gart grinned and gently laid a hand on her shoulder. Kiran gasped as his power flowed through her and repaired her wound, just as it had healed Layton. When he removed his hand, Kiran moved her arm around, testing her shoulder and wincing.

"You're right," she said. "That's nothing like Alyssa's Jidaan of Healing...it still hurts!" Everyone laughed and she continued, "That said, it only hurts a little. Thanks, Gart, I owe you one."

Gart shook his head. "No one owes me a thing. I've been," he paused a moment and sighed before he spoke again. "I've been a completely self-absorbed, pig-headed fool, I think. For a long time." He glanced at Reyanna and smiled. "But I feel like I've got another chance, and I'm not going to waste it." He looked back at the Guardians who had trekked across the continent, ultimately to help him. "I've got a lot to make up for. I never realized how much you three cared about me. I was always only looking out for myself." He cast his eyes downward, thinking of all the years in which he had been so stand-offish, and regret filled him. "I'm sorry. I've been such a fool. I've ignored my friends and my responsibilities for too long." Gart sighed. "Gennie said I'm better than that, and I need to show it." He looked at them again, his friends. "I'll not forget what you all did for me here. I'm sorry for all the trouble I've caused you."

A groan interrupted the discussion and all eyes went to Layton's supine form. Grimacing, the waking warrior slowly pushed himself up to a seated position. Both hands went to his face and he rubbed his eyes as though he had awakened from a long, deep sleep, and then he opened them. He squinted to focus as he looked around and struggled to regain his bearings. He looked first at Kiran, then Nessar, and then his eyes widened in surprise as he saw Gart, Beauty, and Reyanna, all staring at him expectantly. He registered the fact that they were all smiling, and he asked the first question that popped into his mind.

"Did we win?"

Chapter 29

The trip home was, indeed, much easier than the one that ended up in the middle of the Poravian Mire. Kiran Warded them all easily as they traveled through the ancient portal Gart had found, fending off only a few attacks by the scarlet-scaled lizard creatures before they retreated in frustration. Once the group emerged in the forest near Old Caldea, they went north and into the Shadowed Forest, making for the mission therein.

When they arrived at the mission run by the Sisters of Rowann, they were warmly greeted by the nuns that lived there. Ginn was there with Teryn, who had been living in the nearby Rowook Home while convalescing from her wounds. The priestess' magick had sped her healing, and she was thrilled to see Reyanna again, as was Ginn. Reyanna saw the way Ginn looked at Teryn, and thought rightly that something might have blossomed between them during her absence.

The Sisters at the Rowook home took care of Beauty with great eagerness, although the news was not all that Gart had hoped for. "We were able to help her heart beat on its own again, but Beauty is far, far older than any dog we know of," Sister Marisen gently informed him. "The next time it stops, it will likely not work again, no matter what you do. For now, though, she is healthy." Beauty looked up at Gart and *whuffed*, just happy to be at his side. Gart wiped his eyes and thanked the Sisters for all they had done.

Layton's Gates helped them all make the trip to Allinshae in relatively short order, and finally, Reyanna was home. Rask and Shrya were overjoyed to see Reyanna again, and threatened to crush her with their tearful hugs. Gart was nervous at first, feeling very much like an outsider in the Weya village, but when the entire story had been told, both Rask and Shrya stood and wrapped their arms around him as though he had always been family.

"I was there," Rask said gravely. "At the place you call Tiller's Grove. I saw what the foul folk did to your

185

people. It was a miracle she even survived. She still carries the marks from it."

Gart dropped a hand to Beauty's head, scratching her ears and neck and feeling thick lines in her flesh, remembrances from old battles. He sighed, "Yes, I saw. It seems that our family tends to gather scars." He turned to Reyanna, looking at the few visible marks on the side of her jawline. "I must say, though...where mine are frightful, yours actually enhance your beauty."

Reyanna blushed. "That's kind of you. I never really think of them, to be honest."

"And you shouldn't," Gart said. "What you are is far greater than just your scars." He smiled and his eyes misted. "Gennie was always trying to teach me that."

Reyanna's eyes, too, shone with unshed tears. "Will you tell me of her? Of Gennie?"

"Of course, Reyanna. Of course."

Just then, the door opened, and LorMage Calliana entered, out of breath from running. "You're here!" she exclaimed when she saw Reyanna. The LorMage quickly looked for Rask and Shrya and apologized. "I beg your pardon for my intrusion," then her eyes found Reyanna once more, "but one of the children told me that you had returned..." Her voice trailed off as she saw Gart standing next to Reyanna. The pommelgem of the Jidaan of storms jutted up over one shoulder, its emerald gleaming in the firelight. Beauty lay at his feet with her head on her paws, wagging her tail at the newcomer. Calliana looked from Gart to Reyanna and back again, and her eyes widened. "I knew it! I knew I saw something!" She turned with a smile to Reyanna, excited as a little girl. "Right before you left, I saw something in your eyes that seemed familiar, but I could not define what it was at the time." With a flourish, she gestured at Gart. "I know now that it was the sight of Gart's eyes that did it. You favor each other! I could not see it at the time because the vision was so fleeting, but there it is."

"He is my birth father, LorMage," Reyanna said.

Calliana's eyes widened. "Well, that would explain quite a bit." She turned to Gart, who bowed respectfully to her.

"LorMage Calliana," he said simply.

"Guardian," Calliana replied with a slight bow of her own. "Welcome to Allinshae. I would hear the tale in full, if you would tell it."

An hour later, Calliana shook her head in wonder. "That is astounding." She fixed a stern eye on Gart, who had the good grace to look somewhat embarrassed. "You are extraordinarily powerful, Guardian," she leaned closer to him, "and extraordinarily foolish."

Gart sighed but smiled. "That's a nice way of saying I was a complete idiot, thank you."

Everyone laughed, and Calliana softened. "That said, I have a strong feeling that events played out as they were supposed to." When Gart and Reyanna's expressions showed confusion, she continued, gesturing to Reyanna with one elegant hand. "Her powers were just starting to manifest more strongly. We Weya are strong in our lore, but who is to say that one of us, even her adoptive parents, would have been able to recover her once the power overtook her as it did? You might well have been the only one alive to be able to reach her, Gart. And how would you have known to do that, if not for Gennie telling you that she was your daughter?"

Gart's face went blank with surprise, and Calliana continued. "And how would you have been able to talk to Gennie had you not become suddenly obsessed with seeing her again recently, so driven to do so that you spent years figuring out how?"

Gart's head swam with the implications. "Do you mean that all this time, I've been moved around like a token in a game of *okha*?" His frown deepened. "I don't know that I like that at all."

The LorMage placed a gentle hand on his forearm and Gart relaxed slightly. Her voice was sweet and calming. "What I know of the higher beings tells me that the nobler ones do no such thing. They hold free will in high regard. At most, they may...nudge...a person here and there when the stakes are high enough, the same way we might offer advice to a friend who appears to be struggling. The Goddess Rowann has ever been a loving and helpful presence in her way, and it would be like her to guide gently and then simply hope for the best possible outcome.

187

And that's if she even had a hand in it at all. Although the vision makes it seem so."

Nessar chuckled and spoke up from his chair. "Gently? That vision knocked my boots *and* socks off! I'd hate to see what happens if she decides to be more, ah, *insistent*."

Calliana laughed merrily at that. "Indeed, Nessar, though I think she would prefer not to upset the natural order that much."

Gart looked over at Reyanna, who had sat next to him at the table, and squeezed her hand. He sighed. "Well then, if the Goddess put the idea into my head to find Gennie so that I could ultimately help my daughter, then I owe her thanks." He smiled at his daughter, and she smiled back.

"As do I," Reyanna agreed. She had found not only her birth father, but kinship with the Guardians. Somehow, she felt that she had known them for years, rather than only a few short weeks. Reyanna looked at Layton, who sat nearby, eating an apple. He had been so kind to her, and had already been teaching her new fighting skills. Reyanna's gaze found Kiran at the window with a faraway look in her eyes. Kiran, too, had been teaching her, treating her both as a warrior and as a normal person instead of some kind of oddity. The young Ranger felt again a strong sense of rightness surrounding them, a sense of family almost as strong as what she shared with Rask and Shrya. She fit in perfectly with them. "I feel it was meant to be this way."

Calliana smiled at Reyanna and said, "I have a very strong sense that your destiny will be important to a great many people, maybe even the entire Realm. I would have you train with our LorMages. Should you agree, I can have word sent to them immediately. One such as you has not come along for millennia."

"Yes!" Reyanna replied instantly. "Yes, please! My power is quite fearsome, and I want to learn how to control it as soon as possible."

"If I may," Gart interjected politely, "I would very much like to take part in training her. Also, if the LorMages do not object, I would like to learn from them as well. Our power is very similar, Reyanna's and mine, and although I have learned much over the last two decades, I still feel like I know next to nothing. And to be honest," he looked at Reyanna again, smiling, "I want to be close to her." Reyanna smiled her brightest smile back at him and Gart's heart melted a little more.

"I'm not only sure the LorMages won't object, I'm sure they would have asked you to stay in any event." Callianna looked around at the other Guardians. "What of you three? Do you wish to stay as well?"

Kiran turned from the window and replied with some reluctance, "I'm sorry, I just want to get home." She wiped one of her eyes as though dust had gotten into it. "I'm pretty sure my Oswald is chewing his nails to the quick waiting for me to return, and I hate to have him worry any longer." She knew she was not fooling anyone. She missed Oswald so much it made her heart ache, but she was not about to say so. Fortunately, Layton spoke up.

"I can take you home, Kir," he said amiably. "And Nessar, too, if you like. I'm sure the Academy has been running along just fine in my absence. They can do without me a while longer."

"You can take me back to Guardians Keep if you don't mind," Nessar said. "I've got some work to finish up there."

Layton grinned. "Happy to help, Vanessa." Nessar glared at him, but could not suppress a smile.

Reyanna glanced at her parents, who nodded encouragement, then she stood up and addressed everyone. "Before you go, please do us the honor of staying one more day and night. Let us host you all and celebrate what's important: friends, family, and new beginnings."

The celebration lasted a week, all told, and when the sun rose on the eighth day, some of the Weya saw a burst of opalescent light on the road leading out of the village. They said it looked like a circular sheet of energy that stood taller than a man on a horse. Three riders disappeared into it, and the glow vanished, leaving no sign that it had been there at all.

189

Epilogue

The fountain burbled merrily in the otherwise silent room, water cascading down through each of the cunningly constructed descending stone bowls until it finally found its way back into the structure's base. The room had been quiet and dark for many centuries, save for a few brief minutes over two decades ago. Except for that unexpected intrusion, all had been still.

At some point, a spark of pale, white light had awakened. Tiny at first, over the years, it chased away the darkness little by little. It had taken decades, but each day, the brightness had increased a tiny bit. Now, the inside of the huge domed chamber was clear to see, had anyone been there to view it.

Arrayed behind the fountain in neat rows, twenty kneeling figures offered eternal loyalty to one already long-dead. Full-face helmets of black iron sat upon their heads, crested with golden-dyed horse-hair. Fashioned with long and ferocious wolf-masks, the helmets displayed each warrior's prowess with notches along the iron snouts. Most were covered with tiny nicks, evidence of hundreds of battles. Ebony-bladed swords hung from each belt, each still razor-sharp within its gold-chased scabbard. Warriors all, they had once been fearsome in battle, the best of the best.

At one side of the wide, circular chamber, a tall throne sat upon a raised platform. Upon that throne was an enormous being, eight feet tall if he could stand. Although the creature on the throne had died thousands of years in the past, it still commanded respect.

It wore a robe of forest green and brown, edged in glittering gold. Dark, leathery skin covered its body, and close inspection would reveal a short pelt of fur, almost unnoticeable against its mummified epidermis. A wide belt with a rune-inscribed gold buckle encircled its waist. The enormous figure had shoulder-length, dark hair, held back by a golden torque on the being's forehead. It wore no helmet, instead revealing that the helmets were not an affectation, but functional in design. Its facial bones were astonishingly canine, with a snout that pushed forward like

190

a wolf's, its dried lips pulled back to expose vicious fangs. He had been king, once, of this land and others. His might had been legendary, as had been his kindness and fairness.

Then he had found the wand. In retrospect, maybe the wand found him. Either way, it had been the beginning of the end.

Eons later, the wand sat in the dead monarch's lap. It was a simple spiral-carved piece of wood the length of a man's forearm, but it was also much more than that. It was from this that the pale light emanated. It was this, also, that had once taken a good and just ruler and slowly perverted him, changed him into something darker and malicious. Something evil.

Over the constant trickle of the fountain, a faint scrape echoed from the stone walls and ceiling of the domed chamber. For hours, there was nothing more. And then again, a faint noise that should not have been there.

On the throne, desiccated fingers slowly clenched around the glowing wand. The light brightened, as if the wand, itself, were pleased.

THE END

Afterword

Thanks for journeying along with my characters! The good news is that there's an awful lot of stuff rolling around in my head that will likely end up on the page at some point. As I type this, I've seen images of Gart suddenly discovering that new Guardians have been Chosen, Reyanna becoming something amazing, and then there's some noise about Layton becoming King. I mean, what's up with that? Questions keep popping up in my mind, and when I start wandering down those paths, I just find more images, more scenes playing out before me. At some point, my fingers find the keyboard and new tales begin to emerge. I do love when that happens. I can feel something rolling around in there, now, way in the back of my mind. I know from experience that I'll be writing again soon. And I hope you'll be there when the next story rolls out, dear reader. Thanks for coming with me this far...I'll do my best to make the rest of the journey worth your while.

For updates about new releases,
exclusive promotions,
and a complimentary short story,
visit the author's website
and sign up for the VIP mailing list
at

http://www.whitmcclendon.com

Also By Whit McClendon

Mage's Burden, Gart's Road, and A Mage Awakens, all in one action-packed volume!

Look for it on Amazon, iBooks, and BarnesandNoble.com!

About The Author

Whit McClendon was born on October 31, 1969 in Freeport, Tx. He grew up in Angleton Texas and was active in martial arts, track and field, and playing the clarinet in band. One year at Texas A & M proved that lacrosse was far more fun than electrical engineering, and he eventually graduated with a degree in Engineering Design Graphics from Brazosport College. After working in the petrochemical field as a CAD drafter for many years, Whit finally realized his life's dream of becoming a full-time martial arts instructor. He now lives with his family in Katy, Texas, plays lacrosse as often as possible, and runs Jade Mountain Martial Arts. He laughs a lot more now than he did when he worked at the engineering firm.

whitmcc@jidaan.com
www.jidaan.com
www.jmma.org

www.ingramcontent.com/pod-product-compliance
Lightning Source LLC
Chambersburg PA
CBHW072104170626
46813CB00004B/1456